"CULLEN'S BRIDE is a winner on all levels—
it taps into our sense of truth, our need for
justice, and the entire story keeps building
towards the kind of love that puts real meaning
into our lives—a deeply satisfying read."
—International bestselling author Emma Darcy

Cullen turned toward her, and Rachel drew in her breath.

She had the definite impression he was going to
touch her, maybe place his arm around her waist
and help her upstairs.

But even as she watched, a subtle change took
place, a closing-out of emotion, and she realised
he was deliberately distancing himself from
her. She should have been prepared for
Cullen's coolness.

Despite that kiss outside the church, he'd
made his position clear when he'd proposed
this marriage.

The baby was his, and he was trying to be
a gentleman. But did that include a future
with her?

Dear Reader,

We've got a special lineup of books for you this month, starting with two from favorite authors Sharon Sala and Laurey Bright. Sharon's *Royal's Child* finishes up her trilogy, THE JUSTICE WAY, about the three Justice brothers. This is a wonderful, suspenseful, *romantic* finale, and you won't want to miss it. *The Mother of His Child,* Laurey's newest, bears our CONVENIENTLY WED flash. There are layers of secrets and emotion in this one, so get ready to lose yourself in these compelling pages.

And then…MARCH MADNESS is back! Once again, we're presenting four fabulous new authors for your reading pleasure. Rachel Lee, Justine Davis and many more of your favorite writers first appeared as MARCH MADNESS authors, and I think the four new writers this month are destined to become favorites, too. Fiona Brand is a New Zealand sensation, and *Cullen's Bride* combines suspense with a marriage-of-convenience plot that had me turning pages at a frantic pace. In *A True-Blue Texas Twosome,* Kim McKade brings an extra dollop of emotion to a reunion story to stay in your heart—and that Western setting doesn't hurt! *The Man Behind the Badge* is the hero of Vickie Taylor's debut novel, which gives new meaning to the phrase "fast-paced." These two are on the run and heading straight for love. Finally, check out *Dangerous Curves,* by Kristina Wright, about a cop who finds himself breaking all the rules for one very special woman. Could he be guilty of love in the first degree?

Enjoy them all! And then come back next month, when the romantic excitement will continue right here in Silhouette Intimate Moments.

Yours,

Leslie Wainger

Leslie Wainger
Executive Senior Editor

Please address questions and book requests to:
Silhouette Reader Service
U.S.: 3010 Walden Ave., P.O. Box 1325, Buffalo, NY 14269
Canadian: P.O. Box 609, Fort Erie, Ont. L2A 5X3

CULLEN'S BRIDE

FIONA BRAND

Published by Silhouette Books

America's Publisher of Contemporary Romance

SILHOUETTE BOOKS

ISBN 0-373-07914-1

CULLEN'S BRIDE

Copyright © 1999 by Fiona Walker

This edition published by arrangement with Harlequin Books S.A.

® and TM are trademarks of Harlequin Books S.A., used under license.
Trademarks indicated with ® are registered in the United States Patent
and Trademark Office, the Canadian Trade Marks Office and in other
countries.

Printed in U.S.A.

Dear Reader,

Have you ever had a moment in your life when everything finally clicks into place and you know exactly what you want to achieve? In 1993 I *knew* I was going to write a romance. I was energized, confident and so eager to write that when I started out, I didn't care that all I had was a pen and notebook. I gave myself two years to get published.

Five years and several rejections later, Leslie Wainger from Silhouette Books called. She wanted to buy *Cullen's Bride*. The date in New Zealand was April 2. It briefly occurred to me that it was April 1 in the States—April Fools' Day. But it was no joke. I'd finally achieved my dream! Later on that same day, I had another phone call, telling me I was a Romance Writers of America Golden Heart finalist. The good news didn't stop there. It seems I'm not the only one who fell in love with Cullen and Rachel's story, because it kept winning prizes—three in all Down Under, including the Emma Darcy Award.

I hope you enjoy reading about Cullen and Rachel and the small town of Riverbend as much as I enjoyed writing about them. They came from my heart, and they live there still. And I can't wait to visit them all again. Soon!

Regards,

Fiona Brand

For Mum

Chapter 1

Cullen Logan slammed on the brakes and swung out of his truck all in one smooth motion. He was dead tired, every muscle he owned ached, and his thigh throbbed where one of the bawling, bad-tempered steers he'd spent the day drenching had caught him a glancing blow.

At ten o'clock on one of Northland's humid summer evenings, most people wouldn't have noticed the frantic movement down the narrow side alley.

Cullen wasn't most people. It was second nature for him to probe the shadows, searching for a darkness he knew too much about. Swearing a low litany beneath his breath, he grabbed his keys, stuffed them in his jeans pocket, then loped across the deserted street. He would be damned if he was going to let another violent bastard get his rocks off by cornering a defenceless woman.

Defenceless? A gritty black humour surfaced as he entered the alley. The woman was holding her own, a spray can clutched in one hand, a big straw bag swinging from the other like a primitive bludgeon. She'd succeeded so far in keeping the guy at bay, but she was too small, too slight, to come out the winner.

Cullen didn't bother speaking. In the murky half-light, he touched the man gently on one shoulder. The variety of ways he could end this encounter slid through his mind as smoothly as a well-honed knife gliding from its sheath. But when the man jerked around and Cullen got his first look at the glazed wildness in the overgrown youth's eyes, he bit out a curt Anglo-Saxon phrase and clipped him with surgical precision on the point of his chin.

It was no contest. The boy stumbled back against a concrete block wall, then slowly subsided until he was sitting in a crumpled heap on the dusty gravel drive.

The woman's jerkily expelled breath had Cullen turning in time to see her stumble. She cursed in a low, rich contralto as she overbalanced and landed on her rear.

"You all right?" he asked quietly, offering his hand.

"Apart from the piece of me I landed on," she muttered with surprising humour, "I'm fine. Thanks to you."

She gave him a smile that was a little shaky around the edges. Her fingers closed on his, baby-soft against his work-calloused palm, but there was a capable strength in her grip as he pulled her up. Cullen released her the second she was on her feet.

The woman barely reached his shoulder. She stared up at him, gaze steady in a darkness that had taken on an odd intimacy.

"I'm Rachel Sinclair," she announced huskily.

Cullen's eyes narrowed. The name Sinclair was more than familiar—Cole Sinclair's expensively manicured acres eased right alongside his own wild piece of dirt. Sinclair wasn't that uncommon a name, but, in a town as small as Riverbend, the chances were better than even that she was some kind of relation.

"Will he be all right?" She nodded in the direction of the boy who still hadn't stirred, then grimaced as a wave of dark hair slipped from its knot and flowed half over her face. She pushed the hair away, then began uncoiling and recoiling the silky mass with an unconscious, natural grace. Against the crude background of the alley, she was startlingly feminine and delicate, and with every movement of her arms and hair, her scent wove around Cullen—flowers and freshness and the subtle earthy warmth of woman. It sank into him and hardened him with a primitive fierceness he hadn't experienced since his early teens.

Oh, man... Cullen almost groaned the words out loud as he backed off a step. Clamping his jaw tight, he forced himself to breathe evenly. Oh, baby, he forced himself to *breathe.* He was riding hell's own adrenaline rush. Nothing more. This was just some kind of weird reflex. He'd been alone too long and hadn't talked to a woman in weeks in any personal sense—let alone one who sounded like she could make a fortune just fueling men's fantasies with the sexy, honey-warm flow of her voice.

"I chin-tapped him," he growled. "He's staying down because he's already wired on something else."

"Something else? You mean he's—?"

"I don't know what he's taking," Cullen stated, then instantly regretted his curtness. He could feel the adrenaline fading, leaving him twice as tired but just as edgy. If he wasn't careful, he was going to end up scaring Rachel Sinclair more than the guy on the ground had. "I'm a little out of touch with what kids use to blank out the misery these days."

Rachel stared at the man who'd despatched the youth with such ease. His cool statement had temporarily defused the nervous reaction twisting in her stomach, and she supposed she should be grateful for that. But the coldness in his deep, rasping voice was like a slap in the face, reminding her that he, too, was a stranger.

A raw shudder swept through her as she relived the moment when the boy's slurred demand had penetrated her fog of tiredness and she'd realised he'd wanted her bag. It had taken her precious seconds to assimilate that what was happening was real, that she *was* being attacked in her safe, sleepy little home town. She still felt dazed, disoriented. And in the confines of the alley, the man who'd saved her seemed inordinately big. Six foot four if he was an inch, maybe even taller, and all of it hard muscle barely contained by tight, faded denim. The streetlight outlined the long, powerful shape of his body, the mane of hair that grazed his big shoulders. The rest of the stranger was...darkness. Shadows clung to him, obliterating everything but the narrow glitter of his eyes, the skim of light across one harshly sculpted cheekbone and the strong sweep of his jaw. He smelt of horse and hard work and, with the restless prowling grace of his movements, looked infinitely more dangerous than the young guy he'd just decked.

But his touch had been...more than gentle. Her palm still held his warmth beneath her tightly curled fingers.

The breath lodged in her throat at the ridiculous notion. Deliberately, she opened her fingers to dispel the vital heat of the stranger's touch—the small act vanquishing the even more ridiculous urge to reach out and stake another claim on the hot strength that flowed through him with an almost visible force. Either she was going crazy or she must be more shaken than she'd thought; if there was one thing in life she'd learnt, it was how *not* to cling.

But now that the immediate danger had passed, the tiredness that had had her falling asleep over the day's accounts rolled over her again. Her tailbone throbbed from her heavy landing, and her palm began to sting where she must have scraped the skin off it. Logically, she knew she should pick up her bag, walk to her car, seek out light and safety. But she was loath to leave the security the stranger represented as he squatted beside the boy and checked his pulse with the calm efficiency of someone who'd had medical training.

Another shudder of reaction moved through her as her gaze skittered over the unconscious figure. "I'm glad you showed up," she said tautly. "Even if he looks too young and thin to do anyone any damage now."

The man shifted the intensity of his gaze back to her. The streetlight cast his features in frustrating shadow, but she didn't need light to see his impatience; it radiated from him, infusing his deep voice with a cutting edge.

"He was going to hurt you. Don't make the mistake of assuming that small towns are safe just because the big cities aren't. The next time you have to work late, leave by the front door and stick to the lighted areas."

Methodically, he began gathering up the various items that had flown out of her bag and slipping them into the straw holdall she'd dropped when she'd fallen over. His unexpected consideration confused her. Especially since now that her dazed disbelief was fading, she was working up a healthy temper. She was twenty-seven, and the brand-new owner of her own hair salon. The only crime she'd committed tonight was stupidity. *She* hadn't tried to hurt or rip off anyone. "He was after my bag," she retorted. Ignoring her stinging palm and the swimmy sensation in her head, she snatched up her wallet and a crushed lipstick. "Maybe I should have given it to him, but I didn't think. And if I *had* taken time to think, I *definitely* wouldn't have handed it over. I've lost too much to give anything up easily, and I'll be damned if I was going to let him rummage through my personal things!"

Her words sank into silence. Mortification at just how much of her inner vulnerability she'd revealed burned through her. How on earth could she have let something so intensely personal slip out? The answer was more than obvious. On top of the physical exhaustion of uprooting her city existence and moving to Riverbend, she was now probably suffering from shock.

The glitter of his gaze swept over her again, and she felt an unsettling sense of being examined with stillness and patience and, oddly enough, empathy. Rachel blinked at that last notion. Oh, yeah. Now she *knew* she was going crazy. Next thing you know, she would be asking the guy for counselling services and sobbing her life story onto his considerable shoulder. Only somehow she didn't think her rescuer wanted to chew over just why it was that the people she loved could never seem to love her quite enough.

She swallowed, fiercely squashing the unwelcome urge to wallow in self-pity, recognising that the rigid control she'd garnered so carefully over the past two years was dangerously shredded. "Don't worry," she said, injecting maximum frost into her voice. "You won't be called on to rescue me again. If I make a mistake, I only make it once. Then I learn from it."

He straightened and handed the holdall to her, carefully avoiding brushing her fingers with his.

For some reason, his detachment and unwillingness to touch her added to her distress. "I don't know your name. How can I thank you?"

His face, half in light, half out of it, froze her off. Something about the distinctive line of his profile, the slant of his cheekbones, tugged at her memory. But the recognition was as elusive as it was fleeting. She'd never met him before; she was sure of it.

Striding over to the unconscious boy, he picked him up and draped him over one broad shoulder as if he weighed no more than a child. "You can thank me by going home before something else happens that your can of Mace can't handle."

"It wasn't Mace, it was hair spray, and I didn't invite—"

"Hair spray?" He made a sound, halfway between amusement and disbelief.

Rachel's jaw clamped tight against a whole list of seductively horrible insults that she would normally never dream of using. But anger was better than vulnerability. If she could keep her anger simmering, she could get through this. "It was better than the alternative."

"Next time, Rachel Sinclair," he growled in his shiveringly deep, rough-velvet voice, "try a little prevention."

His footsteps echoed down the alley. Rachel stared after him, waves of temper pulsing through her as she watched him cross the deserted street with a stride that wasn't as smooth as she'd expected it to be—as if he were favouring one leg. He dumped his limp burden in the passenger seat of a dusty truck that was loaded down with fencing materials, climbed in behind the wheel and drove away without a backward look.

As the sound of the truck diminished, she glanced around the alley. The anger drained away, leaving her cold, almost dizzy with exhaustion and oddly bereft. While the big, objectionable man had been there, he'd blocked out the shock and terror of the attack. Now that he'd gone, she began to shake.

Squaring her shoulders, she forced herself to traverse the narrow length of the alley, eyes raking the pooling darkness either side of her in case there was another wild boy crouched ready to spring. The turn of the stranger's head replayed itself through her mind, and that maddeningly elusive sense of familiarity tantalised her again before dissipating as abruptly as the shadows did when she walked into the warm yellow glow of the streetlamp.

Damn it all. She still didn't know his name.

* * *

Cullen drove a couple of hundred yards down the road, made a U-turn and parked far enough down from the alley that Rachel Sinclair wouldn't notice him. Switching off the engine and lights, he waited while she gathered herself together enough to get in her car and drive home.

The click of her high heels sounded on the pavement as she hurried toward a small, classy hatchback, unlocked it and tossed in her bag. The creamy-coloured dress she was wearing crept up as she bent, revealing even more sleek, pale thigh. Her legs were smooth and long, like the dark hair that had slid out of the knot at her nape.

She made him think of silk and moonlight. Of delicious coolness coupled with a startling inner heat. God knows how, but some of that heat had sunk into him, leaving him hungry for more.

And she hadn't been all sweetness and light. Once he'd started in on her, her eyes had narrowed and the languid flow to her voice had been replaced by a clipped coldness that had been exactly what he'd needed to remind him to move his butt out of there before he did something he would have cause to regret. Like find out whether she was married or single, where she lived, and what her telephone number was.

Her keys jangled as they hit the road, and he heard another one of those muffled, completely unladylike curses as she retrieved the keys before slipping into her car, starting the motor, then accelerating way too fast down Riverbend's shotgun street.

Cullen's fingers tightened on the wheel. Despite her capable front, she'd been distressed and he'd wanted to comfort her. He wanted to follow her now and see that she got home safely. Closing his eyes, he drew a measured breath. Damn, he must be tired, because he had no business even thinking about reaching out for a woman like her. Rachel Sinclair would demand a lot more than the casual liaison which was all he could ever offer. He doubted the lady had a casual bone in her body.

Grimly, he assessed the slumped form of his passenger. The glow of the streetlight washed over the too thin features that would have been handsome if the boy had ever had a chance at a life. Dane Trask. Cullen had seen him around town, strutting cockily with a couple of other local down-and-outs, and several weeks back he'd pulled Dane out of a ditch where he'd collapsed after drinking himself senseless.

He checked the boy's pulse and respiration again, relieved to find both steady. He *hadn't* hit Dane too hard.

Relief shuddered through him, and for a moment everything shimmered out of focus. Intellectually, he knew he'd used minimum force. The short, sharp blow had barely registered; his knuckles weren't swollen, and the boy's chin showed only a faint red mark. His training and discipline had held, despite his fury that a woman was being cornered and threatened. Despite the corrosive backlash of memories that just being back in Riverbend inspired.

With a last brooding glance at his passenger, Cullen turned the key in the ignition and headed for Dan Holt's place. Riverbend was too small a town to have a permanently manned police station, but they were lucky enough to have an officer living there.

It took Rachel almost twenty minutes to drive the ten winding kilometres from town to her family's farm. Nearly twice as long as usual. But then, she *was* still shaking, and she wasn't stupid enough to have a car accident as well as get attacked by a deranged teenager all in the same night.

The house was in darkness except for the porch light. She and her half brother, Cole, were the only ones in residence at the moment. Cole was managing the sheep-and-cattle station while her father was down south in the Waikato, dabbling in his favourite pastime of raising race horses. Her other three half brothers, Ethan, Nick and Doyle, could be in any of a half-dozen cities or countries, pursuing their various business interests.

The dogs barked as she slotted her car into the four-bay garage, then settled down when she called their names. She'd only been back home for a week, but the adjustment from city living to country was unexpectedly sweet. After the break-up of her marriage, she'd needed the change more badly than she'd been prepared to admit to herself or any member of her nosy, overprotective family.

Music drifted up from the common room, which was down by

the single men's quarters, signalling that a group of the men who worked for Cole were still up and socialising, probably playing pool. But Cole's BMW was missing. Rachel locked her car, then let herself into the graceful old house. She didn't know whether to be upset or relieved at Cole's absence. Her older brother would have comforted her, but he would have dressed her down just as thoroughly as the stranger in the alley had.

She couldn't get him out of her mind.

Or the danger that had appeared out of nowhere, shattering her image of small-town New Zealand—and Riverbend in particular—as a safe, cosy haven. After all the normal security precautions she'd taken for granted while living in Auckland, she still couldn't believe how naive and careless she'd been.

Rachel was pouring coffee the next morning when Cole padded into the big, sunny kitchen.

Typically, her older brother didn't bother with pleasantries. "Dan Holt just rang. He said you had some trouble last night."

Rachel set down the coffeepot and leaned against the bench, cradling her cup and deciding that today she was going to need every last ounce of caffeine kick she could get. Despite her exhaustion, she hadn't slept well. The scene in the alley had played itself over and over in her mind, and her reaction to the dark stranger had permeated what sleep she'd managed to get, making her toss restlessly until finally she'd given up trying and had lain with her eyes open, waiting for dawn. "I was accosted by a drunk when I left the salon. Fortunately, someone stopped and helped me out."

Cole's jaw tightened as he busied himself at the stove frying bacon. "The drunk who attacked you is a seventeen-year-old kid named Dane Trask, and that 'someone' who helped you out was Cullen Logan."

Cullen Logan.

Shock jerked through Rachel, almost making her spill her coffee. Every town had its bad boy—its outlaw. Cullen Logan just happened to be Riverbend's.

Rachel had seen him once, years ago, when she'd been home

from school for Christmas. She'd been standing on the sidewalk, soaking up the warm summer morning, waiting for Ethan and Cole while they made some purchases in the supermarket, when a biker had pulled up at the adjacent petrol station. The big, leather-jacketed man had straddled the throbbing monster of a bike while he eased his helmet off, peeled gauntlets from his hands, then slipped a pair of dark glasses onto the bridge of his nose. He'd killed the engine, then made a leisurely survey of Riverbend's Saturday-morning-busy street.

Rachel hadn't been close enough to describe exactly what he'd looked like, but even at the tender age of twelve, she could see the hot wildness in him. His hair had tumbled to his shoulders in a thick, black mane, and as he'd swung one long denim-clad leg over the bike, his unzipped jacket had parted, revealing a broad, naked chest. He'd moved with a powerful grace that had riveted her young gaze as he ignored the garage owner, Sal Tremaine's, halfhearted offer to pump the gas, filling the bike himself before prowling inside to pay.

She'd seen bikers from a distance before, but she'd never seen such a darkly, insolently beautiful male. She'd stood on the sidewalk with her eyes wide and her mouth dry, suddenly feeling the gulf between childhood and maturity, and unable to tear her fascinated gaze from him.

Ethan and Cole had walked out of the supermarket, talking and laughing, until they had noticed the biker.

"Cullen Logan," Ethan had said, jerking his head in the direction of the garage just as Cullen had mounted the bike and kicked it into pulsing, growling life.

The flat of Cole's hand had connected with the small of Rachel's back as he began herding her toward the car. "Yeah," he'd muttered. "With any luck, he's on his way out of town."

Shock had washed through Rachel then, too, because she'd heard her brothers talking about Cullen Logan before, and she knew he was eighteen, the same age as Ethan.

Even then, she'd realised that Cullen Logan hadn't looked like a teenager.

There had been a hard, seasoned quality to him, an edge of

danger you would have to be plain stupid to miss. A shiver had eased down her spine, thrumming in time with the roar of the big bike as it accelerated out of town in a shimmering heat haze.

If Cullen Logan had been eighteen then, he'd been eighteen going on thirty. Not counting last night, Rachel hadn't seen Cullen since. His property abutted the eastern corner of Sinclair land, but for years now the Logan holding had been leased out to whoever had the money and the inclination to eke a living out of the several thousand acres of rough hill country that had reportedly been one of the reasons Cullen's violent, womanising father, Ian Logan, had given up farming in favour of drinking.

Rachel gulped at her too strong coffee, her mind struggling to absorb the two conflicting images of Cullen Logan; the bad-to-the-bone outlaw, and the cool, sternly controlled man.

"Okay, shoot," Cole said impatiently. "What happened last night?"

She lifted one brow at the outright demand in Cole's voice. "I was accosted, but the boy didn't touch me. He didn't get the chance. Cullen Logan arrived before anything much could happen."

Cole let out a breath and came to stand in front of her. He took the coffee out of her hands and placed it on the bench, then awkwardly pulled her close for a hug. "And in your first week back, too," he said softly.

"It's all right, Cole," she protested, returning the hug briefly, grateful for his gesture, but knowing that if she gave in to the urge to tell him that the attack had shattered her idyllic image of Riverbend and she was still struggling to regain her perspective, she would only confirm what he already thought; that she should have stayed in her tidy apartment in Auckland, kept her old job, and given herself time to get over her failed marriage.

Firmly, she pushed free and retrieved her coffee. As far as she was concerned, all discussion about her reasons for wanting to live in the hometown she'd never really had a chance to belong to since she was seven was closed. The abrupt end to her marriage had left her feeling like she'd been the victim of a hit-and-run. When she'd been able to think beyond getting through each day and had taken stock of how unsatisfactory her life had become, she'd instinctively grasped at the idea of moving back to River-bend. The thought of returning to live here permanently had sustained her through those dark, lonely months.

Riverbend was home, and she was determined to stay.

"If anyone got hurt," she said calmly, "it was the boy."

"If the Trask kid touched you—"

"He didn't. Cullen took care of me, and he took care of the boy."

"Did *Cullen* touch you?"

There was a coldness in Cole's eyes, a bite to his enquiry, that made her bristle. "He helped me up after I tripped over some of the stuff that had fallen out of my bag. I guess if you call a helping hand 'touching,' then yes, he did touch me."

"That wasn't what I meant."

Rachel controlled a flash of anger. After the loss of Rachel's mother at her birth, Cole and her other brothers had taken more than the usual brotherly interest in her, even after she'd been sent to live with her Aunt Rose in Auckland. Looking out for her had got to be a habit with them. Unfortunately, their methods were often blunt and heavy-handed; they generally didn't try to understand her point of view so much as manage her. "Cullen Logan extricated me from a situation I couldn't handle. He was kind enough to gather up all my things, then he dealt with the boy who attacked me. That was all."

"Did you tell him who you are?"

Rachel frowned. "I told him my name, but I don't see why that should mean anything other than that I could be some relation to you."

Satisfaction took some of the chill out of Cole's expression. "If he knows you're a Sinclair, he won't waste his time even thinking about you."

"I don't believe you said that!"

Cole shrugged and busied himself turning his bacon over. "The only reason Cullen's back in the area at all is because Carson, the old guy who leased his land and ran his stock for him, has died. Word is that Cullen's only staying long enough to get his farm into a fit state to sell, then he's out of here for good. So far he's had the good sense to keep to himself. He's also not stupid. You're way out of his league. Do you want me to give you a lift to the police station this afternoon? I'm going into Fairley around two. While I'm collecting weed spray and feed, you can make your statement."

Rachel's half-empty cup hit the bench with a snap. Her nerves were still humming from last night, and now, on top of that, she was mad. "I'm quite capable of driving into Fairley myself and doing whatever is required."

Cole shot her a wry glance. "I just want to make sure you do the right thing and don't end up feeling sorry for the guy who attacked you."

"If I were you, I'd concentrate on that bacon. Smells to me like you're burning it."

Cole's hands shot up in the traditional sign of surrender, but Rachel wondered what his reaction would be if she told him that his suspicions were all twisted the wrong way. When Cullen had strode into the alley behind her salon, he'd radiated a clean strength and purpose that were still imprinted on her mind. If anyone had wanted to do any touching, it had been her. *She'd* been the one who had wanted him to stay.

And Cullen hadn't been able to get out of that alley fast enough.

Chapter 2

Cullen parked his truck across the road from Rachel Sinclair's salon just before closing.

He'd timed it carefully. He needed to speak to Rachel about Dane, ASAP, and with any luck, most of her customers would have gone, granting them some measure of privacy.

Especially since he now knew just exactly who she was.

Even before he'd known for sure that she was old money—the oldest in town—and Cole Sinclair's pampered only sister, his instincts had told him to leave her alone. Cullen wasn't big on backing away from trouble, but he wasn't about to walk smack into it, either. And Rachel Sinclair, with her sexy voice and lush, vulnerable mouth, had to be the most trouble he'd seen since the last time he'd taken up residence in Riverbend.

The door buzzer sounded. Rachel automatically glanced in the mirror. Cullen Logan. Heat bloomed on her normally pale skin, intensifying the uncomfortable humidity of late afternoon.

He was standing by her reception desk, a sleek, hot panther of a man with shockingly light, winter grey eyes that calmly met her gaze in the mirror. A five o'clock shadow darkened his jaw, and his jet-black mane of hair was rumpled by wind and sweat. With his big shoulders stretching the hell out of what looked like an old army fatigue shirt—minus the sleeves—and his long, powerful legs moulded by a pair of faded denims, he looked like he'd just finished a hard day's work and hadn't bothered to pretty himself up to come into town.

Cullen eased some of the tension from his shoulders, keeping his expression carefully blank. Oh, man. Rachel Sinclair was a lady, all right. Her features were pale and delicate—not pretty, exactly, more patrician. Like something out of a French impressionist painting. A Renoir. Yeah, that was the one. She should be in a garden, wearing one of those graceful straw hats to protect her complexion. And a flowing white dress. She was the kind of woman who was born to wear white.

Her dark gaze was steady on him, and unusually direct. There was an intensity there that caught and held his attention more strongly even than the waves of attraction thrumming through him. This was a lady who said what she meant and meant what she said, and right now she was taking him apart, piece by dissected piece, and examining each rough-and-ready part of him.

A grim smile almost succeeded in tugging at the straight line of his mouth. He should tell her not to bother. If she went over every rough edge he had, they would be here until doomsday, and he wasn't planning on staying *that* long.

He almost grinned at the shocked quiet in the place, which was saying something. He'd never thought he would find anything to smile about in Riverbend. Aside from the steady hum of a blow-dryer, no one was saying a word; he felt like the wolf who'd just wandered into the henhouse, and the occupants were all still too stunned to squawk. And he couldn't blame them. He looked like hell. His jaw was as rough as Hades, and he'd ripped the back out of his shirt straining at a broken fence post he could swear had been cemented in. And he needed sleep bad. He'd been skimping on sack time, pushing himself for weeks now to get through the mountain of maintenance work the farm needed. His eyes had that familiar gritty feeling he'd got so used to on combat operations.

After the episode in the alley, he would be surprised if he'd got two hours, max, last night.

Rachel flinched as her assistant, Helen, snapped her blow-dryer off. The profound silence that followed was broken by the click of Helen's high heels as she sauntered across to the front desk.

Even though Rachel knew Cullen wanted to talk to her, and that letting Helen deal with him was just a delaying tactic, she found she needed a few seconds to shake off her response to him.

It hadn't taken long for gossip about what had happened last night to spread like wildfire through Riverbend, and she'd been plied with stories about Cullen all day long—whether she'd wanted to hear them or not. According to local legend, Cullen's mother, Celeste, had drifted into town and almost immediately plunged into a wild affair with the broodingly handsome Ian Logan. The affair had culminated in marriage, despite predictions to the contrary. Just when people were adjusting to the permanency of the relationship, a pale, bruised Celeste had abandoned both her husband and her newborn baby shortly after giving birth. She'd never been heard of since.

With a start like that, it was assumed that Cullen would be as wild and unmanageable as both his parents. In this, at least, the townspeople hadn't been proved wrong. From age seven, Cullen had run away more times than anyone could count; then, when he'd stopped running, everyone had wished he would take it up again. Foster homes and reform schools hadn't held him, and when he was too old to be institutionalised, he'd turned up in Riverbend again—a wild, angry teenager, not just looking for trouble, but making it. The whole town had held its breath, waiting for all that badness to explode.

They hadn't had long to wait. When Cullen's father's battered, whiskey-soaked body was found half-submerged in a roadside ditch, everyone was certain the next stop for Cullen was a cell in a maximum security prison.

But Cullen hadn't gone to prison, he'd gone into the army. And, as far as she knew, he hadn't been back. Until now.

The level of interest in a man who'd been absent for a good fifteen years was bizarre, to say the least. But right now, the only thing that registered on Rachel was that the man taking up her mirror space emanated a raw, hot vitality that battered her senses. Heat poured from him, radiating from the sweat-sheened copper of his skin, leashed in the cold crucibles of his eyes. Handsome was way too weak an adjective. He was beautiful in the way she imagined ancient warriors must have been. If he ever smiled, he would be sinful.

Rachel didn't think Cullen Logan was about to smile—not around her, anyway. He looked like he didn't want to be here at all.

"Well, join the club, cowboy," she muttered beneath her breath, willing away her blank fascination, the disturbing awareness she wanted no part of. Even though she was grateful for the way he'd helped her out last night and still felt the need to thank him, for her own peace of mind, she wasn't sure she wanted him around either.

"Rayyychel."

Helen's mocking summons came too soon. Rachel set her scissors down, drew out the ends of both sides of the bob cut she'd just completed and smiled at her client. "All done," she said a trifle huskily. "I'll get Helen to finish off."

Helen lifted both brows as Rachel crossed the small distance to the reception area. "How come you get all the men?" she said cheekily, giving Cullen a flirty look that bounced off him like a rubber ball hitting granite.

"It's a curse," Rachel retorted drily. "Try starting life with four brothers. Will you dry Janine for me, please?"

Rachel looked Cullen Logan straight in the eye, not bothering to try for a smile. "What can I do for you, Mr. Logan?"

He showed no surprise that she knew his name.

"I need to talk to you about last night."

The salon, already quiet, grew as silent as a confessional. Mrs. Reese, who was sitting waiting for her daughter, Eleanor, put her magazine down and began adjusting her hearing aid. Eleanor swivelled around in her chair and was unashamedly watching and listening. Helen hadn't moved to switch on the blow-dryer.

Rachel felt like saying, "Go away, Cullen Logan, you're making more gossip, and I'm already in up to my neck." But she didn't, and the blow-dryer finally whirred into life, followed by a huffy exclamation from Mrs. Reese.

Rachel stared into Cullen's unnervingly light eyes with a calm she didn't feel, and suddenly she wanted to disturb him, to dent that impervious male assurance. "If you want to talk to me with any degree of privacy, you'll have to let me do something with your hair. I still owe you for last night. I'll listen while I'm cutting."

Reaching up, she touched the thick, glossy black strands grazing his shoulders. It was a normal hairdressing gesture—she did it all the time—but this didn't feel like business. She felt like she was touching fire, playing with fire—and the banked look in his eyes told her that he knew it, too.

Gritting her teeth against his censure, she injected the kind of reckless challenge into her voice that she just knew she was going to regret. "How would you like it?"

The look he returned her was, for a stretched moment, as blank and clear as stone seen through water, but Rachel realised she'd crawled in way out of her depth when a dark humour surfaced and the faint twist of his long, brooding mouth turned sensual.

"How many ways are there to have it?"

Rachel's hand jerked back from his hair. The gesture *had* been too intimate; it had taken her too close to his work-hardened body, to the waves of heat pulsing off his sleek skin. Her chin came up—a useless gesture, as it didn't afford her enough height to make any kind of difference. "Short and fast," she drawled back, "or long and slow."

Something that could almost have been shock flared in his eyes before they narrowed with a speculation that made her want to take her words back and bite her tongue off before she got herself any deeper into trouble. For a minute there she'd forgotten the rumours and the stories. She'd forgotten that Cullen Logan had probably killed a man.

The silence lengthened, gathering tension with every drawn out second, then he let out a long, slow breath.

"Short and fast...for today."

Rachel almost closed her eyes at the next question she had to ask. "Wet or dry?"

"Are you doing the washing?"

She glanced at Helen, who was putting the final touches on Janine's hair. The other hairdresser was very pretty, with a shiny blond elfin cut and pert features. A lot of the male customers came in because she worked here. "Helen's busy, looks like you'll have to put up with me. Is that a problem?"

This time the amusement spread all the way across his mouth, although the faint uplift at the corners couldn't be classified as a smile. "No problem."

Rachel led the way to the basins, suddenly wishing the caramel-coloured shift she was wearing could grow another couple of inches. And her hips and breasts could lose a few. It was an illogical and inappropriate response. She knew she was no more than ordinarily attractive; her clothes were practical and well cut rather than alluring, and she had no outstanding talents to her name.

And the man following her into the private alcove where the basins were situated, making her salon seem small and claustrophobic, didn't have the slightest interest in her other than to discuss something about last night's attack.

Briskly she seated him, fastened a waterproof cape around his neck, then guided his head onto the concave basin rest. He watched her, and, despite her resolve, she felt herself getting hotter. It was a relief when she started washing his hair, because she didn't have to acknowledge what was in his eyes.

He hadn't wanted Helen to wash his hair. He'd wanted *her* to do it, and now it felt unbearably intimate to put her hands on him.

Abruptly, her mood changed. Every ounce of irritation and heartache this situation had caused her surged back, redoubled. Mr. In-Control had had her on the back foot from the first moment. Literally. But he was on her turf now. She began to lather his scalp, taking her sweet time about it—her fingers sliding and massaging with a sinuous expertise.

He groaned, a reluctant rumble of sound. "God, you're good at that."

''Best hands in the business.'' She kneaded the tight muscles at his nape. ''Now, what did you want to talk to me about?''

''Have you laid a complaint with the police?''

''I just made a statement.''

Some of the tension went out of his face, and she realised that at least a part of Cullen's grimness was caused by worry. Worry for the boy who'd attacked her.

''Thank you,'' he said, a dark warmth filtering into his deep voice. ''If you'd made a formal complaint, Dane wouldn't have stood a chance. With his record, they would've locked him up.''

''But he does need help.''

''He needs a lot of things, but at the moment it's all academic. He's in hospital. His father beat him so badly he can barely walk.''

Rachel could feel her eyes widening, her system responding to the sudden dousing shock of such brutal violence. She knew this stuff happened—in cities it was a given. But in Riverbend? Cullen's rebuke about small towns and big cities came back to her. It stung to realise that she was still reacting naively. That he'd been right about her. Vaguely, she heard Helen hustling the reluctant Reeses and Janine out the front door, the bustling, tidying sounds the younger woman made as she swept the floor clean. ''Will he be all right?''

''Physically, he'll heal.''

Rachel released a breath she hadn't been aware she'd been holding and began working the tight skin at the edge of Cullen's hairline, just above his temples.

Cullen wondered if Rachel realised just how long she'd been washing his hair, or how sleekly sensual her fingers felt sliding across his wet scalp. He almost sighed with relief when she began rinsing him off, glad for the candy pink plastic cape covering his lap. It had been a mistake succumbing to the temptation to bait her, to have her touch him. He'd never had his hair washed so well or for so long, and he wondered if Rachel Sinclair got this close to all her male customers. If she did, there must be a town full of frustrated men.

She'd implied that Helen was the draw card. And he supposed that if short, tight dresses and a slick line in sexy banter was what you were chasing, then she could be right. But Cullen had had his fill of women who wanted nothing more from him than stud service and the chance to fulfil their bad-boy fantasies.

As if he'd conjured her up, Helen sauntered into view.

"Everything's shipshape." She fixed Cullen with a considering gaze. "Unless you need a hand with something out here?"

The water went off. Rachel reached for one of a half-dozen bottles on a shelf. "Mr. Logan's only in for a cut."

"If you say so," Helen murmured, shooting Cullen another lazily assessing look as she wiggled her fingers at Rachel. "See you in the morning."

Cullen heard the sound of a bottle being squeezed, caught the scent of something resinous, masculine. He clenched his jaw against another groan as Rachel began weaving her elegant hands through his hair again. After an eternity the water thumped on, and he would have sold his soul to immerse his body in the lukewarm wetness.

The water went off with a shudder of pipes; then she began to towel his hair dry with firm regular sweeps that shouldn't have been sexy. Aside from the scalp massage, it was about the sexiest thing that had ever been done to him. She hovered over him, her loose dress tightening across breasts and hips that were unexpectedly full for her petite build. And as she worked, her feminine warmth and scent wrapped him, her thigh brushed against his, and more times than he could count, her breast came whisper-close to his taut bicep.

"Short or just a trim?" Rachel asked with a brisk professionalism that was just a little too bright, too impersonal.

Cullen concluded that either she was physically scared of him, or the raw, sexual awareness that was tying his gut into knots cut both ways. As soon as he'd considered that Rachel could be afraid of him, he discarded the thought. She hadn't shown any fear in the darkness and confusion of the alley last night, and her actions since he'd stepped into the salon had reflected curiosity and challenge, and more than a little irritation.

Which left the second option.

Every muscle in his body tightened as he absorbed the possibility that Rachel Sinclair was just as attracted to him as he was to her. Cursing savagely beneath his breath, Cullen tore open the Velcro fastening at his nape and jettisoned the cape. Having her touch him had been an even bigger mistake than he'd first thought. And judging from the unruly response of his body, it was way past time he left.

Rachel stifled the urge to back up a step as Cullen flowed up and out of the chair, his wet hair falling sleekly to his shoulders. For the briefest moment she'd had the clear impression he was going to slide his hands around her waist and bury his mouth against hers. The vision was so graphic that she could almost feel the clasp of his hands, the tingling warmth of his lips pressing hers apart. And then he was walking away as abruptly as he'd done in the alley last night, and leaving her just as disoriented.

Disoriented enough to follow him a few dazed steps, as if caught up in a violent slipstream. "Cullen?"

Even though she was sure her voice had been so low he couldn't possibly have heard, he stopped just short of the door, his back to her—a rip in the sleeveless shirt giving her a glimpse of bronzed, heavily layered muscle. Numbly, Rachel searched for a reason to have stopped him. And it certainly wasn't going to be the truth, that touching Cullen *had* been like touching fire, and that the physicality of her own response shocked her. "Will anything happen to that boy's father?"

Cullen half turned, as if reluctant to stay in the same room with her any longer than necessary. "Dane would have to complain to get his father charged, and then his mother and his brothers and sisters would be left on welfare."

"But surely—"

"Ever lived on welfare, Miss Sinclair?"

"No."

Cullen's scuffed riding boots made surprisingly little sound on her polished wood floor as he covered the remaining distance to the door. He paused, one hand on the jamb. "Thanks again, on Dane's behalf."

Rachel lifted her chin at his determined dismissal of her and her own obscure, untenable hurt at that dismissal. "What's going to happen to him when he gets out of hospital?"

Cullen's jaw tightened at the question, and this time, when he met Rachel's gaze, he reneged on looking away. Her eyes...he hadn't known what colour they were in the alley. He'd guessed blue. He was wrong. They were a soft, dark honey—unexpectedly fierce and just a little untamed, with the kind of fire a man could sink right into. And her scent... Her scent was driving him crazy, urging him to step closer and seek out all the shadowed places where her silky, delicate heat flared and burned.

Need shuddered through him again, and he locked his muscles tight against it. She was five foot five at most, small and feminine compared to his build, but he didn't think she would refuse him— not at first, anyway. Rachel Sinclair, like a lot of women, was curious enough about him to at least try a taste. And for the first time in his life, Cullen knew he wouldn't be able to stop at a taste. Something about Rachel shook him to the core. She was finely built, almost fragile, and utterly feminine. He wanted to hold her, to protect and care for her, to see the somber intensity in her eyes dissolve into laughter. He wanted...everything that a past rooted in violence and despair had taught him he could never have.

"Dane's going to stay with me," Cullen said, just when Rachel was certain he wasn't going to answer her question. "And I'm going to give him exactly what he needs—a job fixing my fences." His voice dropped, roughened. "Thanks for washing my hair. It'll probably stay clean for at least a month."

A car barrelled past, breaking the moment. A horn blared, and someone called out, laughing, and with that small interruption, Cullen stepped out into the sweltering stillness of early evening and strode across the road to a dark green four-wheel drive. When the vehicle pulled away, Rachel gave in to the compulsion to step out onto the pavement, under the overhang. The humidity had become unbearable, and it registered somewhere in the recesses of her mind that she needed a long, cool drink. Badly.

A distant rumble sounded. The unmistakeable smell of rain hitting parched, dusty pavement wafted on a hot gust of wind as the truck accelerated down the main street and out of town. Rachel touched her palms to her cheeks and closed her eyes. She was trembling, her hair clinging damply to her brow and nape. I must be coming down with something, she thought dimly. Or maybe it's the time of month.

Or maybe it was that she suddenly felt more lonely than she'd ever felt in her life. Lonelier even than when Adam had walked out on her and she'd spent two weeks of the holiday they'd planned to take together staring at a tropical sea, unable to believe her husband didn't love her.

She closed her eyes on a familiar burst of pain. Correction. He *did* love her. That was the supreme irony, and the one fact she still hadn't come to grips with. After three years of what Rachel had considered a perfect marriage, he'd suddenly met someone. She still remembered his exact words. They'd burned into her, sinking to the centre of her being. "I love you," he'd said, "but I can't stay with you. I've met someone, and I can't get her out of my mind. I don't know what it is that I feel, but I can't bear to be in the same room with her and not touch her."

Water slammed onto the tin roof of the covered way. Rachel's eyes snapped open at the violence of the sound. After only a few seconds the guttering overflowed, and a shift in the wind drove the rain under the shelter, pelting her with big, stinging drops. She knew she should move away, but the pounding rain after the still heat of the day was somehow cathartic. Stepping closer to the edge of the pavement, she lifted her face, tasting the rain in her mouth, the cleansing coolness of it. The salt.

She wasn't crying. It was the rain wetting her cheeks, and not the weak, useless tears she'd given up long ago.

And the tremors moving through her body were from the shock of dealing with Cullen Logan's uncompromising maleness. Somehow—God knows how, for he'd gone out of his way to be cool and abrasively dismissive—he'd stirred something in her that she'd thought had been burned away for good, a sexual need that was more intense, more overwhelming, than any she could ever remember feeling.

It shook her that she could feel a sexual response to any man other than the man she'd chosen to marry. Maybe she was reacting naively again, but she knew her own nature. She was naturally intense and single-minded, and her feelings had always run deep. She'd learned to guard her emotions over the years and didn't trust easily, which was one of the reasons her failed marriage had hit her so hard. When she'd made her vows, they'd been the old-fashioned 'til-death-us-do-part kind.

Logically, she knew that two years had passed since her marriage had effectively ended, that she was still human, still female. She'd expected to participate in sex in order to satisfy a man she could come to love sometime in the misty, uncertain future. But not now. Not with this burning immediacy. And certainly not with a man—a stranger—who didn't even like her.

The rain stopped as suddenly as it had begun. Rachel looked blankly around, finally becoming aware of just where she was and that she was wet through. Thankfully, the street was deserted. Anyone with any sense was inside out of the rain, or at home relaxing after a hard day's work.

She began locking up, grimacing at her sodden shoes, dripping hair and clinging dress. When she'd collected her holdall and the day's takings that hadn't been banked, she finally allowed herself to think about the letter she'd received in with the salon's mail that morning. The letter which was the final culmination of the lengthy legal proceedings that had neatly reduced her lingering hopes and dreams to a tabulated column of figures.

Her jolting awareness of Cullen Logan might have been the catalyst to the draining outburst of emotion, but it was that cold, official sheet of paper which still lay folded in the bottom of her bag that had tipped her so far off balance—even though she'd known it was coming, had expected it for days now.

After all, it wasn't every day she got divorced.

Chapter 3

Cole slotted his BMW into one of Fairley Hospital's narrow car parks. "I still think this is a dumb idea," he growled.

"We've already had this argument," Rachel retorted, stepping out into the soft evening light.

Cole's door closed with a thunk. "Do you really think you should get mixed up with the guy who tried to attack you last night? You don't know Dane Trask. Hell, you don't know the Trasks! The father, Frank, is a mean drunk who's already done time for assault and battery, and Dane's gearing up to be just like him."

Rachel hitched the strap of her holdall over one shoulder. "I'm not denying that what Dane Trask did was wrong."

"Then why waste your time going to see him?"

She suppressed a sigh. There was no way she was going to tell Cole about the lawyer's letter. That she hadn't been able to bear the thought of her own company tonight and would have grasped at any reason at all to go out. If he had the slightest inkling that she was lonely or depressed, his protective instincts would slip into overdrive, and she'd already faced enough opposition from her family about her move back to Riverbend. Frustration welled up in her. Her father and brothers loved her, of that she had no doubt, but they loved her on their own terms. Sometimes Rachel felt as if a glass wall separated her from her family. They cared for her, but they pushed her away at the same time—for what they considered her own good. Every time she'd tried to change the relationship, to demand unconditional love, she'd run smack into that glass wall...until she'd learned to protect herself.

Of course, her protection hadn't been one-hundred-percent perfect. Rachel's mouth curved bitterly. She hadn't thought she'd needed to guard her emotions with Adam; she hadn't known that particular glass wall existed until it was too late.

"I want to see the boy who attacked me in a lighted room," she said coolly. "And maybe I want to find out just what kind of town it is that I've moved back to."

"I'm coming with you."

"No."

Cole's attention shifted. Rachel followed the direction of his glare. Cullen's truck was parked nearby.

A shiver of something very like anticipation eased down her spine, and she frowned at her reaction. So what if Cullen was here, too? He wouldn't be pleased to see her, and after the turmoil of this afternoon's meeting, she wasn't exactly jumping out of her skin to see him again, either. "If you're still concerned with warning me off Cullen," she declared irritably, "you're wasting your time. He's not the slightest bit interested in me, and I don't imagine I'll see him again except in passing."

But even as she said it, she knew it was a lie. Cullen *was* interested in her, even if it was only on the most basic, sexual level, and as hard as she tried, she couldn't dismiss him from her mind.

Cole eyed her from across the bonnet. "You used to look like that when you were too little to reach the toy you wanted but you didn't want any of us to get it for you."

"Right before I used to throw a screaming fit," she agreed.

He tossed the keys. "I'll wait here," he conceded. "In half an hour's time, I'm coming in."

Rachel was tempted to argue, but Cole had an enduring look to the set of his jaw. It was the same trademark Sinclair stubbornness that had had her brawny father and brothers hustling her out of their "rough country life" when she was barely seven years old, because they were certain she needed her Aunt Rose, a city school and "cultural opportunities" more than she needed their love. Arguing hadn't changed a thing then, and she knew it wouldn't shift Cole now. "Half an hour should be plenty of time."

The receptionist gave her directions, and after dropping off a magazine for one of her clients, Edna Simms, who'd just had surgery on her hip, Rachel located the men's surgical ward. Most of the patients had visitors. Dane was in an end bed against a wall, and the only person visiting him was a restlessly pacing Cullen, who, even in a white T-shirt and jeans, looked as out of place in the hospital ward as a big predatory cat would have been.

His head swung in her direction the instant she stepped through the doors, and Rachel had to mentally brace herself against the impact of his light metallic gaze.

She came to a stop at the foot of the bed. "How is he?"

If anything, Cullen's grim, implacable expression became even more remote. "As well as can be expected." He gestured her toward a chair.

Rachel shook her head at his offer of a seat. "I won't be staying long."

Dane was awake and watchful, if slightly groggy. There was a glimmer of intelligence in the one eye that wasn't swollen closed. His mouth was puffed up and cut, and most of his face was discoloured. His ribs were taped. Even though she'd been prepared for him to look like he'd been run over by a truck, the reality was still shocking. "Hello, Dane."

"'lo," he said rustily. He glanced at Cullen. "She the one?"

Cullen inclined his head.

Dane groaned. "Don' remember."

"It doesn't matter," she said automatically, and suddenly it didn't. The incident in the alley faded when compared with the brutality that had been perpetrated on Dane, and Rachel's throat closed up at the abuse the boy had taken from the one man he should be able to trust. Instead, it appeared the only person who cared enough to look after Dane was the man everybody assumed didn't care for anyone or anything.

There was an awkward silence while Rachel searched for something to say. "I...brought you some fruit." Setting her holdall down on the bed, she retrieved a bag of grapes she'd bought purely as a reflex. It wasn't until she was walking out of the shop that she'd realised she was buying her attacker a gift. But now she was glad she had. The contrast between Dane's lack of visitors and Edna Simms' overflow was startling. She stepped closer in order to show Dane what she'd brought. In the process, she had to move within inches of Cullen, and while they didn't actually touch, she could feel the animal heat radiating from his body, scent the faint but distinctive male musk of his skin overlaid by the civilised mantle of soap and freshly laundered clothing. That disturbing awareness overwhelmed her again, making her skin tighten and prickle, her senses become almost painfully acute. A shiver raised goose bumps, increasing the sensitivity of her skin until she could actually feel the rough weave of her linen trousers and vest.

Rachel swallowed on a surge of anguish. She'd been so sure her reaction to Cullen this afternoon had stemmed from her own emotional vulnerability, that the soulless lawyer's letter had been the key. When she next saw him, she'd expected to feel embarrassed by her adolescent overreaction. She hadn't expected the attraction to deepen. A tendril of fear curled in her stomach. She'd barely recovered from Adam. The thought of plunging headlong into another relationship, when she knew she wasn't anywhere near ready to try again, turned the fear into a tight, cold knot of panic.

"Hey, Cul," Dane croaked. "How 'bout that? Grapes."

Rachel straightened and moved back a step, resisting the urge to put even more space between herself and Cullen. Resisting the urge to snatch up her holdall and flat-out run. "You probably won't be able to eat them yet," she said in a voice that was too husky, too abrupt.

As if sensing her uncertainty, the raw panic churning in her stomach, Cullen took the bag of grapes from her without so much as brushing her fingers with his and placed it on Dane's bedside cabinet. "He'll appreciate them in a day or two."

Rachel took another step backward. "If there's anything else I can do…?"

Cullen tracked her retreat, and, if anything, his expression became even grimmer. "You've already helped more than most people would ever dream of doing."

Rachel stiffened. Despite her need to escape, the dismissive quality of Cullen's voice rankled. Evidently he'd pigeonholed her as thoroughly as Cole thought he had—as a soft city creature playing at living in the country. The kind of woman who needed to be protected from anything too rough or earthy. Rachel checked her watch, and relief that she could leave warred with the sudden inexplicable need to prove to Cullen that she wasn't made of spun glass. But the thirty minutes were nearly up, and while she had no qualms about ignoring her brother's dictates, she didn't want a scene in front of a ward full of sick people. "I have to go. Can I come see you again, Dane?"

Dane tried to smile and ended up wincing instead. "You don' have to bring anything nex' time."

"But I will," she said firmly, resisting the urge to glance at Cullen, to challenge his assumptions about her. "What do you need? Books? A magazine? Some more fruit?"

"Maybe a magazine. 'Bout horses."

"Horses?" This time Rachel did glance at Cullen, and even though she was prepared, the cool power of his gaze still sent a minor shockwave rippling through her. "If you don't mind back issues, I can bring you a whole pile. Cole's got an office overflowing with them."

Dane thanked her, but she hardly heard him, her awareness was so attuned to Cullen. With a blank goodbye and an even blanker smile, she retrieved her holdall and turned, only to be confronted by a beefy, older man who'd just come to a halt at the foot of the bed.

"Trask," Cullen said in a rumble so low it lifted all the hairs at her nape.

"Logan," the man snarled in return. "What the hell are you doin' here?"

Rachel felt Cullen's heat all down her back. "Making sure your boy's all right."

"Dane doesn't need your kind of help. He's got his family to look out for him."

Dane's father switched his attention to her. The cold aggression of his stare had Rachel's hand tightening involuntarily on the strap of her bag. Almost without conscious thought she twisted the strap once around her wrist and firmed her grip again.

"Who's she?" Trask snapped.

He didn't speak to Rachel but directed the question at Cullen, as if he disdained women. As if she belonged to Cullen and he answered for her. Rachel's chin shot up, but Cullen moved before she could, brushing past her and planting himself directly in front of her so his broad back obscured most of Dane's father from her view.

"None of your business, Trask," Cullen replied. "Just like the boy in that hospital bed is none of your business."

"She's the one, isn't she? The bitch who's getting my boy into trouble."

"Get out," Cullen said softly. "Before I call the police and lay a complaint of harassment."

"You wouldn't do that," Trask said with a sneer, but he backed off all the same. Weight for weight, there probably wasn't much to choose between them, but Cullen was a good six inches taller, and his body was tightly, sleekly muscled, while Trask wore his weight mostly around his middle.

"Dane may have let you off the hook," Cullen warned coldly, "but don't make the mistake of believing I will."

Trask backed off another step. Rachel could see him clearly now. His gaze kept darting from the door to his son's bed. "I'm entitled to see my own son!"

Cullen shifted again—trying to block her from Trask's view she

realised, as if he didn't want the man to see her or to even remember she'd been here. "Not if you've come to threaten him."

Trask swore loudly enough to alert anyone in the ward who
wasn't already aware of the tense situation. "I'll see you when
you get home," he snarled at Dane, stabbing a finger toward his
son; then he turned on his heel and swaggered out.

Rachel let out a shaky breath as Cullen's hands curled around
her upper arms. She knew what he was seeing, the same white-
faced bewilderment she'd shown him in the alley.

"You all right?" he asked, a disturbing intimacy in the rasp of
his voice, the way he kept holding her.

Just when Rachel wondered if he was going to release her, his
hands tightened, then slid away, as if he'd liked the texture of her
skin and hadn't wanted to let her go.

"I'm fine." She forced a smile.

"Were you going to use that?"

She followed Cullen's wry glance. Her holdall strap was still
looped taut around her wrist, her fingers clenched on the rough
braid, ready to swing the makeshift weapon if she needed to. She
eased her grip. "It worked once before."

The wryness disappeared from Cullen's expression. "It won't
work on him, babe. Trust me. Frank Trask brawls just to fill in
time. He's as poisonous as they come and knows every dirty trick
there is. Promise me you won't ever get yourself in a situation
where you're alone with him."

"I'm not likely to—"

"Promise me."

Rachel shivered at the raw demand in Cullen's voice. She didn't
think he even realised he'd called her "babe." "I promise."

Cullen held her gaze for a moment longer; then, as if realising
how intense they'd got, he gestured toward the chair. "Maybe you
should sit down. There's water on the cabinet if you need a drink."

Rachel checked her watch again. More than thirty minutes had
passed now, and the last thing any of them needed was for her
possessive older brother to come striding down the ward. "I

should go. Cole's waiting. Besides, Dane's the one who needs the attention.''

Beneath all the bruising and bandaging, Dane looked even paler, and he was carefully refraining from meeting her gaze.

''I'll walk you to your car,'' Cullen said curtly.

It was a flat statement, delivered with complete male assurance that his protection was required and she would submit. Rachel almost made a tart comment at the familiarity and the exasperation of it, but in this case she fully agreed. Trask had scared her. There had been a feral coldness to him, a lack of humanity, that had disturbed her more than she liked to admit. Cullen would walk her to her car.

On the way through the ward, he waylaid an orderly, sending him along to sit with Dane in case Trask came back while Cullen was away.

''What will you do when you can't be here?'' she asked as Cullen held a swing door open for her.

''The ward sister's already aware of Dane's situation.'' His mouth twitched in an almost smile as he fell into step beside her. ''If he gets past her again, he's a better man than I am. In any case, I don't think Trask will risk anything in front of witnesses. He prefers to use his fists when he knows he won't have to answer for it.''

Rachel dragged her gaze from Cullen's mouth. It had been a near thing, that twitch at the corners, and she'd wanted to keep watching, certain that he was on the verge of smiling. But then, maybe not, she amended fiercely. All brain function had almost ground to a halt as it was. If he smiled, she would probably turn into a full-fledged idiot.

As they passed the women's surgical ward, Rachel recognised the Reeses, mother and daughter, walking toward them. No doubt visiting Edna Simms and her new hip. Her stomach tightened. She was doing her best to desensitize herself to the gossip that was as much a part of Riverbend as any of the local shops, but the process was unexpectedly difficult. It was unfortunate that the Reeses carried such clout. Isobel Reese was related to half the influential people in town and liked everyone to know it. She'd made a point of informing Rachel that Richard Hayward, the local solicitor Rachel had used when purchasing the salon, was her nephew.

"Murphy's law," she muttered in resignation.

"What *can* go wrong, *always* does," Cullen affirmed in a soft aside, the amusement in his slanting look startling her. She had a sudden vision of him as a wild, go-to-hell boy thumbing his nose at anyone who tried to put him down.

"Mrs. Reese," he drawled, as both ladies were about to sweep past them without any visible signs of recognition, then with an ironic tilt to his straight, dark brows, "Eleanor."

Mrs. Reese replied with stiff correctness, flustered colour forming on her plump cheeks. Eleanor muttered a hello, not bothering to acknowledge Rachel's greeting—her attention was all for Cullen, and she was so busy taking in the view she scarcely noticed that her mother was recovering from Cullen's full-frontal, bad-boy charm attack and was doing a rapid shift into high dudgeon mode.

It wasn't until Isobel Reese hustled her daughter into the women's surgical ward with an almost ludicrous haste that Rachel realised she'd been holding her breath. "Does she always treat you like that?"

"Don't sweat it," Cullen murmured. "Isobel Reese is something of a character around here. Everyone knows what she's like."

"It doesn't bother you? You don't get angry when she's...when she's—"

"Bad-mouthing me all over town?" His eyes still glittered with an unholy amusement. "Why should I?"

Rachel buried the impulse to step even closer to Cullen than she was and jab an annoyed finger at his chest. If he didn't care about what Rachel considered to be outright slander, then why should she? Besides, the last time she'd tangled with Cullen physically, she'd been the one who was sorry. "Maybe I'm too sensitive," she allowed bluntly, "but I don't like gossip. And I don't believe some of the wild stories flying around this town."

Surprise registered in Cullen's eyes, then his expression settled back into what Rachel realised was habitual grimness. "Believe them," he said roughly, taking her elbow in the tingling hot grip of his fingers and urging her toward the foyer as if he were suddenly in a big hurry to get rid of her.

Rachel pulled free, jolted by the simple touch and furious with herself for reacting in any way at all. "I don't believe you killed...a man."

Cullen stopped abruptly. His expression held none of the fragile rapport they'd shared before; he looked big and dangerous, more wild than tamed. And fall-down tired, as if he hadn't slept in days and didn't anticipate getting any sleep in the near future.

"I work for the military," he said in a low, flat voice.

Rachel was certain Cullen had deliberately misunderstood her statement, just as, on a purely instinctual level, she was suddenly certain he hadn't killed his father. "That's different."

"There are degrees of killing?"

"You know what I'm talking about," she said calmly. "If you want to keep the bad-boy image up, you're going to have to stop saving people."

A muscle flexed along his jaw. "I don't foster any kind of image at all. And I may not have done everything they accuse me of, but I sure as hell did some of it. I'll leave you to figure out which crimes I'm guilty of committing."

Rachel drew a breath at the bleak acceptance inherent in his statement. Most people looked for excuses for any wrongdoing. She got the feeling that Cullen judged himself more harshly than anyone. "I don't believe you're capable of committing murder."

Emotion flickered in his eyes, surprise again, and a dark throb of despair quickly cloaked in shades of grey. Then, before she could speak, before she could do something as revealing as reach out and touch him, Cullen spun on his heel and pushed open the main foyer doors.

Cole loped up the steps just as Cullen held the door to allow her through. The door closed behind Rachel with the hushed sound of compressed air. She could feel the tension in Cole's silence, see the fury in his expression.

"Logan," Cole offered grimly.

"Sinclair," Cullen acknowledged.

Her brother eased up another step and laid his hand on her arm, and Rachel kissed any claim on adulthood goodbye. The past twenty-four hours had been too disturbing, too disruptive, for any kind of logical reaction now. If her brother thought the tantrums she used to throw when she was three years old were wild and memorable, then he had a thing or two to learn. She was way more irritated now than she'd ever been at the tender age of three.

"Get your hand off my arm," she warned. "I'm not a juicy bone to be guarded."

"Rachel—"

"Don't talk. If you talk, you'll make it worse. I'll scream." She wasn't actually about to throw a screaming fit, but Cole, like every other member of her all-male family, was as thick as a plank when it came to women. He would believe her.

Cole froze. Rachel stepped away from both men. They watched her warily, then looked at each other. It was a male look of complete understanding, a look that said all women were crazy, and men were crazier to even try to understand them.

"See that taxi over there?" Rachel nodded in the direction of the rank. "I'm going to get in it, and I hope the driver is a woman, or I may just decide to walk."

She strode down the steps. The silence behind her was audible. As she bent to look in the car window, she heard footsteps. Her head shot up, and she glared at Cole. He swivelled abruptly and walked to his car. Rachel knew what he was up to; he was going to follow the taxi if she got in it.

Unable to deny the compulsion, she glanced at Cullen. He was standing at the top of the steps, and his gaze hadn't left her. She'd felt the force of it leveled between her shoulder blades as she'd marched toward the taxi. Even through the encroaching darkness she could discern the slitted heat in his eyes—the same heat that had burned her so badly this afternoon—and her stomach muscles jerked with the impact of all that hot, hungry approval.

The now familiar response shimmered through her, along with

the tightening knot of panic that was equally familiar. It frightened her that she had so little control over her reaction to Cullen, that she was so open and vulnerable to a man who hadn't given her the slightest sign that he wanted even the most superficial of friendships.

Rachel bent down to the taxi window again. "Are you a woman?" she demanded.

A laid back, definitely feminine voice replied, "Some men might dispute that fact, honey, but last time I looked, I was."

Rachel let out a relieved sigh. "Well, good." Opening the front passenger door, she slid into the seat and dumped her holdall on the floor between her feet. "I wasn't going to let you drive me home unless you were a woman," she explained.

"I'm not about to complain about discrimination." The woman chuckled. "I wish I had more customers like you."

Cullen waited until Rachel had left before he started checking the carpark to make sure Trask's rusted-out Ute wasn't still in evidence.

He'd barely been able to trust himself not to go after Rachel while she was still there. When her eyes had flared and she'd stood both him and Cole back on their heels, he'd wanted her with a fierceness, a longing, that stunned him.

And his body had responded with a hair-trigger lack of control that alarmed him. If he could lose control, shed fifteen years of hard-won discipline, because Rachel Sinclair traded a bold look with him, then he could lose control in other areas. The thought made him break out in a cold sweat. He'd never tested his resolve to remain outside of the normal man-woman relationships, mostly because he'd never been tempted. Well, God in heaven, he was tempted now.

It had been bad enough that he'd given in to the compulsion to comfort Rachel after Trask had done his low-life act on the ward. The second he'd wrapped his hands around her bare arms, he'd known he was going to have trouble letting her go. Her skin *had* felt like silk. The texture had instantly reminded him of an exquisite silk velvet he'd once handled in an Asian warehouse his assault team had searched while trying to locate an illegal arms cache. According to one of the guys, the bale of cloth had been French and worth a fortune. But it had been the way the silk had clung and warmed against his skin that had entranced Cullen, not its monetary value.

His eyes closed on a sudden vision of Rachel clinging to him as softly, as sweetly, as the silk velvet had, and he swore beneath his breath at his stubborn arousal. The heavy ache throbbed with a low-level intensity that was both distracting and kept him constantly on edge. He could control it if he kept away from Rachel. If she kept away from him.

The only real question was, how long would it take for her to realise that this town, the whole roughness of country living, just wasn't for her? Not long, he decided, with an odd mixture of fury and relief. Despite that surprising temper and her ideals, she was a city creature, too sensitive and delicate to survive for longer than a few months in Riverbend.

He just hoped he would survive until she left.

Chapter 4

Rachel would have dropped the tray of prime steaks she was ferrying to the barbecue if a strong, tanned hand hadn't reached out and steadied it for her.

She knew who her saviour was without looking, even though she hadn't seen Cullen since the hospital incident over two weeks ago. Ever since she'd arrived at the Hansons' barbecue, which was an annual event and as much a business meeting for the various farmers and stock buyers as a social get-together, she'd been aware of Cullen.

"Thank you," she muttered, jerking at the heel of her shoe, which had gotten wedged between two pavers. She'd been so surprised and distracted to find Cullen all but blocking her route to the trestle tables that she hadn't watched where she was stepping. She should have remembered how uneven the Hansons' patio was. She should have remembered she was back in the country, where dressing for a barbecue meant jeans or cutoffs and sturdy footwear, not a silky dress and barely-there Italian shoes.

Of course the shoe wouldn't budge. Cullen took the tray from her and set it aside, and before she could protest, he went down on his haunches and wrapped one big calloused hand around her ankle as he eased her foot from the shoe. The heat from his palm seared her skin.

He looked up, straight into her eyes, his gaze faintly sardonic, cold and light against his olive skin and the midnight-sleek hair he'd pulled into a ponytail at his nape. "Are you going to take the other one off, City Girl? Or are you going to risk a broken ankle?"

Flushing, Rachel jerked her ankle from his hands. Why hadn't she done that before? She slipped out of her other shoe while Cullen prised the stuck heel from the paver. He straightened, handing both shoes to her.

Rachel accepted them, resisting the urge to snatch them back. "Saved again," she said coolly. "This is getting to be a habit."

His mouth curled at one corner, but she sensed that this time the mockery was directed inward. "Only with you."

"And Dane Trask. I hear he's staying out at your place."

Cullen shrugged, the movement straining the light shirt he was wearing. "He's moved into the old shearers' quarters. It's hardly the Ritz."

She stared down at the shoes she still held in her hand, then, without compunction, tossed them into a corner. "You gave him a break when no one else would."

"He doesn't need another beating, that's for sure."

She looked him squarely in the eye. "You're a nice man, Cullen Logan, no matter how hard you try to convince people otherwise."

"Nice doesn't come into it. I need a hand, and I've had trouble getting casual labour. Dane's going to work harder than he's ever done in his life, first painting the shearers' quarters, then fencing."

"And then the horses."

"And then the horses," he agreed. "He's read every one of those magazines you dropped off to him twice over."

Rachel couldn't help but smile. Dane had been embarrassed when she'd walked onto the ward, but as soon as he'd spied the magazines, he'd lost all awkwardness and talked nonstop about quarter horses and thoroughbreds until she'd had to leave a half hour later. According to Dane, he was more than happy to fix fences as long as he got to work with the prime horseflesh that had been left to run wild on Cullen's land. "Will you be able to keep him off...whatever he was on?"

"It won't be easy. I can't control what's in his mind. He has to do that."

The breeze lifted, blowing hair across Rachel's face and making the skirt of her dress float, then catch in a drifting shimmer of apricot silk as it snagged on Cullen's thigh. His long brown fingers closed on the silk, detaching it from the coarser, rougher denim; then he opened his hand, dropping the silk as if it had burned him.

With a curt nod of dismissal, he returned to his lounging position against a shady pergola and continued his discussion with a local stock buyer.

Rachel retrieved the tray of steaks from the chair Cullen had set it on. Her pulse was too rapid, and after being reasonably content and looking forward to a relaxing evening of socialising, she now felt brittle and tense, overwhelmed by a heightened awareness. The party was suddenly too loud, the laughter too brash, and the sharp scent of the charcoal barbecue ruined what little appetite she'd had. Despite her bewilderment and panic at her response to Cullen, she hadn't realised how badly she'd wanted him to follow up on the attraction she'd been sure was mutual.

He'd just made it as clear as ice he wasn't going to.

"Nice," Russ Jones drawled as he handed Cullen a beer. "Thinking of trying your luck?"

The beer frothed, ice-cold where Cullen tore the tab away. He regarded Russ narrowly. "Not my type," he said, resettling his shoulder against the pergola and watching as Rachel placed the tray on a trestle table near the barbecue.

The wind pressed the fabric of her halter-neck dress against her feminine curves, reminding Cullen of exactly why she wasn't his type. A man could grow addicted to a body like that and forget everything that mattered—including who he was and, most especially, who he could never be.

Russ lifted one blond brow in disbelief. "Mate, you're still breathing, aren't you? Judging from the conversation, every single man here who still has a pulse reckons she's exactly his type. *And* some who aren't single." He took a long pull at his beer and grinned. "Think I might get my hair cut next Friday."

Cullen's jaw tightened. He wished with a sudden impatient savagery that Russ would go back to talking about beef prices and look the hell away from Rachel. That dress was worse than her being naked. She looked lush and fragile at the same time, the kind of combination that drove most men wild with lust—especially country boys who'd been staring at the ass-end of cows all day.

He swallowed a mouthful of beer, willing his muscles to unlock, willing the ache in his groin to dissipate. When he'd arrived tonight, it had taken just one look at Rachel's silky hair and that beautiful stubborn mouth and the expected heat had slammed into him, putting paid to any plans he might have had of smoothing the restless edge off his mood. When he'd wrapped his fingers around her slim ankle, he'd wanted to do a lot more than just take her shoe off.

Somebody started some dance music going. Cullen scanned the gathering of farmers, work hands and their families, all gathered to celebrate the successful end to Riverbend's annual stock sale. Rachel was at the centre of a lively group—most of them men— and one of them was Richard Hayward, a walking, talking advertisement for *Gentleman's Quarterly*. Hayward was senior partner in the law firm that did the lion's share of the legal work for several small country towns, including Riverbend. Just the thought of him putting his elegant, manicured hands on Rachel's pale skin filled Cullen with an irrational fury.

He didn't trust Hayward. Fifteen years ago, the lawyer had offered to represent Cullen free of charge when Cullen had been pulled in for questioning about his father's death. But something about the smoothness of the offer, the casual assertion that Cullen *needed* representation, when he knew damn well there was no case the police could bring against him, had made Cullen instantly wary. The subsequent offer to dispose of Cullen's land for him had grated, too, even though at that point in time—in the cold anonymity of the police interview room—he'd had no desire to retain the land, no desire to do anything but get out of Riverbend and never come back.

Hayward had changed Cullen's mind just by being nice.

Nice hadn't sat easily with the coldness in Hayward's eyes. Especially when he'd never offered anything other than contempt or indifference before.

A woman insinuated herself into the group, and Cullen recognised Hayward's wife, Caroline. She was no less elegant than her husband—her silk blouse and matching pants moulding a body that was as expensively well looked after as her carefully tended face and blond hair.

Cullen's jaw tightened. He wondered what the couple were doing at a simple country gathering like this. The Haywards had moved out of Riverbend years ago, when Richard had taken his father's place in his practice in Fairley, and from all he'd heard, city lights and city vices were more to their taste than a farm barbecue.

As if the intensity of his scrutiny had pulled at her, Caroline Hayward paused in her disinterested perusal of the crowd. Her eyes flew wide when she finally spotted him. She jerked her gaze away just as her husband handed her a glass of some clear liquid. Lifting the glass, she took a long swallow. From the hectic colour that spread across her cheeks, Cullen deduced it wasn't water she was knocking back.

Hayward looked at him then, and something about the bland lack of reaction in his glance sent cold warning snaking down Cullen's spine. Beside him, Russ crumpled his now empty beer can. The sound was preternaturally loud, even against the considerable background noise of the party.

"Here comes the cavalry," Russ murmured.

Cullen barely acknowledged Russ's comment, but a cold smile touched his mouth as Cole Sinclair, six-foot-two of mean, hard muscle, insinuated himself into Hayward's group and slid an arm

around Rachel's waist. The man might as well have hung a Don't
Touch sign around his sister's neck.

It was crazy. Cullen hardly knew her, and she wouldn't tolerate
it, but he'd wanted to do the same thing himself. "They'll have
to get past Cole and maybe even some of those other big brothers
of hers," he commented. "Now I'd *really* like to see that."

"What were you doing with Logan?" Cole asked in clipped
tones as he walked Rachel far enough away from the socialising
groups to ensure privacy.

"It's none of your business," she retorted, "but my shoe got
stuck in a paver. Cullen caught the meat tray before I dropped it
and ruined everybody's dinner."

"It didn't look like the tray he was holding to me."

Rachel stepped away from Cole's hold, perversely wishing she
had her two-inch heels back. Closer to eye-level contact might just
remind Cole she was out of school. "He was giving me a lecture,
not a come-on."

The grim set to Cole's mouth told her that he didn't believe a
word she'd said. "Stay away from him, Sis. You've had enough
grief. Cullen's a hard man. The only thing I've ever heard of him
doing with a woman is taking her to bed."

Rachel didn't bother to disguise her incredulity. "Isn't that a
bit like the pot calling the kettle black? And how can you possibly
know how Cullen treats women? He hasn't been in Riverbend for
years."

Cole had the grace to flush, but his eyes were hard. "Cullen's
old man was a violent drunk, and for a while it looked like Cullen
was headed down the same road. I'm not saying Cullen's the same,
but the history's there. I just don't want you building him up in
your mind. He saved you from being hurt, but he's trained for
combat. Cullen's spent the last fifteen years in the army, most of
that in the Special Air Service. He could probably have killed the
guy who attacked you without breaking sweat."

His words dropped like stones into her mind, blocking out all
the good-natured revelry, the too loud music. For a few seconds

she was back in the alley, smelling the acrid scent of Dane Trask's sweat, along with something else sharper, more disturbing—glue or another potentially lethal substance. Then Cullen had been there. In contrast to the corruption and ruin of the boy, he'd been clean and strong.

And that was what she couldn't forget. Cole could tell her how "wrong" Cullen was, but nothing could change the clarity of that first impression. Rachel might be as dumb as a post where relationships were concerned, but she knew gallantry and honest care when she saw it. When she'd needed it to be, everything about Cullen had been "right."

Rachel talked and danced her way through most of the evening, but she felt as if she were playing a part. No matter how hard she tried, her mind remained attuned to the tall, broad-shouldered figure propping up the pergola beside another shorter man. She knew exactly when Cullen filled his plate with steak and salad, and that he preferred plain rolls to garlic bread, ice-cold beer to hard spirits, and not too much of it.

He spoke, he socialised, but there was an aloofness to him that repelled any but the most determined overtures. In such a physically powerful and attractive male, his intense aloneness was riveting. If he'd so much as smiled, women would have been all over him.

Rachel tossed the paper plate with her barely touched meal into one of the conveniently placed rubbish sacks, and when she glanced up, she found herself staring at Cullen's profile. The now familiar jolt that just seeing him sent through her was replaced by an inexplicable wave of hurt. There's no reason to feel like this, she told herself fiercely. You don't know him. And he's made it plain he doesn't want to know you. Just when she was about to look away, Cullen turned his head. His eyes locked with hers. The movement and the glance were precise and deliberate. He'd been aware that she'd been watching him, and this was his way of telling her so.

Rachel met his challenge with one of her own. He held her gaze, then inclined his head, granting her the minimum of courtesy before dismissing her. As snubs went, it was devastating. All the overheated blood drained from beneath her skin as swiftly as summer rain leaching through cracked, drought-stricken soil. If Rachel had one skill in life, it was communicating with people. It was the reason she enjoyed hairdressing, the reason she loved the whole concept of the family she'd never fully been a part of, and why she needed so much to put roots down in the hometown she'd never been given a chance to belong in. This man had blocked her as effectively as if she'd run into a solid wall.

And not glass this time. Granite.

Rachel turned back to the group of people she'd been eating with and plastered a smile on her face. It hurt that Cullen kept shutting her out. She'd tried to convince herself that she was simply suffering from the throes of a strong physical attraction. But she knew it was more than that, knew the single-minded intensity of her nature. Somehow, despite her wariness, Cullen had reached past her defences. Whatever was happening to her was out of control, and more dangerous, more compelling, than mere attraction.

Rachel danced some more, talked with a woman who ran a local craft cooperative, and told herself she'd done enough. Rachel Sinclair had had the time of her life. No one would miss her if she walked off and grabbed herself some much needed solitude.

The Hanson property was big, with well set out buildings, manicured lawns and gardens, and a view of the high country they all shared. Rounding a corner, she came to an abrupt halt. Cullen was leaning against a wooden railing, looking out over the newly cut hay paddocks, which stretched away like bleached, rough-cut velvet beneath an almost full moon.

A little of the fighting spirit she'd once taken for granted welled up inside her, and she lifted her chin against the shadows that made his face look even darker, more dangerous, than it usually was. "Getting ready to do a little howling?"

He made a soft sound that might almost have been a laugh. But she didn't believe that for a minute. She'd never seen Cullen smile; a laugh was beyond imagining.

"You trying to get me run out of town?" he asked in a low voice. "The locals already give me a wide berth."

She strolled closer, wondering if he could see through her pretence of casualness to the uncertainty that racked her. But his eyes revealed nothing; they still looked about as cold and giving as tempered steel. She set her hands on the top rail of the wood fence, the rough grain abrasive against her chronically sensitive hairdresser's palms. "Maybe if you smiled once in a while they might smile back."

"I'm not much on smiling."

"Or dancing."

"You did enough for both of us."

The way he coupled them together in the same sentence, his voice low and raspy, sent waves of heat through her. They could be lovers discussing the party, secure in the knowledge that when they lay down at night it was only with each other. Her fingers tightened convulsively on the fence, and she felt the sharp sting of a splinter sliding into her flesh. "I would have liked to have danced with you."

"Didn't Cole read you the riot act?"

Cullen hadn't even bothered to look at her, to acknowledge the enormous risk she'd taken in exposing her desire to dance with him. And for Rachel it was an unheard of exposure. She'd been brought up to accept her role as passive in the male-female relationship. Men chased; women waited. But suddenly that passivity infuriated her. It hadn't brought her the kind of marriage she'd needed, and it hadn't allowed her to keep her husband.

With a deliberate movement she withdrew her hands from the fence and turned to face him, curling her fingers in on the small pain invading her palm, using the needle-sharp sting to remind her of everything she'd lost and the reasons why. "Cole's my brother, not my keeper."

"But he warned you off."

"Cole warns me not to burn my toast," she said with raw exasperation. "I don't see the point of this—"

She stopped abruptly as his gaze pierced her. Impatience and restless energy vibrated from him, along with something else, a tension that was completely male. "I'm not a charity case, Miss Sinclair. I came to the barbecue to conduct business, and because these are my neighbours and I'd like their goodwill while I knock my property into shape. If I want a woman, I can get one."

"And if I want a man, I can get one on *my* own." She paused. "For a time, anyway."

He let out a slow breath. "I'm trying to save us both some strife. You don't know what you're getting into."

She tilted her head, challenging him. "I was only talking about dancing. This doesn't mean we're engaged."

His very stillness sent a shiver through her. She was staring into bright moonlight, while his face was eclipsed by shadow, and she was achingly aware of how alone they were.

He shifted, and his shadow slipped over her, casting her into a darkness that held a sudden suffocating intimacy. His nearness made her acutely aware of his solid muscularity, the sheer density and power of his male body.

"I wouldn't want to stop at a dance."

The simple statement sent a jolt of pure feminine fear down her spine, but it wasn't enough to make her back off, because a dizzying elation came with it, too. "What makes you think I'd allow you anything more?"

For a moment she thought he was going to touch her; then he turned back to the undulating fields, back to the velvet ebb and flow of the breeze. "Because you'd want it, too."

"You don't have the first clue what I want," she returned quietly. She wanted to yell at him, to release the fierceness rising inside her, the terrible aching need to love and be loved. The need for a man who would see only her, want only her. It was a futile desire, but she was riding that emotional roller coaster again, and she'd lost her perspective the same way she'd lost her husband. Fast.

"I know what you *don't* need," he said with a destroying gentleness, "and that's a few sweaty hours between the sheets with a man who can't give you anything more than that."

Her heart almost stopped at the image of Cullen's muscled body entwined with hers in dampness and tangled sheets. The image was crude and utterly sexual, brutally ripping away any possibility of softness or tenderness. "You're going to a lot of trouble to scare me off."

"I'm no Prince Charming," he admitted flatly. "I'm big and hard, and so hungry it feels like I haven't had a woman in years. I wouldn't court you, Rachel, I'd just take you."

The shock of his words slapped coldly at her, but something about his body language, the careful distance he kept from her, his refusal to let her see his facial expression, made her stand her ground. "I'd have some say about that. I don't believe for one minute that you treat women like objects."

The silence closed in around them; the music and laughter of the barbecue seemed to lull and recede, making his voice sound deeper, harsher, on the still night air.

"You're right," he admitted. "I don't." He turned so the moonlight skimmed his face, so she could see the compassion softening the brooding line of his mouth, stealing the glitter from his eyes. "But I also don't intend to take the daughter of a neighbour and family I respect just to relieve my physical needs. And I especially don't want a woman who thinks she can change me."

Rachel stiffened at the tender cruelty of his brush-off.

Damn him, he was feeling sorry for her.

Nothing could have made her more furious. Not his calm indifference, not the knowledge that somehow he'd seen right through her, seen her desire to put things right for him, to change the mystifyingly strong opinion of the town and somehow melt all the hard reserve he used to distance himself from people. From her. "You could almost convince me you're genuine if you weren't trying so hard to put me off."

And then she did what she'd promised herself she wouldn't. She reached up and touched the satin-rough line of his jaw.

His fingers closed on hers, calloused and hard as he wrenched her hand away on a soft, succinct curse that should have shocked her. She wasn't shocked—his touch burned her as she knew it would, sealing them together with a jolt of pure sexual energy that turned the coldness in his gaze to hot metal. Cullen was all the things he'd said he was, and he could probably hurt her very badly indeed, but the one thing he wasn't was indifferent.

She winced as the splinter dug deeper into her flesh.

"What is it?" Cullen rasped.

Without waiting for her reply, he turned her hand over in his grip and unfurled her fingers, letting the cold light of the moon wash across her palm. The splinter was long and thin, jutting darkly from the mound of flesh below her thumb. Just seeing how big it was made the wound sting even worse.

Cullen cupped her hand with both of his and unexpectedly lifted her palm to his mouth. His teeth flashed whitely as they closed over the splinter and tugged it from her flesh. He turned his head, jaw rasping against her skin, and spat the splinter out. Then, instead of letting her go, he bent his head, and his mouth closed around the small wound. His teeth pressed into her soft flesh as he sucked out any remaining debris; his tongue laved her skin in a hot, wet caress that rippled through her. She couldn't move, could barely breathe. Her whole world had shrunk to the circumference of his mouth and the heat radiating from her palm.

"Damn," he said, releasing her hand, then reaching out to touch her hair. "This isn't working."

She drew a shuddering breath at the light stroke of his fingers as he sifted them through an errant tendril. "If you're talking about your plan to scare me off, then I'd say it's doing the exact opposite."

His mouth curved into a wry smile, and Rachel caught her breath. She'd been right in thinking he would be sinful if he smiled. Sinful and bad, good enough to eat, and dangerously, wildly sexy.

"Baby, I may not scare you, but you sure as hell scare me."

And then he bent his head, blocking out the moon. His hand

curved around her nape, his palm rough against her skin, holding her still as his mouth brushed hers. His lips were firm and unexpectedly tender. She'd braced herself for a hard, plundering, ravaging assault, but the sweetness of his caress was butterfly-soft and so beguiling that she ached for him to deepen the pressure. Her hands lifted and settled on the incredible warmth of his chest as she parted her lips and tilted her head to grant him easier access. She was as guilty of misjudging Cullen as everyone else was—he looked every inch an outlaw, but he was kissing her like an angel. A fallen, dangerously beautiful angel.

Cullen groaned when Rachel opened her mouth for him. He hadn't expected that. But then, nothing about Rachel Sinclair was predictable. He should have run the second she stepped up to the fence. Come to that, he should have left the party as soon as he saw her arrive. But he hadn't. He'd stayed, and he'd ended up touching her. Worse, he'd let Russ fill his ear with the kind of small-town gossip he should know better than to listen to. He hadn't wanted to know about Rachel's failed marriage, or that her mother had died when she was a baby and her father had been too sunk in grief to hold his daughter. He definitely hadn't wanted to know that when Sinclair had finally surfaced from mourning, he'd been at a loss for how to deal with the girl child who looked so much like his too fragile second wife, beyond paying for other people to care for her.

And most of all, Cullen hadn't wanted to hear about how Rachel had been sent away to school when she was still so small she should have been cuddled up on her mother's lap. He didn't want the image of Rachel, desperate and alone, haunting him. He had enough of his own ghosts and demons.

Her tongue touched his tentatively, almost shyly, and Cullen groaned. Damn. Who was he trying to kid? He'd come to the barbecue because he wanted this. Because watching her from a distance was better than nothing. And suddenly he was more concerned with cradling her close, soothing and stroking her with his hands, than making her believe how impossible it was that they could ever be together.

His tongue mated gently with hers, and she sighed, melting against him. Her arms crept around his neck, fingers drifting through his hair, sliding it free from the leather thong that bound it, then knotting her fingers in it to pull him closer.

Cullen shuddered with pure pleasure at the insistent tugging sinking his own fingers deeper into her hair, coaxing her tongue farther into his mouth, deepening the kiss with every second that passed, until they were welded together so tightly that her heartbeat shivered through him.

His hand drifted over the warm, silky skin of her back, grazed her zipper and, before he could think, eased it down so he could trace the hollow at the base of her spine and the lacy line of panties that were just as flimsy, just as silken, as her dress. Cullen shuddered again as Rachel continued to pet him as if he were a big muscular cat, her fingers flexing, stroking, raking through his hair. He wanted to do the same to her, and more. He wanted to push all the silk aside and slip his hand lower, test the sweet moisture he knew he would find....

Rachel made a low sound in her throat and moved, fitting herself more closely against him. She wasn't wearing a bra, and just the thought of releasing the tie behind her neck, then taking the weight of her breasts in his hands, almost tipped him over the edge. He had to remember where they were, who she was....

Who he wasn't.

When he took her it was going to be long and slow, not a rushed, hurried fumble in somebody else's backyard. The thought hammered through him, twisted in his gut, and gave him the needed discipline to slide her zip up and ease her away. "Rachel," he said hoarsely. "We've got to stop."

She blinked at him, eyes clouded and soft, hair tangled, mouth so sensually swollen that a fierce growl of male possession started deep in his throat.

Cullen pulled in a breath, fighting the hunger that pulsed through him as he deliberately put space between them. He wanted her mouth again. He wanted the cool glide of her hands on his skin, her moon-pale body and silky dark hair wrapped around him—but the tight, hard rise of his flesh was warning enough. It was almost a relief to hear Cole's voice, edged with a cold, unmistakeable menace.

"It's just as well you did that, Logan, because if you hadn't, I would have taken you apart."

Rachel stepped out of Cullen's shadow, placing herself firmly in bright moonlight. "Back off, Cole," she declared. "Cullen wasn't doing a thing except turning me down."

She moved again, sideways this time, placing herself directly between him and Cole. Cullen clenched his jaw against a powerful surge of emotion. He wouldn't have believed it if he wasn't seeing it with his own eyes. Rachel was protecting him from her brother.

Cullen stepped out from behind her pale, drifting dress and wondered how he'd got himself into a situation where a woman was ready to do battle for *him*. "What Rachel means is that we just got a little carried away by the moonlight," he stated with cool deliberation. "Nothing more. I was just leaving."

Cole met his gaze for a long moment, then nodded curtly. He shot Rachel an uncompromising look. "Get your bag. We're leaving, too."

Rachel didn't respond to her brother's order; she was too busy watching Cullen, her jaw set stubbornly, revealing that the fierceness she'd displayed at the hospital wasn't just a flash in the pan. She was used to fighting with her brother—hell, with anyone she took a fancy to square up to.

"I'll leave when I'm ready."

Cullen took another step away, deliberately distancing himself from her. It was unexpectedly difficult to do. The instinct to catch her around the waist and move her behind him so he could take care of big brother himself was so strong that every muscle in his body was tensed against a retreat. "Cole's right. You should go."

"Don't bother trying to tell me what to do," she said with dangerous softness. "It's bad enough I have to put up with him!" She stabbed an accusing finger in Cole's general direction, not taking her gaze off Cullen for a second.

The passionate fury in every line of her body made Cullen go still. The sudden vision of Rachel locked beneath him, her leg wrapped around his waist, that wild gaze linked passionately with his as he pushed himself inside her, flooded his loins with a throbbing, painful heat. A groan rolled through him, and he broke out in a sweat. Sweet hell.

He wanted her. Here. Now.

And God help them both, but she wanted him, too.

Cullen unclenched his jaw by slow degrees, but he couldn't do a thing about the guttural roughness of his voice. "Listen to your brother, he knows what he's talking about."

"Cullen…" Rachel reached out to him, but he'd gone, turned on his heel and strode away, leaving her shattered and confused, achingly bereft and more than a little angry at Cole. "You went too far," she declared in a voice that trembled with temper. "Don't interfere again, Cole."

"I'll interfere if I have to," Cole said stubbornly. "You've been hurt enough, and getting involved with a renegade like Cullen isn't going to improve your odds of that happy-ever-after marriage you claim you're looking for."

Cullen reached his truck and leaned against it, taking several deep breaths. He was shaking with pure, burning need.

And other emotions that were too complicated to unravel.

If he had any sense at all, he would head back to Auckland for the weekend. Three hours of driving and he could find the kind of woman who wanted nothing more than satisfaction on a physical level and wouldn't demand anything he wasn't prepared to give. But the thought filled him with distaste. There was only one pair of legs he wanted coiled around his waist, only one pale-silk body twisting beneath his.

His teeth ground together. And he couldn't take her. He wouldn't. Having sex with Rachel Sinclair would destroy her and ruin him. And sex was all he could ever offer a woman. He'd found out who he was fifteen years ago, and that person couldn't risk intimacy on any but the shallowest level.

Once the farm and his half-wild stock were fit for sale, he would sell up and return to barracks and his military career. He couldn't conceive of staying in Riverbend any longer than it took to cut every tie he'd ever had with the place.

Having any kind of relationship at all with the town's equivalent of a princess wasn't going to happen.

Chapter 5

Rachel checked her watch as the last customer finally walked out the door into the perfect Saturday afternoon weather. "I'm out of here," she muttered to herself, snatching up the letter that had arrived in the post that morning and locking the salon with relief.

For the past month she'd spent every spare moment painting the flat above the salon and hanging wallpaper, working until her shoulder and arm muscles ached and her eyes burned with tiredness. The decorating wasn't so urgent that she had to exhaust herself getting it done, but she'd needed the hard work, the satisfaction of bringing order to her life, to balance out the unexpected chaos of her emotions. And most of all she needed a place of her own. The next big effort would be shifting in the furniture she'd stored out at the farm. That was for tomorrow. What was left of today was for her, to fill some of the empty spaces inside her with a little sunshine. When she was good and relaxed she would read the letter, which was from Sandy—her ex-boss—and catch up on all the gossip about her friends and Sandy's large, rambunctious family.

She drove out to the farm as fast as her city thoroughbred of a car could take the dusty, winding back road, thinking for the hundredth time that she would have to switch to a model that didn't mind bucking from one pothole to the next. Maybe she would get a four-wheel drive. It would be part of her general toughening-up campaign. Since the Hansons' party she'd vowed to see sense. The final dissolution of her marriage had upset her more than she'd bargained for. She'd been on some kind of crazy emotional seesaw, and Cullen had somehow triggered her to tilt in the one direction she didn't want to go.

Into the arms of another man who didn't want her.

Cole came toward her as she strode purposefully across the lawn to the stables, a duffel bag crammed with her towel, a cold drink and the letter slung over her shoulder. She already had her swimsuit on beneath her shirt and denim cutoffs.

"Swimming at the water hole again?" He shook his head. "Why don't you just use the pool?"

"I can swim in the pool any time. I like the water hole because it's so peaceful."

Cole followed her into the tack room. She could feel his scrutiny like a laser playing over her features.

"You're having trouble sleeping again," he accused. "Maybe you should give the riding a miss today."

Rachel grabbed a bridle, looped it over her shoulder, then pulled her saddle down, bracing herself against its weight. She wasn't sure whether Cole's concern was attributable to the shadows beneath her eyes or her own rusty riding skills. She didn't really care. She was living in the country now, and she was going riding. "I'll sleep better if I get some exercise and sunshine."

He eyed her warily. "At least let me carry the saddle."

"It's not heavy." Rachel walked past him and out into the sunlight.

Cole continued to shadow her. "I suppose you could take Jessie, but she's not going to be too impressed."

Rachel gave him an amused look. "She never is."

She saddled and mounted the sleepy mare, then clicked her

tongue, urging Jessie to greater speed as they made their stately way through the gate and down the tree-shaded farm road, then onto the track that led to the water hole. The dusty bay stock horse flicked an ear. Her ambling gait didn't alter.

"Damn," Rachel muttered resignedly. She'd squeezed with her legs until they ached almost as much as her rear, but the horse knew she had a rank amateur on her back and refused to lift her pace beyond a plod. And Rachel didn't have the heart to kick her. In truth, she felt guilty taking Jessie out. The only time she ever saw the old mare move voluntarily was to put more food in her mouth or to escape capture.

Cullen guided the big stock horse through the trees with his thighs, shrugging out of his shirt as he went. The sun beat through the sparse branches arching overhead, sending bands of heat sliding like hot chains across his sweaty skin.

A sudden sense of being home assailed him, a rightness in the muscular horse between his legs, the rugged, challenging country he was riding through, and the sheer physical effort it took to bend the wildness around him to his will.

His jaw tightened against the renegade emotion. The stock horse, Mac, had belonged to wily old Alistair Carson—another casualty of the rough demands of Logan land. Alistair—who'd owned a small adjoining farm—had run Cullen's stock along with his own. The brutal workload, along with the old man's stubborn persistence, had finally killed him.

The only way Cullen could make a success of such a big, diverse spread was if he committed himself to the challenge. To do that, he would have to stay.

Cullen urged Mac on at a faster pace. He smelled the river before he saw it; the resinous scents of bush and fresh water were strong in the brassy stillness of the afternoon. The water level had dropped with the dry, leaving the banks cracked and eroded where the cattle came down to drink. Debris from last winter's floods was snagged high, some of it caught on low tree branches—a stark reminder of how quickly and how high the water could rise. Despite Mac's objections, Cullen bypassed the first tributary, heading lower down the gully toward the main watercourse and its deep, green swimming hole. After allowing the horse to drink, Cullen left him amiably munching the spindly clumps of grass that grew beneath the feathery manuka and kanuka trees, and climbed down the bank before shedding his boots, dusty denims and finally his battered leather Akubra hat.

Impatiently, he drove his fingers through his damp hair. The cool river current would slide over his skin, washing away the sweat and dirt, and maybe, just maybe, it would wash away some of the impossible heat that had taken up permanent residence in his loins.

But he wasn't counting on it. Cold showers hadn't made a difference. And he doubted the lukewarm river water would succeed where his ice-cold bore water had failed so miserably.

His hands locked into tight fists as he waded into the water, deeper, then deeper still. The skimming current tugged at him, stroking his skin, making his muscles harden with a sudden, reckless need, a wildness he usually kept firmly under control. Flinging his head back, he gazed up at the wide, endless sky, a low curse grating from between his tightly clenched teeth. The days when he'd taken what he wanted and damned the cost were gone. He'd paid for that wild streak more times than he cared to count. Paid for it, and brought it under control.

And he wasn't about to let it rule him now.

Rachel stared at the man swimming naked in the river.

If she had a shred of decency, she would go quietly back to where she'd tied Jessie, ease her sore backside into the saddle and ride away. The trouble was, whenever Cullen walked into the picture, she lost any of the ladylike graces her very correct and formal guardian, Aunt Rose, had instilled in her.

He surged out of the water at the far side of the swimming hole. Hair streamed over his broad shoulders; sheets of water slid off his heavily muscled back and ran in a rivulet down the long, deep indentation of his spine to his tight, muscular buttocks and powerful thighs. The sun struck, harsh and merciless, rippling like fire over his sleek, coppery skin. In the cool green setting Cullen burned with a primitive barbarism that made her mouth go dry.

Heat speared through her—part mortification that she was actually spying on Cullen, and part the alien, disturbing excitement that frightened her with its intensity. Abruptly she relived the kiss at the Hansons' barbecue, the way he'd settled his mouth against hers and eased her against his long, hard body—the possessive stroke of his hand on her back. He'd been fully aroused and had made no effort to hide it. The strength and heat of his arousal pressing against her had made her go weak. Closing her eyes briefly in an attempt to shut out the too vivid images, she grabbed for a handhold and began pulling herself up the bank. She still couldn't believe the way she'd thrown herself at him.

Her foot slipped, dislodging a small avalanche of pebbles, and she went down painfully onto her knees. Berating herself, she scrambled back into the stifling dusty confines of the manuka scrub. Damn, damn, damn. Her heart was pounding, and her skin was so clammy her clothes stuck to her where they touched.

Backtracking with feverish haste to where she'd left Jessie, Rachel stuffed her towel into her duffel bag and searched frantically for something to use as a mounting block. At a pinch, she *could* haul herself on the tired creature's back. It didn't help that she was panicking, that she was certain Cullen would know someone was here, and that she would die of embarrassment if he found her.

A trickle of sweat ran down her spine as she jerked the duffel closed. Rachel shrugged, irritably trying to unstick the back of her bathing suit from her spine. It was so still and quiet. Except for those annoying cicadas. The relentless chirruping sawed at her nerves, stretched them tight.

A harsh, ripping sound had her spinning around, breath suspended in her throat. An irridescent gleam of peacock blue and glossy black with a flash of white shot past her. A bird. She let her breath out. A native tui. An array of sonic beeps sounded from high in the canopy above her head, followed by squawking and finally a series of loud, glottal clicks. The sheer indignant volume of the bird had her smiling in relief. With the birds and cicadas making such a racket, maybe Cullen hadn't heard her after all.

But if she tried to ride out of here now, he would hear her for certain.

Pulling in a calming breath, she forced herself to sit and wait. With fingers that shook annoyingly, she fumbled the duffel open and searched out her letter. No way was she running like some frightened virgin out of a fifties melodrama. She would read Sandy's news, and by the time she got through the usual marathon of lively gossip, Cullen would have finished his swim and gone.

Curiously, there was only one sheet, which enclosed a smaller, formal, cream envelope. The envelope slipped to the ground as Rachel concentrated on the letter, gripped by a sudden apprehension. For once Sandy was to the point. Adam had asked her to write and enclose his letter and the invitation in the hope that this way it would cause her the least upset.

Rachel's hand tightened on Sandy's trademark, extra thin onionskin, crumpling the delicate paper. Now that the divorce was final, her ex-husband was inviting her to his wedding. Vaguely, she heard the tui scolding overhead, brushed absently at a sand fly, and felt perspiration gather and trickle between her breasts. Adam had tried to talk to her several times over the past few months, but Rachel hadn't let him, hadn't been able to bear having a conversation about his plans for the future. He'd written, but she'd thrown the letters away unopened. But it wasn't as if she hadn't expected this. It wasn't as if she didn't *know*—

A snapping sound had her jumping to her feet. The letter fluttered to the ground.

Cullen was leaning against a tree about six feet away, a broken stick held between his hands. He'd pulled on worn tight denims and scuffed riding boots, but moisture still slicked his shoulders and dampened the dark pelt of hair shadowing his chest.

"You're trespassing," she said, her voice unexpectedly harsh.

He tossed the twig away. "You're on my land."

Rachel wiped her palms down the side seams of her cutoffs. He followed the movement, then let his gaze slide the length of her legs and back up again. There was an edgy glitter in his eyes that made her stomach tighten.

"I've been swimming here all my life. There's no way *I'm* trespassing."

He shrugged. "This has always been Logan land. It's just that my *neighbours* have never been too particular about observing the boundaries."

"Then maybe you should fence the boundary."

"And make the Sinclairs and the Hansons pay for what they've been taking for free all these years? Now there's a thought."

Her chin came up. "My family doesn't need to take anything. I'm sure that if Cole was aware of the boundary he would be more than happy to pay for the right to water his stock here."

"Cole knows. So does Hanson."

"So why don't they—"

"Don't sweat it," he growled softly. "If I was that concerned about my neighbours using water when there's more here than I'll ever need, I'd be knocking on their doors with a contract in my hand."

Rachel's mouth settled into a stubborn line. Cullen wasn't saying it, but it was clear this was just another example of the general prejudice against him, and this time her own family was involved. Well, despite his lack of interest, she wasn't going to let it go. As soon as she got back, she was going to have a piece of Cole.

Cullen straightened from his lounging position, his expression back to the hard, impenetrable mask he usually wore. "You look hot. I'll leave you alone so you can have your swim. I presume that's what you came for?"

Rachel's eyes locked guiltily with his. The silence drew tighter, relieved only by a faint breeze rattling through dessicated trees. The forgotten letter flipped over on the ground; she snatched for it, but it skated along, ending up snagged on Cullen's boot. He retrieved it, then gathered up the cream envelope, which still lay where she'd let it fall. He handed the mail back to her with the discreetly embossed words *Wedding Invitation* right side up.

"Anyone I know?"

Her fingers closed on the invitation. "I don't believe you ever met my husband."

Before he could answer, before that rock-hard impassivity could change to something as damning as compassion, she grabbed her duffel, spun on her heel and scrambled with as much dignity as she could muster down to the river. When she was alone she sat on the bank, the invitation with its letter scrunched in one hand, staring at the water for long minutes. Finally she let out a breath and felt an inner tightness relax. Sighing, she tossed the scraps of expensive paper into the flowing water and watched them float away.

She wouldn't go to that wedding and watch her ex-husband marry someone else. But she didn't feel as devastated as she'd thought she would. She wasn't exactly over the moon about Adam's impending nuptials, of course. Maybe ten years from now she could think of Adam and his wife-to-be with relaxed civility. But she was only human, and right now her only regret in throwing the invitation and letter away was that she was littering the stream.

The soothing sounds of the river closed around her. She stared determinedly at the water until she was certain Cullen had gone. When she couldn't stand the inactivity for a second longer, Rachel peeled off her shirt and shorts and dropped them onto the mossy bank, revealing the old cream one-piece swimsuit she wore beneath. It seemed somehow symbolic and cleansing to dive into the deep green centre of the pool. But when she surfaced and pulled herself up onto the diving rock on the opposite side, Cullen was there, still minus his shirt, sitting atop a big, black stock horse with all the smooth, easy grace of the natural horseman.

Anger at his calm arrogance overcame her instant awareness that once again he'd caught her at a disadvantage. "Like what you see?" she demanded coolly.

His head came up, eyes narrowed and intense. "I'm male."

"Well, hallelujah for that!"

"And what about you? Did you like what you saw?"

Rachel gritted her teeth. So, he did know she'd watched him. "I only saw half."

"You haven't answered my question."

Her own eyes narrowed at his persistence. She was too unsettled to do anything other than counter his bluntness with bluntness of her own. "I couldn't comment honestly until I'd seen all of it."

The horse jibbed as if Cullen had suddenly tightened his hands on the reins. He brought the animal under control, his shoulders flexing and glistening with the movement. "Is that an invitation or a challenge?"

"Take it whichever way you like."

The small silence that followed had all the hairs at her nape lifting and her skin quivering with every brush of the breeze, every trailing droplet of water. Cullen's chest rose as if he'd just filled his lungs to capacity, but when he spoke his voice was completely devoid of inflection.

"Feel free to swim here any time you like. Have you got another swimsuit besides that one?"

Her jaw loosened. "Several. Why?"

"Because when it's wet, it's the same colour as your skin."

It wasn't what she'd expected to hear. The suit was an old one she'd left behind in her room and, apart from the high-cut legs, was very modest. She'd never dreamed the fabric had become so thin and faded that it had become transparent.

"I can see everything," he growled. "You might as well be naked."

Wheeling his horse, he urged the big black animal up the bank. It took the steep grade with all the agile grace of a big cat before disappearing from sight.

Exit stage right, she thought shakily, staring down at the dark peaks of her breasts, easily visible through the light material of her suit, then farther down to the shadow at the apex of her legs. She wrapped her arms around her middle, embarrassment washing through her, along with another emotion, one not easily admitted to.

He didn't want her.

She'd been standing almost naked in front of him, and he still wasn't tempted. His rejection somehow seared more deeply than the wedding invitation she'd just disposed of. Sinking down onto the rock, Rachel let her head drop onto her drawn up knees. She'd already learned that her feminine assets were ordinary at best. They hadn't been enough to hold Adam. And compared to the sheer magnetism of Cullen, Adam seemed as tame and ordinary as a sleepy house cat next to a hungry Bengal tiger.

Cullen got far enough away from the river that the scents of damp earth and water had been replaced by dry vegetation and dusty cattle. His hands curled on the reins, drawing the horse to a standstill. Mac snorted, his neck flexing against the reins.

Cullen couldn't leave her.

The revelation unfolded slowly within him, locking up his muscles until the horse jigged forward at the unintentional pressure of his thighs. Cullen curbed the sudden movement with the reins, making the gelding toss his head, then peer around at him with an enquiring look.

"Damn," Cullen said softly, running a reassuring hand along the satiny line of Mac's neck and staring at the distant, brooding hills, then closer in, at the flood-damaged bridge he was supposed to be checking over preparatory to getting an engineer in. Always before he'd been able to concentrate on whatever goal he assigned himself, to control his emotions—to not allow this kind of intimacy to develop.

Rachel's personal life was none of his business.

Her ex-husband was a damned fool, and that was also none of his business.

He swore in the roughly eloquent patois of one of the several different languages he'd learned in countries that were just as harsh and damned as the syllables that leaped from his tongue. Then he wheeled Mac and sent him at a fast easy-moving lope back to the shady grove they'd just vacated.

A faint sound had Rachel scrambling to her feet as Cullen appeared, minus his intimidatingly large horse. He came down the bank and onto the rock shelf with the smooth animal grace that was as natural to him as breathing.

Crossing her arms over her breasts, she watched him warily. "I thought you were leaving?"

"I meant to leave. I guess I'm not as good at it as I should be."

Rachel swallowed hard on the hysterical desire to laugh. The flippant remark, "I wouldn't take any bets on that, buddy," trembled on the tip of her tongue, but instead she found herself saying, "So, why did you come back? Maybe you wanted to offer the poor abandoned wife—or should I say ex-wife?" she amended, "a consolation prize?"

"You still love him."

For a moment she thought she'd misheard his flat statement. His sheer effrontery forced an answer from her. "I don't know what I feel for Adam," she admitted, surprising herself. "He wants to be friends."

"And you weren't made to be any man's friend. With you, it's all or nothing."

Rachel stared through the harsh sunlight into his eyes, into a molten darkness that threatened to pull her in. She must have made a small sound. She registered it vaguely, just as she registered the smooth, purposeful way he moved toward her. His hands settled on her shoulders, rough-textured, warm, the touch so featherlight it made her shake. The breath left her on a jerky sigh, half delight, half a shimmering tensile awareness of danger, as she stepped up against the muscular strength of his body. But instead of the kiss she expected, he wrapped his arms all the way around her and pulled her in close.

His breath left him on a low vibrating rumble, his chin came to rest on the top of her head, and he pressed her face into the pad of muscle at the curve of his shoulder. Rachel closed her eyes briefly against the wonder of his gesture, the incredible heat surrounding her, and something only just realised—a quality that had been there all along with Cullen, but which she'd never fully defined—a sense of rightness. Of finally coming home. The thought drifted, settled, but she was too tired, too momentarily content, to examine the curious dichotomy—that there was nothing in the least secure or domesticated about the man who was holding her with such care.

"Didn't he get to know you at all?" Cullen mused in a voice that was little more than a rough purr. "You're so fierce and wild beneath that ladylike exterior. If you were my wife and I left you for another woman, I'd spend the rest of my life wearing a flak jacket and watching my back."

"Adam's not like that," she mumbled, a strange, hesitant joy filling her at the teasing note in his voice. She tried to picture Adam. His hair was brown, he was a little above medium height, leanly muscled, assured and good-looking in a completely urban way. "He runs a successful advertising agency and prides himself on not having enemies. It would never occur to him that anyone *wouldn't* like him."

"I don't like him," Cullen murmured, stroking his chin across her hair as if he liked the feel of her against his skin. "Want me to go see him for you?"

"And do what?" She found herself smiling. "Tell him he has to marry me again?"

That surprised a low sound of amusement from Cullen. "Hell, no," he drawled softly. "I'd give him a sympathy card, because one day he's going to realise what a mistake he made in letting you go. But it's not all bad news, because he was all wrong for you anyway."

Rachel breathed in the river-scented musk of his skin, the unnerving delight of being so close to him. "So, tell me," she found herself asking while she braced herself for his answer, "who's right?"

He didn't answer for a long time, just continued to hold her, and she couldn't help but be aware that his hug wasn't purely comfort—she could feel the firm male pressure of him against her belly. He was fully aroused, although he seemed prepared to ignore that fact.

"Not me," he said finally.

Pain sliced through her at the simple denial. Rachel knew that what they shared was little more than an abortive series of encounters, each one of which Cullen had been determined to walk away from without furthering their acquaintance. But even knowing that, and despite every attempt to armour herself against the attraction, Rachel hadn't been able to stem her feelings. She felt an attachment, a bond with Cullen, that went beyond logic or sensibility. When she was with him she felt more alive, more vital, more *female,* than she ever had before.

With an effort of will she freed herself from his embrace, suddenly hating the comfort he was giving her, the notion that Cullen was letting her down gently, that he hadn't meant to come back at all and was probably regretting it. "You should wait to be asked before you turn a lady down," she said in a voice that, despite every effort at control, shook.

The breeze stirred the feathery branches above them, sending shadows sliding across his skin. "If you asked, I don't know if I could refuse. I don't want to put my resolve to the test."

She looked blindly away. "You won't have to."

He touched her jaw, bringing her gaze back to his. The lingering stroke of his fingers was so indescribably tender that she drew in her breath against the light tingle of it, closed her eyes against the shiver of need that rippled through her.

"Don't," he muttered thickly.

His warm palm slid possessively around her nape, his long strong fingers rasping gently against her skin, slipping into her hair. He dipped his head, his teeth closing over the sensitive flesh of her lobe, and the sharp pleasure-pain tore a small sound from her.

He lifted his head but didn't take his hands off her. Both hands now, cupped around her throat. "If you've got any sense you'll slap my face. Now."

He was going to kiss her. And Rachel knew with a sickening twist in her stomach that she shouldn't let him do it. Not again. I was bad enough standing here while he rejected any possibility of a relationship—while he expressed his frustration at even being attracted to her—and at the same time made love to her with every rasp of his work-hardened fingertips, every warm brush of his breath sliding across her cheek. If he caressed her with his mouth, she wouldn't want him to stop.

But she didn't have the strength or the will to stop something she wanted so badly, and that stark realisation filled her even as his breath filled her mouth. She'd never felt this aroused, this *alive*, with Adam, and Cullen had barely touched her. Her marriage had been happy, satisfying, everything she could have wished for, but she hadn't felt this consuming hunger, this deep wrenching sensation, as if the man fitting his firm, brooding mouth to hers had reached down inside her and taken possession of everything she was, everything she could be.

And then she couldn't think. Cullen's hands shifted, tilting her head as his lips stroked across hers in a slow, tantalising caress. She could feel the sun heavy on her eyelids, hear the slow, deep passage of the river flowing over smooth rocks, and then everything receded as her senses focused on the increasing intimacy of the kiss. His mouth parted hers, and his teeth closed on her lower lip. Rachel gasped out loud. Then his tongue pushed inside her, and his taste exploded in her mouth, hot and male, as deeply disturbing as the strong, complex man cradling her with such restraint against his big body.

Once again she'd expected him to ravage her mouth, and his tenderness tore away the last of her defences. She couldn't fight this attraction when he was kissing her with more attention, more simple sweetness, than she'd ever had from any man, including her husband.

Cullen almost groaned out loud when he finally lifted his mouth from Rachel's. The breeze sifted against his skin, cooling the moisture dampening his lips. He needed to kiss Rachel again more than he needed his next breath. "We've got to stop." The words were harsh, guttural. His hands curled around her upper arms, forced some space between them.

Rachel's mouth was wet and red from his. Her eyes confused. Cursing inwardly, Cullen grabbed her hand and drew it to the heavy wedge of flesh straining the front fastening of his jeans, demonstrating as graphically as he knew how just why they had to stop. He took his hand away, leaving hers there, pale against sun-hot, faded denim. But instead of rejecting his crude gesture, her fingers tightened around him.

A hoarse sound ripped from his throat at the sinuous caress. Cullen's head went back, the sun searing his closed lids with a fire that was a pale facsimile of the fire streaming through his body. With a hungry growl, he closed his hands on her waist and took what he needed: her mouth, her breath, the moonlight-cool imprint of her body fitted tight against his. And in the damp, thin swimsuit, she didn't just look naked, she felt naked. His tongue drove into her mouth, and she parted her legs over his thigh, altering the way she was leaning against him so that he was cradled between her hips. It was an instinctive movement, one a woman made to accommodate her lover. One a woman made when she wanted to be made love to. And he doubted she was even aware she'd done it.

Her hips swayed in small, subtle movements, stroking him in time with the rhythm of his tongue, and the ache in his loins turned savage. With fingers that shook, Cullen pulled down one shoulder strap of her swimsuit. The round whiteness of her breast, with its delicate, surprisingly dark tip, brushed his palm. She cried out, her back arching at the brief contact.

Cullen swore, his breath coming harshly. She was so responsive, *too responsive*. With a groan, his mouth closed over one breast, his hand over the other. Her breath came in a gasp as he pulled her into his mouth, tongue swirling tightly around the lengthening bud of her nipple. With a gulping cry she freed herself from the swimsuit straps and clasped his head, holding him against her breast.

When Cullen released her, the sight of her breast, wet and swollen from the attention of his mouth, sent such a powerful surge of desire through him that for a moment he couldn't breathe. His control wasn't just shredded, it was damn near nonexistent. If he touched her again...

"No," he said from between clenched teeth.

Rachel was momentarily paralysed by Cullen's sudden withdrawal. She could barely take in his denial. The reality of him against her—her hands wrapped in his thick, strong hair, holding him against her breasts—sank in, and mortification washed through her with a peculiar piercing pain that leached all the blood from the surface of her skin. She felt it go, felt the pale chill that replaced it. How could she have lost herself so thoroughly that she'd forgotten he didn't want her?

Correction, she thought shakily, he wanted her; she could feel his arousal. What male wouldn't want a near naked woman who'd made her willingness, her availability, clear? He was simply reacting as any healthy male would, on a purely physical level that didn't include any of the side benefits of love or commitment, or even friendship.

"I'm sorry," she whispered. She stumbled back, jerking at the straps of her swimsuit.

"Sorry?" His hands shot out to grasp her wrists, stopping her desperate attempts at covering up. His mouth was wet and sensually full, his eyes dark, almost frighteningly intense. "What do you mean 'sorry'?"

She shook her head. The sun beat down on her bare breasts, and she felt the humid moisture on her skin drying, her skin tightening. How could she explain that she was sorry she'd given in to her need to touch him, that she was sorry she'd been stupid enough to run straight at a granite wall?

His voice dropped. "Are you apologising for this?"

His hands cupped her breasts. The sight of his strong fingers cradling her much paler flesh sent fresh heat spearing through her, driving the humiliation in even deeper. "Don't," she snapped huskily. "Don't touch me unless you mean it."

"Oh, I mean it," he retorted grimly.

And then his mouth was on hers again, his tongue plunging deep as he hauled her so tight against him her breasts were flattened against his chest. The world tilted as he lifted her, then he was pulling her down, easing her on top of his long, muscular body as he settled himself against the unforgiving rock. With gentle hands he stroked her skin and smoothed the hair from her face, and she could no more stop the soft sounds deep in her throat than she could stop herself responding to him. Cullen's hand moved between them, stroking the damp apex of her thighs; then he eased the thin barrier of fabric aside. She cried out again as his fingers gently explored her exquisitely sensitive flesh. Then he was murmuring to her, soft words, endless words, coaxing her closer, telling her how beautiful she was, how desirable. Telling her how much he wanted her, *needed* her.

His mouth found hers in a deep kiss as one long finger penetrated her, and the world shivered and rippled out of focus, then came apart in a sweet, rending sunburst of delight.

After what seemed like hours but was probably only minutes, he stirred, gathering her in his arms and lifting her as he surged smoothly to his feet.

"Where are we going?" she mumbled sleepily.

His voice wrapped around her, deep and rough-velvet as a purr. "Shh, just relax. I'm going to bathe you."

Cullen ignored the fact that he still had his jeans and boots on as he waded thigh-deep into the river, too intent on the woman in his arms to even register that after the radiant heat of the rock shelf, the water was icily cold. He shifted Rachel in his arms, letting her slide against him until her feet found the riverbed; then he began to lave water between her legs, over the soft hollow of her belly where the cream swimsuit bunched, over the alabaster perfection of her breasts and down the elegant, sculpted curve of her spine.

He wanted her more with every stroke of his hand, every trailing stream of water silvering her delicate skin. He was still fully, painfully aroused, his breathing was too rapid, and sweat kept dewing his skin despite the cool water that swirled around his thighs. But he kept his touch gentle, restoring the straps of her swimsuit to her shoulders with as much care as his fumbling rough fingers could manage. When he was done, he cradled her in his arms again and waded across the shallowest point to the far side, carrying her back to where she'd left her clothes. "Are you all right to ride?"

Rachel's eyes snapped open. She was startled by the flatness in Cullen's voice as he set her on her feet, and for a moment the world spun out of control. She was still caught up in the tender care of his touch as he'd bathed her. But the arid lack of expression on his face grounded her with a thump. If he'd expressed his regret at touching her out loud, he couldn't have been clearer. "I got here," she said, as evenly as she could. "I expect I can make it back."

"I can double you on my horse if you need help, or if you're prepared to wait, I can go get the four-wheel drive. There's an old stock trail farther up in the foothills that will take a vehicle in the dry."

"I said I can manage. I don't need your help."

Cullen's jaw hardened, and for the briefest moment she thought he was going to ignore what she'd just said, pick her up and carry her back to wherever he'd left his horse. His reaction was at odds with the lack of emotion in his voice and the cool offer of help which had successfully relegated the shattering intimacy they'd shared to a one-sided sexual encounter that he had no desire to repeat.

Rachel raked her chin up a notch. Cullen could backtrack as much as he liked, but he couldn't take back his barely leashed response to her, his hoarse declaration of need as she'd come apart in his arms. "Don't expect me to pretend that what...happened, didn't."

His gaze met hers, and there was nothing cool in it. He looked hot, and so hungry that the hairs at her nape stirred. "It would be better for both of us if you did." With a last brooding glance, he strode back the way he'd come.

Rachel listened to the fading sound of his footsteps, the splash of water as he forded the river, the thud of hooves as he rode away.

Her body still throbbed from her release, and her mind reeled from the sharp immediacy of her response to Cullen, the shattering completeness of her surrender. How could she be so drawn to a man who wasn't even remotely interested in commitment?

Chapter 6

Rachel moved into her flat the next day. Cole and three of his men helped shift in the furniture she'd had stored at the farm. They also cleared out the tiny garage at the rear, which she'd been unable to use because it was choked with the previous owner's junk and all the leftover debris and building materials from the recent renovations. Helen helped her get the place straightened, hang curtains, and put crockery and silverware away.

"It's nice," Helen said wistfully, looking around. "I like what you've done with it. I never would have thought that clay colour could look so good."

"I wasn't sure, either," Rachel admitted, taking pleasure in the warm honey-glow of the sun on the walls, the way it complemented her comfortable furniture, bright rugs and shelves of books.

"Well, it certainly looks a lot different than when Maisie Jackson had it." Helen glanced around, shaking her head in memory of the last owner of the salon, who'd had a fetish for seventies kitsch and who, judging from some of the wild colour combinations she'd favoured, had been colour blind. "I hope you'll be happy here."

"Oh, I intend to be," Rachel said with a determined smile. Just being in Riverbend answered a need she'd always been aware of—despite some of the unpleasant things that had happened since she'd moved back. "Riverbend is my home."

When Helen and Cole and the farmhands had left, Rachel sank quietly onto a sofa, her gaze touching on all the things she'd gathered around her since she was a small girl exiled to a city that was too big, too impersonal and too far away from her family. She was an inveterate pack rat—or so her father had said. She'd kept every photo, every gift, every book she'd ever enjoyed—hoarding them close in an instinctive search for security and familiarity.

And now, once again, possessions were all she had.

Shaking off the morbid thought, she sprang to her feet and snatched up the grocery list she'd made earlier. If she didn't make it to the supermarket soon, it would close and her cupboards would remain bare until tomorrow.

At this time of night the supermarket was near empty, and Rachel was enjoying the relative freedom of the aisles when she rounded a corner and ran into Cullen. For a frozen moment she stared at him, so shocked at the unexpected encounter she almost missed the unguarded rawness of his expression before he spun on his heel and strode in the opposite direction, a container of milk dangling from his fingers.

Rachel forced herself to keep strolling the aisles as if nothing had happened, staring at her scribbled list and repeatedly walking past items she needed before doubling back in frustration. Just when she thought she had herself back under control, she glanced up to find him looking across his shoulder at her instead of at the girl checking his groceries. The hot darkness in Cullen's gaze sent a melting pain through her bones, followed by a surge of anger.

Damn him. If Cullen Logan crooked his little finger, she would drop the loaf of bread she'd just picked up and walk into his arms without counting the cost. But he wasn't going to do that, and on cue a blankness as familiar as the metallic colour of his eyes closed out every last trace of emotion. He completed his transaction, picked up his grocery bag and strode out.

The glass doors slid closed behind him, and Rachel looked down at the bread she'd somehow managed to crush against her chest. Releasing a tired breath, she dropped the sorry loaf into her trolley. There was no point in shopping for anything more—her concentration was shot. Tossing her list back in her bag, she wheeled her cart to the checkout.

As Rachel left the supermarket, another woman hurried toward the entrance, towing two small children along with her. Emily Trask. Dane's mother.

As the other woman passed, she kept her head down, but even with the avoidance of eye contact and the clothes that wrapped her from neck to ankle in the sweltering humidity, Emily Trask couldn't hide the fact that she'd been beaten black and blue, and a whole lot of other colours besides.

Rachel smiled and nodded, careful not to stare, to make the other woman more self-conscious than she must be about the disfiguring marks, but her mind reeled at the sheer brutality that had put those ugly swellings and cuts on Emily's face. The same brutality that had the two children huddling in tight against their mother, clutching at her skirts as if afraid to let her go.

As Rachel dumped her groceries on the back seat of her car, then returned her trolley to the trolley park, she came to a decision. She was going to do something.

Rachel didn't know what, but it was beyond bearing that anyone should be treated like that, and that the police couldn't do a thing about it. Tomorrow she would take advantage of the small-town gossip and make discreet enquiries, using the grapevine that appeared to flow directly through her salon.

By the next afternoon, the grapevine hadn't turned up anything Rachel didn't know already. Emily Trask regularly sported bruises. Various people had tried to intervene, but they'd only made it worse for Emily and the children. Frank Trask had done time for assault and battery once, but that had been because he'd got drunk enough to make the mistake of hitting someone who wasn't afraid to lay charges. To compound Frank's mistake, the man he'd hit had been his boss, so he'd lost his job, as well. Unfortunately, the construction company went bust a few months later, and when a new crew moved in, Frank got his old job back.

Despite Rachel's reluctance to expose herself to any more grief, she decided there was only one person she could appeal to who could possibly offer a solution that might help the Trask family. After work, she was going to see Cullen.

Frank Trask peered in the window of the shearing quarters. The boy wasn't there, and the risk Trask had taken in driving brazenly onto Logan's land suddenly manifested itself in the burning rage that had been coiling deep in his gut ever since he'd found out his old lady had done a runner, taking the kids and shifting into the Women's Refuge in Fairley that afternoon. Word was that Dane had helped her pack and then driven her over there in Logan's truck.

Frank lurched in the darkness, swearing beneath his breath as he nearly ended up on his butt in the dirt. Maybe he shouldn't have had that last beer before heading out here? He snickered. Make that the last half dozen. Not that it would make any difference when it came to the business end of this little trip. When he caught up with Dane, he would teach the bastard that no one crossed him. He would teach him just as good as he'd taught his mother a couple of days ago. Just the thought of smashing his fist into the boy's skinny ribs made him feel better. The pleasure of thinking about it was almost as good as actually doin' it.

And the boy needed another lesson. All Frank's mates at the pub agreed with him on that point. Family was family, and no half-assed soldier-boy like Cullen Logan was goin' to interfere with Frank Trask's disciplining of his family.

The sound of a car approaching had Trask stumbling back into the shadows. Sweat leaped from his pores as he considered the possibility of an actual confrontation with Logan; then the air whooshed from his lungs as he watched a woman climb out from behind the wheel of a shiny little city car. He recognised her instantly. Rachel Sinclair had been the topic of more than a little speculation down at the pub, not the least that she was carrying on with Logan.

But she sure was a looker.

Trask licked his lips and stroked a hand over his fly, feeling a gloating satisfaction at the bulge growing beneath his fingers. She had a body on her, make no mistake. A little slap around and she would open her legs for him, and damned if he didn't feel like showing her just what she was missing out on.

Anticipation hardened him even further when he saw what she was wearing. Her breasts weren't huge like he really liked 'em, but they stuck out against that silky little top like she was begging for it, and her long pale legs were nice. Yessir, just one yank and he'd have that short skirt up around her waist. Yeah. It excited him to rough up the action a little. Made it better for the woman, too.

A vision of the four Sinclair brothers wavered through his mind, making him frown. They were big, hard bastards, and he'd had run-ins with them all at different times.

But now there was only Cole.

He grinned to himself in the shadows. Hell, if he was ready to take on Logan, he could handle Cole Sinclair. And besides, if the little lady was lying down for Logan, she must like it rough, despite her refined appearance.

Trask licked his lips. And didn't he just know the type? Slick city bitches with a greedy yen for what they couldn't get from those soft office boys.

Rachel knocked at the front door of Cullen's house one more time. The sound echoed hollowly, as if the house was as empty and sad on the inside as it looked on the outside. After waiting another few seconds for a reply, she gave up and walked toward a low building that she hoped was the shearing quarters where she knew Dane was staying. She'd expected to find lights on in the house, to find some evidence of activity, and the air of darkness and isolation was disconcerting. She was almost at the freshly painted building when a man stepped out of the shadows. ''Dane?'' she said on a ridiculous wave of relief.

''Try again, darlin','' a coarse voice answered.

Fear and adrenaline jolted through Rachel. She recognised that voice, even though she'd only heard him speak once. Frank Trask. ''Oh, I—are you visiting your son, Mr. Trask?''

''Mr. Trask,'' he echoed, stepping close enough for her to make out his heavy-bellied form, smell the beer on his breath and the sour sharpness of unwashed clothing. ''I like the sound of that. I like the sound of 'Please, Mr. Trask' even better.''

Rachel swallowed and glanced around, trying to keep her movements considered and normal, trying to keep the apprehension off her face. But Trask moved in anyway, crowding her personal space, sending fear and fury rippling through her. She stepped back, stumbling on her heels. He laughed, taking pleasure in her discomfort, stepping in close enough that her flailing hand brushed against his spongy gut. The feel of him was repulsive, igniting a fierce anger that only seemed to excite him further. He took another half step, invading her space again, and his breath washed over her face. It was hot and moist, unbelievably fetid. She remembered Cullen's warning not to get caught alone with Trask, that any self-defence tricks she had up her sleeve probably wouldn't work on him, but she wasn't going to go quietly. Whatever Trask wanted to do to her, whatever foul violation he had in mind, he would have to knock her out to do it, and meanwhile, she was going to get her hits in—scratch him, hurt him and scream for all she was worth.

Trask's hand closed on her wrist. Rachel jerked against his hold and opened her mouth to scream, when the sharp sound of hooves striking hard-packed gravel cut through the night.

With a desperate swing, Rachel took advantage of Trask's momentary surprise, putting all her force into the blow. She managed to connect solidly with his throat. He made a satisfying gurgling noise, released her wrist, then roared with rage as he lurched toward her.

"Move away from her, Trask," a deep voice rasped from the shadows. "And do it real slow, so I don't get too excited."

Frank Trask froze, then stepped back with a slowness that would have been comical if the situation hadn't been so alarming just moments ago. He craned around, eyes bugging from his head as he tried to pinpoint just where Cullen was.

Cullen decided he wasn't about to let him wait. He prowled into the open. Trask flinched and whipped around, because Cullen wasn't where his voice had just been. But then, Trask's senses weren't particularly keen. By the reek of beer mixed in with the foul odour of his body, he'd spent the day at the pub, liquoring himself up for his next act of cowardice.

"Go into the house, Rachel." Cullen didn't shift his gaze from his twitchy, sweating prey. "The door's unlocked."

"If you need some help—"

"I can handle it."

"He hurt Dane's mother. I saw her in town yesterday."

Rachel's voice wobbled a little, making the fury coursing through Cullen chill down to an icy resolve. He would do his best to ensure that in future Frank was real careful he didn't so much as walk on the same side of the street as Rachel.

"Do you want me to phone the police, Cullen?"

"Just go inside, babe. Let me handle this. The police haven't had a lot of success at slowing this creep down, but Frank and I talk the same language. Don't we, Frank?"

Rachel knew she should move, but the soft rumble of Cullen's voice was hard to turn aside from. There was something mesmerizing about his cool control, the utter confidence in every word he said. He made her feel safe.

Trask backed up until he was flat against the wall of the shearing quarters, and the cold glitter in Cullen's eyes turned even icier. Trask tried harder to melt into the wall.

A shiver went down Rachel's spine. Cullen looked grim and remote on a good day, but with his dark hair slicked back with sweat, a shadow of stubble roughing up his jaw, and nothing on but a pair of scuffed riding boots and tight denims, he looked like hell's own definition of dangerous. A fierce, wholly feminine satisfaction filled her, pushing back the ugliness of Trask's intent, the vulnerability he'd forced on her. She'd always abhorred violence in any form, but Cullen's defence of her touched a primitive chord. Right or wrong, he had the equipment to protect her from everyone and everything.

"Move it, honey," Cullen prompted, still in that same controlled voice.

Rachel flicked a final look at Trask, who seemed to shrink before her eyes, and decided Cullen didn't need her help. "I'll make some coffee," she said firmly. "It'll be ready in just a few minutes."

Cullen waited for the front door to close behind Rachel before he took one long stride toward Trask.

Trask eased along the wall, his hands opening and closing as if searching for a weapon, anything to give him an edge. "You don't know who you're messing with," he snarled. "Lay one hand on me, pretty boy, and you'll go down just like your daddy did. Two hits, one to the nose and one to the gut. *Boom, boom,* that's all it would take."

Cullen grasped the dirty cloth of Trask's shirt, then jerked upward. A burst of bad breath washed over his face, but he'd smelt worse, seen worse, than Frank Trask could ever be. And, like most bullies, Trask was a coward.

"Dream on, Trask," Cullen said in a cool whisper. "My father was a drunk. I'm not. But while we're on the subject of violence, let's clear up a few things that have been bothering me for a while. I hope I never get to hear about you beating up on a woman again, because you're starting to irritate me. And when I get irritated, sometimes I lash out at whatever it is that's ticking me off. Now, I know you're used to fighting women and children, and taking on a fully grown male will be something of a step up for you, but I'm prepared to make allowances. For instance, I won't break any bones the first time around, but I can't make any promises about a rematch. You might have heard that if I get angry enough I could *probably* even kill a man. But you shouldn't believe every bit of gossip you hear, and that particular piece of information happens to be all wrong. Because you see, Trask, if you touch my woman again, I *will* kill you.''

"I won't—won't touch her—'' Trask gasped. ''Didn't realise she was yours— Pl-please—can't breathe—''

Cullen calmly tightened his hold, cutting off the cowardly, stumbling rush at denial. He leaned closer, close enough that he could smell the spittle dribbling down Trask's fat, unshaven jaw and the hot, stinking fear rising up from the man's sweating body. ''Just one more thing.''

Trask's head nearly wobbled off his thick neck in his effort to show how very willing he was to listen to this one last piece of advice.

Cullen smiled coldly. ''If I ever see your wife, or any of your children, with bruises, I'll take it as a personal invitation to call around and see you.''

Trask shook his head, dragging in the tiny amount of air Cullen was allowing him with a tortured whine that almost tempted Cullen to ease back on the pressure. But there really was just one more loose end. ''And, Trask,'' he continued softly, ''don't think you can get away with hitting them in those other places. You know the ones I'm talking about—the soft, hidden places that nobody sees. Because when I was in the army, I did some special training. If you've heard all the other gossip that seems to be so rife around this place, you may have heard about that.''

''You were SAS,'' Trask gurgled.

Cullen showed his approval by jerking just a little tighter on the shirt. ''That's the one. They taught us some...interesting things, mostly for our own protection, you understand. But it means I've got all this knowledge—and, I'll have to admit, not a little experience—and if I ever see any member of your family walking as if they're hurting, or even just not moving right, I'll be looking for you.''

Trask bounced his head.

Cullen opened his hand. Trask dropped like a stone, ending u
splayed out in the dust in an untidy heap. He stared up at Culler
wiping the spit from his mouth, eyes filled with fear and a pur
evil hate; then he turned on his side and vomited. Cullen ignore
the sour smell, the strangled, grunting sounds, as Trask emptie
his miserable gut onto Cullen's dry dirt—gauging instead just ho
effective his tactics had been. A man like Trask just naturally ge
himself into all sorts of unpleasant situations—and he could stan
mer and act with the best of them. Trask retched one last tim
then lurched to his feet, avoiding Cullen's hard, measuring ga:
as he headed toward his utility at a shambling run.

The ignition screamed as Trask worked the starter motor un
the worn, smoking engine finally caught; then he buried his fo
and sent the vehicle fishtailing down the drive. The lumberin
Holden hit the cattle stop with a thump, and Cullen winced :
metal sheared against metal, but his post stood solid, scraping pai
and scoring a long dent in the vehicle's already battered hide.

Trask was panicked but not out, Cullen decided, as the oth
man recovered enough to plant his foot again and spray grav
from hell to breakfast as he headed for the county road. But :
least Cullen was fairly sure he wouldn't go near Rachel again.

The front door opened, spreading light across his barren fro
yard.

"Cullen?" As Cullen strode toward her, Rachel saw with reli
that he wasn't hurt. "Did he...?"

"We didn't fight. We just had a little...discussion."

Rachel could imagine what the "discussion" had entailed; Cu
len's eyes still smouldered with a controlled fury. "I brought yo
coffee."

Cullen stepped up onto the verandah and accepted the mug, bi
he didn't drink; instead he took hold of her hand. "Did he touc
you anywhere?"

"He grabbed my wrist. You didn't give him the chance to d
anything else."

Cullen was silent for a long time. He turned her hand over ar
examined the faint red marks on her wrist. His thumb smoothe

over the sensitive skin with a gentleness completely at odds with his size and strength. The simple caress started an inner shaking, and suddenly she needed to be in his arms and held tight. Rachel stiffened and forced her expression to blankness. She wasn't accustomed to throwing herself in any man's arms, and yet the impulse to do so now was almost too strong to deny. Not that it mattered one way or the other. Cullen had drawn the boundaries of their relationship—he'd made it clear he didn't want intimacy— and she'd already run into his granite wall one too many times.

Cullen released her and began drinking his coffee, half-turned away so that all she could see was the hard, remote cut of his profile, the sheen of light sliding off one bronzed shoulder. "Did he say anything to you?"

"He—wasn't big on conversation. I don't think verbal communication is very high on Frank Trask's list of priorities."

"You shouldn't have come here," he said abruptly.

Hurt washed through Rachel, followed by an incredible dragging weariness. She didn't know why, but after what had just happened, she'd expected Cullen to be different with her. Softer. Her chin came up. "I wanted to talk to you about Dane's mother. I saw her outside the supermarket. She was so bruised.... I thought Dane should know—"

"Dane helped her shift out this afternoon," Cullen interrupted. "Using my truck. The family's moved into the Women's Refuge in Fairley. Dane's staying with a friend who lives nearby until Emily can arrange permanent accommodation. He won't be back until everything's sorted. Trask was probably looking for Dane when you showed up instead. He can't afford to go near his wife. She's taken out a restraining order against him. Hopefully this time she'll go the whole way and start divorce proceedings. It sure as hell can't be any picnic living with an animal like Frank Trask."

Cullen's jaw tightened at Rachel's instant recoil at the mention of Trask. He could never allow himself to forget that if he'd stayed in Riverbend after his old man had died, he would probably *be* like Trask. The army had given him control, discipline, an outward respectability that Trask didn't possess—but it had also harnessed the very violence that was at the core of his soul, honing it to a degree that even a man like Trask couldn't imagine. As bad as Trask was, he didn't even rate the reserves bench in Cullen's game.

Cullen gulped down the rest of his coffee, willing some of the knotted tension in his gut to dissolve. But not too much. He couldn't afford to relax, because if he did, he would touch Rachel, and in his present mood he wouldn't let her go. He would take the sweetness she was offering and damn the consequences.

Fury still vibrated through him that Trask had laid his dirty paw on her, that he'd intended to hurt her. Along with the rage came a savage regret. Cullen wished that Rachel hadn't had to see him dealing with Trask on his own level. He'd tried not to let her opinion—her expectations—become important to him, but they had. He found he wanted to be her white knight after all. Only trouble was, he came from darkness and shadows, and they were all he knew.

He stared into the empty mug before placing it on the verandah railing, steeling himself to meet Rachel's gaze. "Are you okay to drive?"

"Of course."

Her eyes were wide, dark, and her skin was far too pale. It was all he could do to stop himself from reaching for her. "You're shaking."

"It's just reaction. It'll go away. I'm quite capable of driving."

"I don't want to let you drive," he growled. "If Dane was here, he could follow in my truck and I could take you in. But as it is, the best I can offer is to follow you."

"You don't have to do that. You're tired, probably hungry—'

"I'm not leaving you to get home alone this time."

Her eyes flashed at the reference to all the other times he'd walked away. "I can manage. Despite what you probably think, I didn't come out here chasing you. You've already made it clear you're not interested."

Cullen's hands curled into fists at her blunt statement, and he knew he was about to make a huge mistake. He couldn't have her but he was damned if he would let her go on believing he didn't want her. "If you think I'm not interested, you couldn't be more wrong. Baby, I'm so interested I can hardly think of anything else. But it's just not possible. *We're not possible.* When I said you shouldn't have come here, I meant you shouldn't be near me. For your own good. Around Riverbend, I'm bad news—and whether there was reason for the mud that was thrown or not has never made one bit of difference. It sticks. It'll stick to whoever associates with me, and it won't matter how clean your reputation is. You've got a business at stake. If you want to make a comfortable life for yourself in Riverbend, forget about me."

"And if I can't?"

The very blankness of Rachel's expression was arresting. Perversely, her shuttered distance added to his ferocious tension. He found he wanted to know what she was thinking, what she was feeling. He didn't want her to hide anything from him, ever. Heat slammed through him, and between one breath and the next he was fully, achingly aroused, his muscles taut, twitching with the strain of *not* acting. "Lady," he said, his voice harsh, guttural, "you've *got* to try."

Rachel felt the bleakness of Cullen's statement like a blow. But his words were at odds with his expression—it was primitively male, sexual and possessive, and so hungry her heart missed a beat. It was the kind of look that stopped women's lives, then sent them spinning in another direction entirely.

The kind of look she'd been waiting for her whole life.

The thought came out of nowhere, stopping the breath in her throat. Rachel nodded, barely aware she wasn't agreeing to Cullen's request to keep away from him but was simply moving her head in reflex.

She wondered what on earth was happening to her. The seesawing depth of her emotions was completely uncharted territory; she felt as if she'd been cast adrift—that the goals that had defined her life had shifted. That *she* had changed in some fundamental way.

She'd always been so sure about what she wanted from a relationship, and this wasn't it. She'd never imagined she would be so fiercely attracted to a man who both didn't need her and yet was every bit as demanding, as dominating, as any of her brothers. A man who affected her more powerfully than she'd ever imagined one human being could affect another.

Something squeezed painfully in her chest. She knew with a frightening clarity that if she let herself, she could love Cullen, and that what she would feel would be beyond the scope of anything she'd ever felt before. She also knew that he wouldn't allow himself to love her. He'd always been blunt on that point.

She should be happy that he'd been so ruthlessly clear-cut, that he hadn't taken advantage of her. This way she could step back from a potentially hurtful situation, control her emotions before it was too late. But Cullen's stance filled her with a helpless fury. *He* was making all the decisions, all the rules. And she was tired of being shut out, of being forced once again into the passive role she knew too well.

Ten minutes later, after Cullen had quickly washed and thrown on a clean shirt, she was driving down his winding drive with his truck lights glowing behind her. Her body felt odd, disconnected, as if she were going through the motions and her brain had gone on hold. It took all her concentration to keep her car out of the ditch and make the correct turns. Another fifteen minutes and she was slotting her car into the tiny garage at the rear of the salon and rummaging for the keys to get into her flat.

Cullen came up behind her just as she finally managed to get the key in the lock and push the door open.

"I'll check your flat before I leave," he said quietly.

His presence filled her hallway as he stepped around her and started up the stairs.

Rachel closed the door and, out of habit, locked it and put the chain on before following Cullen. She couldn't hear his footsteps; it was eerily quiet, and he hadn't turned any lights on. If she didn't know better, if she couldn't *feel* his presence, she would think she was alone.

When she reached the lounge, he melted out of the darkness and switched on one of her low lamps. A shiver coursed down her spine at his sudden appearance, and the image of Trask emerging from the shadows played through her mind. Suddenly the thought of being alone was unnerving, even in the cosy confines of her own home. But she was used to coping on her own, she reminded herself. *She was used to being alone.* And she was perfectly safe. All she had to do was stand here and wait until the downstairs door shut behind Cullen.

But instead of leaving, he stepped closer. "You need someone with you. I'll call Cole."

The clipped impersonality of his tone was like being hit by an icy cold wave. It rocked her, washed her defences away. Until he'd spoken, she hadn't known how much she'd wanted him to stay. "No," she said quietly.

She didn't want Cole, she wanted Cullen. Maybe she *had* changed in some fundamental way, because suddenly she yearned for the protective qualities she'd found so stifling in her brothers. She wanted Cullen's arms around her, the comfort and peace of just being close to him. And she wanted to offer that comfort in return—to soothe the darkness and despair he'd let her glimpse.

A muscle twitched in the hollow below his cheekbone, and, if possible, the line of his mouth became even grimmer. And then Cullen closed his eyes. The naked intensity of his expression hurt to see, and she knew in that moment that he was torn. He didn't want to leave—and he didn't want to be the one to stay.

The strain etching his features taught Rachel more than she wanted to know about Cullen if she was to keep her distance and her dignity. She'd known she could attract him—arouse him—now she knew he cared for her, even if he would never admit it. Taking a breath, she reached up and touched his jaw. His eyes didn't open, although his breathing altered. Without thought, beyond shame, she rubbed her palm over the stubbled darkness shadowing his skin, slipped her fingers upward to the midnight softness of his lashes. They flickered against her touch, oddly delicate when everything else about him seemed larger than life and so strong.

With a movement that took her by surprise, he captured he hand and brought it to his mouth. "I don't want you to be alone, he said roughly.

"I know," she whispered.

For the barest moment she saw an answering loneliness ope up in his eyes, saw the yawning darkness he usually hid so wel then, in a convulsive movement, his arms were around her, clam ing her in tight against his hard, musky warmth, holding her th way she'd wanted to be held on his verandah. Her arms wer around his neck, fingers automatically seeking out the sleek sk at his nape, the thick silky texture of his hair. He shuddered a her fingers tightened in his hair and, with a slow inevitability, be his head and laid his mouth on hers. She opened for him at th first touch. The taste of Cullen was rich and dark, masculine ar untamed, and the stroke of his tongue made her ache.

Long minutes passed, and he didn't lift his mouth, not com pletely, and suddenly she knew he wasn't as controlled as she thought. The encounter with Trask had pushed him closer to he than he'd wanted to get, and now he couldn't back off.

"Rachel," he groaned when he finally wrenched his mouth fre "Tell me to go."

Rachel dragged in a breath. Her mouth was tingling, her lij swollen, her body lethargic with a drugging sensuality that ma it difficult to think at all. But even so, she understood everythir inherent in Cullen's terse statement. His control was hanging l a thread. If she didn't call a halt, he would make love to her. The would be no promises, no declarations, nothing but a few momen out of time.

Fierceness swept through her, pushing aside caution and dou She could retreat, take the sensible, rational course, or she cou take the few moments out of time. Balanced against a forever th so far held little promise and a past that was measured by failu and regret, there was no contest. Cullen alarmed her, made h vulnerable, but he also made her feel more alive, more richl vibrantly female, than she'd ever felt before.

Her breath caught in her throat as she reached for the first butt of his shirt. It slid free. Another button went the way of the first, and she slipped her hand beneath the soft cotton and felt the heat pulsing off his skin, the coarser texture of hair.

A low sound grated from his throat, but he didn't push her away. Deliberately, she unfastened the rest of the buttons and pushed the shirt off his shoulders. Her arms slid around his lean waist, and she opened her mouth against him, tasting the salt and maleness, breathing in the difference and the shattering familiarity of him.

She'd never seduced a man in her life. During her marriage, Adam had always been the one to instigate lovemaking, but now she couldn't stop touching Cullen. Beyond holding her, Cullen wasn't touching her. The rigidity of his muscles, his odd stillness, finally transmitted itself to Rachel, and as he pulled away, hands settling on her upper arms, she braced herself for rejection. But instead of pushing her away, Cullen sucked in a sharp, uneven breath and bent his head, brushing his lips over the sensitive skin where her neck and shoulder joined. His grip tightened while he stroked her with his tongue and teeth, tracing the quivering cords of her throat until her legs weakened and his hands were the only thing holding her up.

"Cullen," she whispered when she couldn't take any more. Not if he was going to leave.

He made a sound that was half assent, half groan, as his mouth became more demanding, ravaging her neck, the lobe of her ear, her cheek. And everywhere he touched, her skin ignited, sending rivulets of fire to the aching centre of her body. With a gulping moan, Rachel knotted her fingers in his hair and pulled his mouth to hers. A tremor shook him, then his tongue pushed into her mouth, driving deep as he crowded her back until she came up against the wall. The heavy weight of him pinned her, making her skin flush and moisten, sending a shiver of instinctive feminine fear shooting down her spine at the prospect of surrendering to all that raw, sleek power. But she wanted him too much to let him go. On the most primitive level, it was his mesmerizing combination of strength and gentleness that had drawn her.

His hands cupped her breasts through her blouse, and a pang of such intense desire shot through her that for long moments she couldn't breathe. He tore at the buttons and then simply dragged her bra down before taking her breast in his mouth the way he had at the swimming hole, deep and hot and hungry. Rachel's head fell back against the wall, fingers sinking into the taut muscles of his shoulders. Her senses were spinning, drawing her into a whirlpool where there was only feeling, only sensation. She felt the calloused scrape of his hand between her thighs, the sensation of bareness as he rucked her skirt up around her waist, and then he was touching her through the thin barrier of her panties. She whimpered, both at the exquisite relief of his touch and the frustrating hindrance of her clothing. Cullen groaned hoarsely and found her mouth again. Rachel felt his thwarted male impatience in the rhythmic plunging of his tongue, the roughness of his fingers as they hooked around the lacy edge of her panties and tugged. She was dazedly aware of fabric rending, the coolness of air circulating; then his big hand cupped her with intimate pressure, and he penetrated her with his finger.

Rachel gasped, her whole body clenching at the rasping pleasure of the intrusion. Other than the interlude with Cullen at the water hole, she hadn't been touched or made love to for more than two years. And they'd been a difficult two years. She'd missed Adam. She'd missed the intimacy of married life, the sheer animal comfort of skin against skin, of strong arms around her, the sharp, clean scent of male sweat, and the coarser textures of body hair and hard muscle.

Cullen shuddered against her. She heard his harsh intake of air, felt his hands at her waist, then a sense of weightlessness. Rachel's head snapped forward as he lifted her. Her arms automatically clamped around his neck to stabilise the movement. He clasped her buttocks, hoisting her even higher. Instinctively, her thighs parted and gripped his hips. The movement brought her hard against him, and she felt the coarse rub of denim against her inner thighs, the brush of his hand against her female flesh, the rasp of a zipper, then the unmistakeable satin-hot bluntness of his sex lodging against her opening. A split second later, he began pushing himself inside her.

Rachel contracted around him in shock, making his entry more difficult. She couldn't see him, but she knew he was large, stretching her delicate flesh to its limits. When she realised he was only part way in, panic tightened her internal muscles even further.

Cullen's head shot up; his gaze locked with hers. He looked dazed, and she sensed his stunned realisation of how far they'd come, and how impossibly fast.

For an agonising eternity he didn't move, and in those moments her panic, and much of her discomfort, subsided. He felt hot inside her, inescapably muscular and male, and she wanted to feel all of him. But she also felt his hesitation, and that sent panic of a different kind twisting through her. She couldn't bear it if he stopped now, but the dazed look had left his eyes, and now they glittered with a sharp, savage awareness.

"I'm too big," he rasped.

"No." Rachel arched, deliberately parting herself more widely over him, inviting him deeper into her body. She heard his intake of air, felt the raw tremor that shook him. Sweat sprang out on his skin, making him glow copper in the half-light. His lips drew back, baring his teeth as he fought for the control she was intent on denying him; then, with a rough sound somewhere between a groan and a purr, his hips jackhammered, and he thrust himself all the way in.

Time stopped. Rachel registered the wild dilation in Cullen's eyes, her own sense of unreality. She was backed up against a wall, her arms and legs wrapped around Cullen, and he was so deep inside her that her muscles quivered in reaction to his alien heat and hardness.

And then he started to move. Roughly, jerkily at first, as if he were still fighting for control after the explosive shock of entry, then more smoothly, as she softened around him and lubricated the solid male glide of his flesh.

He shifted, pinning her more securely against the wall, one hand gripping her nape with surprising gentleness. His gaze linked with hers as he thrust with a steady, hungry intensity that she met and matched. He might not love, but at the moment it didn't matter; they were man and woman, and he wanted her. Only her.

She could feel the tension inside her building, gathering, with startling speed. His gaze sharpened, moving beyond purely physical absorption, and he thrust harder, short, sharp shoves that made her tighten unbearably. With a shaky cry she let the shimmering delight take her. His mouth found hers, cutting off the small sound, and then he groaned and tensed and drove himself so deep inside her that she could feel him against the entrance to her womb, could feel the pulsing stream of incandescence as his whole body shook with the fury of his release.

Minutes later, Cullen stirred. They were still locked together in a limp sprawl against the wall. Rachel's legs were still clasped around his waist. Reluctantly, he disengaged himself, letting her slide until her feet touched the floor. She lifted her head. Her dark hair was a wild cloud, her eyes heavy-lidded. The pale, delicate skin around her mouth and along her neck was pink, abraded from his stubbled jaw. Possession jolted through Cullen, roughly, arousingly. She looked like a woman who'd just been thoroughly loved. His woman. The thought gathered momentum, hardening him again with a fierceness that took his breath.

His jaw clenched against the needy ache. He wanted Rachel again, but he wouldn't take her. She looked sore and shattered. Her clothes in disarray, she looked like she'd been in a fight. And he'd done it to her. Disgust filled him at his lack of control, the rough way he'd marked her. The blank, stunned expression he'd put on her face.

With careful movements, he fastened his pants, then picked her up, cradling her in his arms with a gentleness he wished he'd shown when they were making love. *Damn it,* he knew how to be gentle. He knew how to make it so sweet and slow she would nearly die of the pleasure before he took his. But he hadn't been able to slow down; he hadn't been able to stop. He hadn't been able to do anything but drag her clothes out of the way and get inside her as hard and fast as he could.

He'd lost control.

His mouth tightened grimly. There wouldn't be a next time.

There shouldn't have been a first time. He hadn't used any protection. He hadn't *had* any protection with him, because this wasn't supposed to happen.

Her arms stayed around his neck as he made his way into the darkness of her bedroom. She was quiet. Too quiet. When Cullen saw the steady way she watched him, the acceptance in her eyes—as if she knew what he was thinking, what he had to do next—his chest locked up with pain. She knew he was going to leave.

Rachel could see the silent battle on Cullen's face. She reached up and stroked his lean cheek as he lowered her to the bed, not bothering to hide how she felt. She wasn't about to embarrass him with words, but she was going to savour every moment with him. Making love with Cullen had shaken her. She'd never felt so utterly female, so vulnerable, but at the same time, she'd held *him,* taken his strength inside her, matched the primitive force of his passion.

Unexpectedly, he bent and kissed her with a slow, destroying tenderness; then he disappeared in the direction of her bathroom. When he came back, he had a damp washcloth in his hand.

Gently, he removed her rumpled clothing, then sat on the side of the bed and began to lave her skin before cleaning gently between her legs. He'd bathed her the last time they'd been together, at the river, and it occurred to her with a sudden chill that he was cleaning his touch from her skin.

His eyes sought hers, cool control restored as if he'd never gone wild in her arms. "I didn't use any protection. Are you likely to get pregnant?"

Contraception hadn't occurred to her. When she'd been married he'd been on the pill, but for the past two years there hadn't been any need for that kind of protection. "I'm not taking anything, if that's what you mean. It's late in my cycle, so it's probably not likely."

He continued to stroke her skin with the washcloth, seemingly absorbed with removing every last trace of their lovemaking, and

even though he didn't mean his touch to be arousing, the sheer
intimacy of Cullen caring for her in such a way made her skin
tingle, made her soften inside. Rachel swallowed on a burst of
anguish and endured the gentle stroking.

Finally Cullen put the cloth aside. "If you're pregnant," he said
in a low voice, "then it's done. We'll face that hurdle if and when
it happens."

He pulled the quilt back and eased her beneath it, his touch as
tender and impersonal as if he were ministering to an unknown
child. Then he astounded her by coming to lie beside her, on top
of the quilt, still wearing his jeans.

She'd never shared a bed with any man other than her husband,
and the intimacy of actually sleeping with Cullen made her mouth
go dry. People couldn't keep glass walls, or even granite ones,
intact while they were sleeping. When you slept, you were wholly
vulnerable, wholly exposed. "You're staying?"

He pulled her back against his chest, settling her head on his
arm. The gesture was gentle and oddly determined. "Do you want
me to leave?"

Rachel didn't bother answering; she just pushed herself back
against him until she was as close as she could get with the quilt
wadded between them. His free arm curled over her waist, drawing
her in even more securely.

She stayed awake as long as she could, soaking in his warmth,
the vitality that didn't seem to dim even when he was lying quiescent. Eventually she felt herself slipping into oblivion, aware
that Cullen wasn't allowing himself to relax, that he was waiting
for her to sleep—and that when she did, he *was* going to leave.

Cullen came up out of sleep fast.

A fine tremor ran through muscles corded with tension. Something was wrong. Different.

The something moved, burrowing into his side.

The breath left his lungs on a silent string of curses, and he
sank back onto the bed, still on edge, still poised for... He grimaced. The enemy.

And here she was, all 120-odd pounds of her, wound around him like a vine, silky head nudging a pillow out of his chest and shoulder, hair spread from moonshine to breakfast and smelling of flowers. He traced his fingertip along a dark strand with a careful gentleness, not wanting to wake her, just needing to touch her incredible softness. He hadn't meant to stay, hadn't meant to let Rachel's warmth seep so far into him that he relaxed his guard enough to fall asleep with her in his arms.

Her hand shifted, brushing down his tense midriff, settling with a soft, warm weight over his navel. Desire pulsed in a hot lava flow, drawing his body tight with a need that was becoming as familiar to him as breathing. Carefully, so as not to wake her from the rest she needed, Cullen eased from the bed. What they'd shared for one night was more than he asked of heaven or earth, and all they would ever share.

He wouldn't allow himself to be this weak again.

His accumulated leave would run out in about two months; then he was due back at the Hobsonville base, back to doing what he was best at. In the meantime, he would use every waking hour to complete the most urgent repairs at the farm, arrange for the stock to be auctioned, then leave the property in the hands of a real estate agent.

Once he left, he would make sure he had no reason ever to come back to Riverbend again.

Rachel woke to the fragrance of coffee and an empty bed.

Rolling over, she smoothed her palm across the place where Cullen had lain. Cold. Disappointment seeped through her, pushing aside her self-condemnation at the way she'd behaved last night, the way she'd more or less begged him to make love to her. But condemnation aside, she'd still wanted to wake in his arms, to be cuddled and stroked—but she'd always known Cullen wasn't the cosy type. He'd warned her that all he wanted was sexual gratification, but she hadn't wanted to believe anyone could separate their emotions so neatly.

"You're awake."

She rolled onto her back. Cullen was leaning in the doorway, barefoot and shirtless, a mug of coffee in one hand. I'm glad I didn't seriously expect a softening in those winter-grey eyes just because we made love, she told herself, because they are just as flat, just as...disassociated as usual.

"Good morning." Jackknifing, she dragged the sheet over her breasts and pushed hair back from her face. He was almost dressed, fully awake, self-contained, and she was...a mess.

"Thanks." She accepted the mug he held out, sipped the aromatic brew and tried for a bright smile.

It was wasted. Cullen searched out his socks, sat down on the side of the bed and pulled them on; then he eased on his boots, before reaching for the shirt he must have picked up off the lounge floor earlier and tossed over the back of a chair. He'd already had a shower, she could smell the clean scent of her soap on his skin, and his hair was still damp.

Rachel set her half-empty coffee mug down on the bedside table. "I'll see you out."

He stood, buttoning his shirt. "There's no need."

Rachel ignored him. She threw the quilt back, deciding she wasn't going to care that she was naked and he was fully dressed. She might as well not have worried at all, because he did a good job of pretending she simply didn't exist as she marched across the room, snatched her robe from the hook behind her door and pulled it on, tightening the belt with a savage twist. So much for behaving in a civilised manner; she found she didn't have it in her after all.

He was watching her now. She could feel his attention, hear the change in the tenor of his breathing. "I take it this is goodbye," she said flatly, as she led the way out of the bedroom. It was still dark, and she saw with an incredulous glance at the clock in her lounge that it was just after four-thirty in the morning. Even though she knew Cullen was going now to protect her much vaunted reputation, the ease with which he was leaving, his sheer organisation—even bringing her a hot drink in bed—hurt.

"It has to be."

She started down the stairs, taking them slowly, carefully, and the anger drained away with every step. Cullen was leaving, as she'd known he would. What they'd shared last night had been, for her, beyond words. She was still stunned by the sheer wild beauty of their lovemaking, the intensity of emotion, the warmth and security of falling asleep with him wrapped around her, even if he'd insisted on sleeping on top of the covers. "I know why you think it has to be goodbye."

She halted near the door. When he joined her, the small hallway shrank to the proportions of a doll's house.

"No, you don't," he countered bleakly. "Besides the other, more tangible, problems, I can't offer the steady relationship you need."

Even though she'd expected Cullen to come out with something like that, his clipped statement hurt. At least with Adam she'd always been aware of his affection and regret. "I didn't expect a declaration of undying love, and I know you didn't want...this, but after last night—" She swallowed, looked down at the warm gold-and-brown tones of the rug beneath her bare feet, then up into Cullen's eyes. "I don't believe for one minute that you're not capable of sustaining a relationship."

His gaze remained damningly steady. "Lady, I don't think you want what I've got to offer. No decent woman would."

Rachel knew that this was it. The granite wall. In some ways Cullen was exactly like Adam and her family—he wanted to make all the decisions about what was "best" for her, regardless of what she wanted or needed. "I don't care about your past," she said flatly.

He stepped back, his shoulders grazing the wall. Rachel realised it was a defensive move, that her simple declaration had rocked him.

"My past is who I am," he replied grimly, "and I won't inflict it on any woman, no matter how much I want to be with her." His voice dropped to a hoarse rumble, and the bones of his face seemed to sharpen, the hollows becoming more pronounced. "And I want to be with you...very badly. So badly I can't bear to be in the same room with you and not touch you. That's why it has to be goodbye. Once I got you in my bed, I wouldn't let you go.''

Shock spasmed through Rachel. She swallowed, then remembered to breathe. Pieces of what he'd said bounced around crazily in her head, echoing, re-echoing, and always coming back to, ''I can't bear to be in the same room with you and not touch you.''

Adam's words.

Adam's words when he'd explained why their marriage had to end. He'd said he couldn't bear to be in the same room with this other woman and not touch her. Now Cullen was telling her the same thing. The words were for her this time, and still he was walking out on her.

''So, that's it,'' she said blankly, still trying to grasp how he could feel so intensely and still leave. ''Even though you feel this...compulsion, a one-night stand is all we'll ever share?''

Cullen's hands closed on her waist. She was lifted, trapped between the cool impervious wall and the hard heat of his body. He'd moved so fast she felt dizzy with it. His mouth dropped down on hers; his tongue filled her mouth. Rachel clutched his arms and hung on, relief and pleasure spiralling through her at the hungry demands of his hands and mouth. For a wild moment hope flared. He would stay. And if he stayed, she would have time. Time to convince him that they had the beginnings of something precious and unique.

Just as abruptly, she was free—bereft—swaying against the wall.

Cullen took the chain off the door and opened it. Damp air swirled in. His voice when he finally spoke was low, thick. ''I won't touch you again, but what we shared was *not* a one-night stand.''

The door closed behind him.

Rachel touched her fingers to her mouth; her lips were swollen and still tingling from his kiss. And it wasn't just her mouth. The rest of her was throbbing, her skin acutely sensitive. She could still feel the imprint of his hands, his body. Numbly, she stared at the wall opposite. Gradually she became aware of the passage of time. She was going to have to shower and change. To somehow pull herself together enough to open the salon and pretend everything was normal. A small moan surfaced from deep in her throat. She shoved her fist against her lips to stop the noise, but the low keening continued anyway.

Coldness seeped into her, and she began to shiver. Reaching out, she grabbed the bannister for support and began to pull herself upstairs. With every step she took, she could feel the small aches of muscles unused to lovemaking, the tender throb deep inside where she'd stretched to accommodate Cullen's raw power.

It was ironic, dreadfully ironic, that the words that had destroyed her marriage should be the same ones that would end her fledgling relationship with Cullen. He couldn't have found a more potent way to hammer home that no matter how strongly attracted he was to her, he would never stay.

Chapter 7

Cullen eased behind the wheel of his truck, slammed the door shut and crashed both fists down on the wheel.

The hell with it.

Damn—*damn*—his lack of control! His complete and utter disregard for anything but the fire in his blood, and his aching need to touch Rachel just once.

He should have let her drive home alone last night.

No. He couldn't have done that. Not with that son of a bitch, Trask, still cruising around, maybe getting liquored up for more trouble. He rubbed one hand over his face, rasping the stubble shadowing his jaw, probing the gritty ache in his eyes. A car drove past, then another one, and he became aware that the sun was cresting the horizon and that he shouldn't be parked so close to Rachel's salon.

And then something Trask had said last night forced its way past his own self-absorption. "You'll go down just like your daddy did," he'd boasted with a sneer. "Two hits, one to the nose and one to the gut. *Boom, boom,* that's all it would take."

Cullen jerked the key in the ignition and pulled out into the silent street, heading for home. The only people who knew where his father had been hit were Dan Holt—who'd been the attending officer at the time—his colleagues, and the coroner who'd investigated the death and pronounced that while the alcohol and physical abuse had contributed, Ian Logan had ultimately died by accidental drowning.

In any event, his father had been hit three times that night, and once again the only people who knew that fact were the officials assigned to the case.

And Cullen had been the one to administer the first blow.

After walking in on a strident argument between his father and Ian Logan's latest woman, he hadn't been able to stand there and watch his brutally handsome, charismatic father abuse his mistress.

At twenty-four, Caroline Hayward had had a youthful dewiness about her, even though Cullen knew that, despite her marriage to one of the district's wealthiest men, she'd been sharing his father's bed for the best part of a month.

Cullen remembered it as if it were yesterday. A cup had shattered against the kitchen door just as he'd opened it; then Caroline had started screaming when Ian Logan backhanded her across the mouth. The noise of the ensuing ruckus had been indescribable, and Cullen's stomach muscles had clenched in distress even though he was eighteen and at least as big as his father.

Caroline hadn't looked anything like the sleek, rich young woman she was. Dressed in one of his father's shirts, her makeup smudged, her hair tangled and a red mark on her jaw, she'd simply looked scared. Even slumming it, whatever her purpose, didn't excuse his father for frightening or abusing her.

"Leave her alone," Cullen demanded.

The low pitch of his voice startled them both into momentary silence. Shards of the broken cup crunched beneath his boots as he advanced another step into the room, underlining his right to be there, to put a stop to his father's madness. Caroline made a gulping sound and ran at him, plastering herself to his side. She cried out, lifting one bare foot. Blood welled from the pad just below her big toe, where a fragment of porcelain had struck deep.

"Butt out, Cullen," his father snarled, looking tough and menacing in faded denims and nothing else.

He was a big man, still muscular and vital—younger-looking than the forty-five years of age Cullen knew him to be. And just as mean as ever when things didn't go his way. But for the first time Cullen wasn't afraid of him. He'd had *disagreements* with bigger men, and won.

"Not this time." He met his father's flat, calculating gaze, then deliberately turned his attention to Caroline, detaching her from his side and sitting her down on one of the motley chairs grouped around the kitchen table. Grabbing a tea towel, grimacing that it wasn't exactly in a fresh state, he went down on his haunches to look at her foot.

Ian Logan stalked to the refrigerator, pulled a beer out, then levered the top carelessly onto the floor as he stood drinking and watching.

The blood welled sullenly where the piece of porcelain was still embedded in her flesh. Ignoring her gasp of reproach, Cullen removed the shard and wrapped the tea towel around her foot. Despite the heat and humidity of the summer evening, her skin felt clammy and cold. "Get dressed, then go home," he'd said.

"She'll go when she's ready."

"Oh, she's ready." Cullen straightened. "After what you just did to her, I doubt she'll be back for more of the same. Am I right, Caroline?"

She didn't answer.

Cullen made the mistake of turning his head and seeking confirmation in Caroline's eyes. He heard his father move, sensed his intention even as the bottle came toward him. Shifting on the balls of his feet, Cullen was able to lessen the impact of the blow, but even so, the half-full bottle of beer connected just below his temple, just missing his eye and making lights explode in his head. Automatically, he ducked and weaved to the side, years of defending himself on the streets coming into play. Wind whooshed by his mouth as his father's follow-up punch just missed connecting. Then, one eye already puffing up and closing, Cullen sent his fist driving forward in a fast, hard punch at his father's jaw, rocking the older man back on his heels. Cullen's knuckles split with the force of the blow.

It was the first time he'd ever struck back at his father. Years of fear and anger washed through him, condensing into a rush of triumph. That one blow had been empowering—the rage spun hotly through every cell of his body, blocking out pain, blocking out everything but the need to hurt back. To hit again and again. But as the adrenaline faded, he just felt sick.

With a groggy, confused look at his father, who was hanging on to the fridge to keep himself upright, and Caroline cowering in the corner watching *him* with a horrified fascination, Cullen stumbled to the bathroom, flipped the lid on the toilet and lost the contents of his stomach.

The ugliness of the scene made him feel tainted. Dirty. He didn't think he would ever forget the pure, hot pleasure of burying his fist in his father's face. A groan scraped past his raw throat as he flushed away the sour smell of nausea. Ah, God, no one should have to feel that! Least of all a son when he was hitting his father. And to cap it off, he was pretty damned sure it was the same brutal pleasure he'd seen on his father's face on occasion. Usually when Ian Logan had been beating the hell out of him.

He spun the basin tap on full. Icy water gushed out, splashing up and over the stained, chipped bowl. His stomach revolted again, and his eye hurt as if there were a knife plunged through the centre of it. It was already swelling and discolouring. Dipping forward, he rinsed his face, then held his bleeding, abraded hand under the cold stream.

Turning the water off, Cullen reached for a towel. His jaw clenched against the stiffening pain in his hand, the steady throb pounding at his head. The scene in the kitchen kept replaying itself in short, violent flashes through his mind, making his head spin with darkness and despair.

Caroline had looked at him with horror and fear. He began to shake. No way was he like his father. *No way.*

When he walked out into the kitchen, the room was empty of

everything but broken crockery and bloodstains and the stench of violence. Of any room in the neglected homestead, he reflected, the kitchen was the most betrayed. It was a large, farmhouse kitchen and should have been the cosy centre of a large, happy family. Instead it was dirty and grey, the windows bare to the blank darkness of the night, the walls in need of another coat of paint, the hardwood floor in need of a sander to take off the layers of grease and dirt. The wide, practical counter was covered in a jumble of his father's dishes, and the smell of countless fried meals was heavy in the air.

A car revved and screamed down the drive. Caroline's bright red Porsche. At least she'd had the sense to get out.

Grimacing at the effort it took him, Cullen swept up the mess on the floor and wiped up the smears of blood. His father was in the lounge, watching television. As if nothing had happened.

Maybe nothing had, on Ian Logan's scale of things. His lover hadn't liked being roughed up and had walked out on him. His son had finally got up the guts to take a poke at his old man. Now he was comfortably sunk on the sofa, nursing his bruised jaw and the ringing in his ears with another beer to act as a general anaesthetic. Big deal. Life goes on.

But it couldn't go on like this for Cullen.

After chucking the cloth he'd used in the bin, Cullen stared at his reflection in the window over the sink. He looked like hell. His eye was puffed up and starting to darken, but that wasn't what held his attention; he'd had black eyes before. In the garish light from the single bulb hanging from the ceiling, the expression in his undamaged eye was old, ancient...accepting. His mouth a bitter line.

Something moved inside him, tightening up his chest, pushing at his throat until a harsh sound forced its way out from between tightly clamped lips. *Sweet hell,* he was crying.

He dashed at his face, stifling a curse at the double beat of pain from his sore hand and swollen eye. Why had he come back here, anyway? What kind of instinct had aimed him back at this nothing town and deadbeat farm?

In Riverbend he was less than nothing. A loser.

The only way he could make something of himself was to leave. He sniffed, cursing the pathetic sound and daring himself to take one more look at his equally pathetic hide in the reflecting blankness of the window. Despite his resolve to leave, another tear coursed down his lean tanned cheek, mixing with the stubble on his jaw. It wasn't as if he were leaving a *home,* he castigated himself. He wouldn't know what a home was if it leaped up and hit him in the face.

He was leaving a violent drunk, a broke piece of dirt and the dream of a mother who had stayed around only long enough to expel him from her body.

It took him half an hour to load the Harley; then he dossed down in the barn beside the bike, knowing he needed sleep before he hit the road, and not trusting his father to leave either him or the bike alone. Besides, it had started to rain—the heavy, tropical kind you would have to be crazy to ride in. Well, he wasn't crazy yet, despite the urge to run as far and as fast as he could. He didn't want to see his father again, to look into cold, metallic eyes so like his own. It was bad enough looking like a carbon copy of his old man; he didn't have the strength yet to face the fact that he *was* him.

By ten o'clock the next morning the skies were clear and he was blasting into town to fill up on gas, the rumbling throb of the bike stirring the locals into more life than they usually showed. He gassed up, ignoring old Sal Tremaine, who always treated him as if he were going to pull a gun and rob his store. The clamp of emotion still pressing tightly around his chest finally began to ease as he left town in a shimmering heat wave. The euphoria of leaving, of the bright summer day, had lasted all the way to Fairley. Right up until he'd been stopped on the side of the road, read his rights and then herded into the back of a police car.

For the murder of his father.

Cullen eased the truck over his cattle stop and pulled up beside the barn. Fifteen years ago, he hadn't stood a chance. With his beat-up face and the abrasions on his knuckles—and the fact that he'd been leaving Riverbend at speed—he'd been the prime suspect. If it hadn't been for the coroner finding that Ian Logan had died by accidental drowning, Cullen would probably still be serving time.

So what exactly had Trask been boasting about? Had he been the one to beat his father up that night? How else would he know what injuries Ian Logan had had? Cullen was still as confused about his father's death as the police had been at the time. While Cullen had been dead asleep in the barn, Ian Logan had driven his battered truck into town. Someone had given him an expensive brand of whiskey he couldn't afford, then, when he was too drunk to retaliate, had hit him twice—hard enough to knock him out—then left him and the empty whiskey bottle by the side of the road just outside town. Evidently Ian Logan had roused himself enough to stumble into a ditch, then passed out again. The heavy rain had done the rest, rapidly filling, then overflowing the ditches for a short period of time. Long enough to drown him.

Any number of angry husbands would have had reason to want revenge—Caroline's husband, Richard Hayward, for one. But Hayward had offered to represent Cullen the next day, waiving his fee. His hands had been elegantly unswollen, with no telltale marks on his knuckles. And Trask had been new in town, moving in with a number of other construction workers who were involved in the shopping mall developments at Fairley and had been attracted by Riverbend's low real estate prices.

Maybe Trask *had* beaten Ian Logan up that night. He was a violent enough man not to need much of an excuse.

Cullen swung out of the truck into the crisp freshness of dawn. He had a natural resistance to seeking any kind of help from the law for himself, but he was going to have to set that aversion aside for Rachel's sake. He would talk to Dan Holt about Trask's threatening behaviour and the possibility that Trask had been involved in Ian Logan's death.

He knew nothing would come of it. Dan was conscientious; he would question Trask, but there was no evidence, only hearsay. Trask might be stupid, but he wasn't *that* stupid. He would clam up or, worse, try to make it sound like Cullen was still trying to cover his own ass for what had happened all those years ago.

Cullen's mouth twisted cynically. And if he hadn't been believed fifteen years ago, why should anyone believe him now?

Chapter 8

Rachel was pregnant.

"Are you sure?" she asked the doctor. It was a silly question to ask when she knew very well that she was pregnant—that six weeks after spending that one night with Cullen, she was most emphatically pregnant.

But then, the intervening weeks had been confusing. She'd had a skimpy period, and when Cullen had rung to check on her, she'd told him curtly that he was in the clear and hung up before she could betray the devastation she felt—and before he could express relief. But for the past few days her body had felt...different, and her next period had failed to appear.

Dr. Dalziel, who had delivered her over twenty-seven years ago, didn't seem to mind her question in the least. "The test is positive, Rachel. Can you give me a possible date for conception, or, failing that, the date of your last period?"

Rachel dug into her bag, pulled out the piece of paper on which she'd noted the date she'd made love with Cullen and handed it to the doctor. "The conception date is...accurate."

As Dr. Dalziel made notes in a file, Rachel sat numbly trying to reach into the future and grasp what was going to happen. How radically her life was going to change.

It wasn't as if she hadn't gone over the possibilities already, but nothing had been real then. This *baby* hadn't been real. Now she had to face the ramifications of being a single parent, because Cullen didn't want any kind of relationship with her. She hadn't seen him since the morning after they'd made love.

And she wouldn't not have her child.

A fierce protectiveness welled up inside her, and she touched her flat stomach with gentle, wondering fingers, barely hearing Dr. Dalziel's advice on diet and rest. She was going to have to tell Cullen—but not yet. Not until she'd had time to come to terms with this herself.

She left the surgery in a daze, stepping off the kerb without looking. Brakes squealed. An angry driver honked his horn. "You got a death wish, lady?" he yelled before driving off, leaving the acrid scent of smoking rubber and exhaust fumes behind.

Rachel stumbled back, legs shaking, hand automatically clutching at her stomach. A wave of nausea swept over her, and she groaned out loud, clapping one hand over her mouth and reaching out to a nearby telephone pole for support.

The nausea receded, leaving her feeling weak and sticky with perspiration. "Oh, great," she muttered out loud, glancing around to see if anyone had noticed her hanging on to the pole for dear life. She straightened, then walked slowly and carefully back to the salon.

Now, not only was she pregnant, but she felt like it, too.

Rachel almost didn't hear the sound of the knocking above her aerobics music. She hit the switch on the stereo and frowned at her watch before pulling an old, soft grey sweatshirt on over her leotard. The knocking came again, and she started down the stairs. It was way too early for Cole to be here. Maybe if she'd been a great cook he would have shown up early to prowl the kitchen, lifting pot lids and generally making a nuisance of himself. But they were having vegetarian. Her mouth lifted wryly. Of course

Cole didn't know what she was going to feed him, although he probably guessed it would be something exotic and spicy—not the plain meat and vegetables that he deemed "proper" food.

She unlocked, leaving the chain on. When she pulled the door open and peered through the gap, she had an absurd impulse to slam the door closed again.

It was Cullen.

Time slowed to a trickle, then seemed to halt altogether. It passed through her mind that she was hallucinating, that lack of sleep and the aching need to see Cullen had finally tipped her over the edge. Then reality kicked in. After seven, almost eight, weeks he'd finally decided to show. He was checking on her as she should have guessed he would. And now that he was physically here, she found she still wasn't ready to face his final rejection of both her and their baby. "Go away," she muttered, and shoved at the door.

It wouldn't budge. She looked down and saw his leather-booted foot wedged in the gap.

"Let me in, Rachel," he said in a low rumble that made her even more determined to get rid of him, because the impact he was having on her was near lethal. Just one glance at his cool grey eyes and the fragile defences she'd worked so hard at shoring up crumbled.

"I'm glad to see you're using the chain," he murmured.

Rachel stopped pushing; there was no point. She couldn't keep Cullen out if he wanted to come in. "I told you before, I only make a mistake once. Then I learn from it."

She only wished that statement were true, because right at this very moment she was staring into the narrowed, glittering eyes of her second mistake.

"Are you going to let me in?"

Rachel was tempted to say no. Unbearably tempted to say yes, then, when he removed his foot from the door, to slam it and lock it tight. But simple honesty compelled her to nod. Five minutes and he would be gone again. Gone for good. And as much as she wanted to avoid his final rejection, she couldn't *not* tell Cullen that he was going to be a father. He had a right to know. And, more importantly, her child had a right to know who his or her father was.

When he removed his foot, she unlatched the chain, then left him to follow her up the stairs. The hallway was too narrow to linger in, and she didn't want to get that close to Cullen again. At least in her lounge she could put the width of the room between them and, with any luck, a sofa or two.

His tread as he came up the stairs was unnervingly silent, and when he entered the small, civilised domain of her sitting room, a shiver that was purely primal in source rippled down her spine. Any progress she'd made in trying to neutralise what she felt for Cullen was abruptly ripped aside by the sheer, untamed force of his masculinity. Rachel was absurdly glad for the oversize sweatshirt she was wearing, because she suddenly felt exposed and uneasy.

She knew too well how much he could hurt her, and there was more at stake now than just her emotions.

Cullen prowled around her furniture, circumnavigated a coffee table and stopped only feet from her. She saw that he'd showered and changed before coming to see her. His hair was still damp and caught back in a ponytail; his jaw was freshly shaven. He smelled faintly of an expensive, subtle cologne and was dressed for the cooler weather in black close-fitting pants and a black crew neck sweater that clung to his shoulders and chest.

"How have you been?" he asked with a gentleness that at first startled her, then made her want to hit him.

Rachel drew a deep breath. "Do you really care?"

He didn't answer, just kept watching her, cool and wary and distant, and Rachel finally gave in to the urge to hurt him, to make him feel some of her shattered devastation. "As a matter of fact, I'm pregnant. Two months pregnant. I guess that means a December baby. It'll be hot then, but apparently summer is a great time for giving birth."

Cullen's heart stopped. Then it thudded to life again, hammering savagely as adrenaline seared his veins and corded muscles that were already locked tight. He felt as if he'd just been kicked in the solar plexus; he was having the same difficulty in getting his breath.

Pregnant. Two months pregnant.

He finally dragged air into his lungs, and with it came a flood of sharp-edged images: a lamplit room and Rachel clinging to him; the shattering moment of penetration; the consuming, rending heat of release. And now a baby, *his baby*. Growing inside Rachel.

A strident screech cut through the early evening quiet as some-one hauled down a garage door, and, more distantly, Cullen registered the plaintive lowing of a cow. The faint scent of wood smoke drifted through one of Rachel's partially open windows, mixing with the flowery scent of the bowl of potpourri on her coffee table. "You said you got your period," he said in a voice so low it scraped gravel.

"I did. But apparently that can happen."

There were dark hollows beneath Rachel's eyes, and, stubborn defiance apart, with her hair tumbled around her pale face she looked haunted and tired and fragile. He watched her reach for a handbag that was nestled on one of the couches. She passed him a slip of paper. It was tattered, as if she'd had it a while, as if she'd handled it repeatedly. The lab report was brief and to the point. And it changed everything.

He noticed it was dated a couple of weeks ago. His chest tightened. "You weren't going to tell me."

"I would have. Eventually."

Cullen held her gaze, absorbing her condemnation, knowing that he deserved everything she wanted to throw at him. He hadn't trusted himself to see her until he was packed and ready to leave town. There were no words he could dredge up that could atone for the hurt he'd caused her, because even while the primitive, possessively male part of him gloried in her pregnancy and the claim on her it gave him, the logical part of his brain knew that now there wasn't just one reason to let her go. There were two.

"I'm going to have the baby."

Cullen's fingers tightened around the lab report, tightened

against the need to reach out and claim her, to demand to see some evidence of the child in the delicate curve of her stomach, her breasts. And suddenly he needed to hold her with a force that shook him. Not in a sexual way—although that desire was even stronger, more overwhelming, than it had ever been—but just to have her close.

But there was a new strength in her tawny eyes, a distance that filled him with an inexplicable fury. A fury he had no right to. Under the circumstances, he should be glad she was so strong, so independent. The complications of their situation shuddered through him, escalating his frustrated anger, his need to take charge, to sweep away all the barriers that made Cullen Logan and Rachel Sinclair so impossible. *Damn it, she was his.*

A knock interrupted the tense silence. And it wasn't just a knock. It was a heavy pounding that demanded entrance.

The sound jolted Rachel out of the immobility that had taken hold of her while she'd waited for Cullen to respond to her news. To ultimately reject her and their baby. She was so certain of his rejection that she could already feel the pain of that final separation seeping through her limbs, tying her stomach in knots.

Cullen's gaze was damnably cool and controlled as her door shuddered under another assault, his voice a low, even growl. "Do you want me to answer that?"

Rachel almost laughed out loud but managed to halt the incipient hysteria before it carried her away completely. And let the whole town know you're sleeping with me? she thought. Let you know that I don't mind that the whole town knows I'm your— She shook her head, grimacing, because the hell of it was she knew that for Cullen their situation wasn't that simple. She'd already managed to hurt him, to shake him, even though he wasn't showing it. She would only hate herself more if she gave in to the temptation to become a complete shrew. "It's my door," she said, moving toward the stairs. "I'll get it."

Cullen padded to Rachel's bedroom window and stared out at the uncharming view of the back alley. Cole's truck was parked across the road, right behind his own.

When he heard the hard male voice demanding to be let in, heard Rachel fumbling with the locks, Cullen's hands knotted into fists. Frustration rose in him again, starting a snarl deep in his throat. He wasn't used to being helpless, and he didn't like it one little bit. *He* should have been the one to answer the door. *He* should have been the one to deflect Cole's aggression. Rachel was too damned fragile to take anything else on right now. And although Cole loved his sister, he couldn't see beyond his own protective role. He would cut her down in his quest to save her.

Unless Cullen staked his claim the only way Cole would understand.

The concept of caring for Rachel and the baby speared through him, sinking in bone deep until he couldn't think of anything else. Common sense told him to leave despite her fragility. But even as he listed all the reasons why his departure would make her life— and the baby's—better, he knew he wasn't going to go.

The raw, possessive hunger to have her with him took his breath away. He just wasn't capable of abandoning Rachel, just as he hadn't been capable of staying away from her in the first place. And he sure as hell couldn't walk out on a child—*his child*—the way his mother had walked out on him. Not until he knew they were both safe and provided for.

Cullen prowled back into the lounge, coming to a halt very near the place where they'd made love. The wild sweetness of the memory made his throat constrict with a longing he still hadn't been able to grind out of his system with hard work and cold plans for the future.

Cole's boots sounded like gunfire on the hardwood stairs. So be it, Cullen thought as he braced himself for the confrontation. Not exactly high noon on Riverbend's main street, but close enough.

"You bastard," Cole said with quiet menace. "You just couldn't leave her alone."

Rachel stepped around her brother, placing herself between Cole and him. "This is none of your business, Cole."

Cullen put his hands on Rachel's shoulders, his stomach lurching at the automatic way she protected him even now, and suddenly the words weren't so very difficult to say. "We're getting married."

Rachel stiffened beneath his touch.

Cole's expression went blank. "Run that by me again?"

Cullen increased the pressure on Rachel's shoulders, urging her back against him. She was still stiff and resisting, but she didn't pull away. Her hair drifted like cool silk against the backs of his hands, and he gave in to the temptation to brush his mouth across the top of her head. "She's mine," he declared in a hard, cool voice. "We're getting married next week."

Rachel still hadn't moved; he felt as if he were holding a store mannequin, and he cursed the inevitable arousal that just being near her caused. With every breath the evidence of his weakness was more glaringly evident, and he fully expected her to spin around and crack him across the jaw with her fist. Right before she told him to go to hell.

"Rachel?" Cole demanded, ignoring Cullen.

She didn't answer for long seconds; then a faint tremor went through her. "I didn't require your...sanction when I married Adam," she said huskily. "I don't intend to ask for it now."

Relief relaxed some of the ferocious tension cording Cullen's muscles. She hadn't exactly said that she was marrying him. But she hadn't turned him down, either.

Cole swore and ran his fingers through his light hair. "Does Dad know?" he asked in a strained voice.

She lifted her chin. "I was planning on ringing him...when I—we set a date."

Rachel's capitulation had Cullen's fingers tightening in reflex, drawing her back until she was firmly lodged against his chest. He wanted to wrap his arms around her, hold her close, drown in the scent and feel of her. He was shaking, dizzy with mingled delight and despair. In a life spent dodging shadows, wading hip-deep in a darkness that sucked and pulled and somehow managed to coat everything, the gift of her trust blazed. He had no right to Rachel or the baby, but she, *they,* were his.

Cole drew a sharp breath, then let it out slowly. "You're crazy,

Sis. How long have you known Cullen? How well do you know him? Damn it, if Adam wouldn't st—'' He stopped abruptly, pale beneath his tan. ''Cullen won't stay,'' he continued bluntly. ''If you expect any kind of long-term commitment you're buying into a world of trouble.''

Rachel flinched. The movement was tiny, almost instantly controlled. Cullen almost missed the betraying flicker as he fought down a surge of fury at Cole's callous statement. If Rachel's body hadn't been so closely moulded to his, he wouldn't have picked up the only visible outward sign that Cole had hurt her—intolerably—and he suddenly realised just how guarded, how controlled, Rachel was. Even if her emotions were tearing her apart, she would still work to hide them, to hold them deep inside and absorb them into herself, where they would do the least damage to anyone she loved. She bore the cost. *She* was the one who paid. It gave him a savage sense of satisfaction that, if nothing else, he could protect her in this now. ''She's moving in with me as soon as we can arrange it. Marriage is just a formality. Or would you rather see your sister just living with me?''

''Hell, no,'' Cole growled, his eyes narrowing with frustrated fury. ''With anyone else it wouldn't matter, but with your reputation, Logan...'' He shook his head, jammed his fingers through his hair again. ''I'll talk to you later, Rachel.'' He fixed Cullen with a cold glare. ''Don't hurt her.''

His booted feet thudded down the stairs. The door slammed behind him, sending a vibration shimmering through the sturdy timbers of the old building.

Don't hurt her.

The words hit Cullen with the same sharp force of the heavy door meeting solid hardwood. Don't hurt her the way his own father must have hurt Celeste, the way Cullen had been hurt before social services had taken him beyond the older man's reach. And then finally, completing the natural cycle of violence that was as inevitable as the turning seasons, in the way Cullen had hurt his father—and enjoyed doing it.

He bowed his head, resting it in the crook of Rachel's neck, allowing himself the luxury of filling his nostrils with her scent, her warmth, before he had to let her go. "I take it that was an acceptance."

"I take it that was a proposal." She wrenched free and spun to face him.

Oh, baby, she was mad.

Now that Cole had gone, the gloves were well and truly off, and Cullen couldn't help the satisfaction that filled him at the tilt to Rachel's chin, the half-wild fury in her eyes. He realised that one of the things that drew him to Rachel so strongly was her strength, the knowledge that no way would this lady ever allow herself to be a victim. She carried her pride and courage deep within her, and while her first husband might have put one hell of a dent in her self-esteem, ultimately she'd used the hurt to make herself stronger. "Yeah," he said warily. "It's a proposal. I'd go down on my knees if it would help, but somehow I don't think that would make any kind of difference. We both know I'm no gentleman."

"You don't have to marry me, Cullen."

"I took a risk, and I accept the responsibility that goes with it. We'll get married as soon as we can arrange it. Is a week long enough for you to get organised?"

Rachel was chilled by the lack of expression in Cullen's voice. He could have been reeling off a grocery list. When he'd declared so unconditionally that she was his, hope had flared. Against everything she'd already decided, against every logical reason there was for refusing him, she'd grabbed at his offer. But the only reason he wanted to marry her was because he felt he had to. "I accepted my share of the risk."

"I should've seen to your protection."

"I should have seen to my own! But I didn't, and I'm pregnant, and *I* take complete responsibility. It's my body, my baby—"

"Mine, too," he growled, stepping so close that his hot, restless vitality seemed to charge the very air she breathed. With a curiously possessive gesture he cupped her abdomen with one big hand, as if he could feel the small pulse of life deep inside her.

"I won't let you do this alone." His hand fell away, and coldness rushed in to replace the warmth of his palm. "When the baby's born, then you can make some decisions."

Rachel hugged her arms across her middle—trying to hold on to the sensation of his touch, she realised with a sharp, exasperated breath. She watched him pace to the window above the street and stare out at the sporadic flow of evening traffic. "What do you mean, 'make some decisions'?" she demanded, caught and held by the tenseness of his posture. And then she realised he wasn't watching the street, he was watching her reflected image.

"Getting you reestablished in the city. Whatever you need to get your life back in order."

"I don't want to live in the city! You'd hate it."

He didn't turn around, and in the darkening room the shadows clung to him, shrouding his shoulders. "I live in barracks when I'm in the country," he said evenly. "And once the baby's born you'll have more chance of meeting someone if you're back amongst your own. On your own."

Rachel blinked; then the full meaning of Cullen's words hit her. He not only didn't want to marry her, he didn't want any kind of relationship with her and was already planning for her to meet someone else. "I don't intend to move away from Riverbend. In case you hadn't noticed, this is my home. And I don't want to meet 'someone.'"

"But you will." Finally he faced her. "After the baby's born we can dissolve the marriage. And if you're far away, and I don't know who's touching you and taking you to bed, maybe, just maybe, I can stand it."

The flatness in Cullen's voice hit her like a blow. If she'd knocked him off balance with her news about the baby, he'd evidently recovered, because he expected her to tamely agree. And then another revelation completely eclipsed most of what he'd said.

Cullen was jealous.

Blindingly, burningly jealous. She repeated it to herself, biting back the furious need to argue with him, to fight and throw things

nd rage at the way he'd planned to neatly cut her out of his life.
or her own good, of course.

He was jealous. Possessive. He couldn't bear to be in the same
oom with her and not touch her. He couldn't bear the thought of
nyone else touching her, either. And she had seven months of
us pregnancy left to run. Seven months.

Rachel lifted her chin, almost disdaining that last, feeble straw.
ut she was beyond shame, beyond anger. Beyond anything but
eling her way through the bewildering minefield of emotion
e'd stumbled into. Time was all she had to hold on to, and she
as going to clutch at it, because she knew with a sudden stunning
arity that she was in love with Cullen. That if he disappeared
om her life, she wouldn't want anyone else. Ever.

She'd got over Adam.

But she could admit now that most of her hurt had been the
ain of failure and lost dreams, and the terrible blow to her fem-
ine pride. She'd let Adam go without a fight—there hadn't
emed to be anything left to fight for.

She stared into Cullen's level metallic gaze and knew she was
oing to fight for him. He felt more for her than simple physical
esire, otherwise he would never have touched her. His emotional
volvement was the reason he'd stayed away from her—and why
e was so intent on controlling the situation now. The baby they'd
ade together was giving them both a second chance, and she was
rabbing it. For all their sakes.

Taking a deep breath, she hugged her arms tighter around her
iddle. "We can talk about living arrangements after the baby's
orn. In the meantime, I'll check to see when we can book the
hurch."

"No church. I was thinking registry."

"Then think again, cowboy, because I won't feel married unless
's done in a church."

She could feel the force of his regard, his desire to control the
tuation; then, abruptly, he ran a hand over his hair. The unchar-
cteristic uncertainty of the gesture filled her with renewed hope.
he was beginning to know him, to be able to read him.

When he spoke, his voice was low and raspy, and it was be
coming so dark she could barely see his face. "If a church is wha
it takes to make you feel married, then okay. But the sooner w
get this settled, the better."

Cullen retrieved his mobile phone from the glove box as soc
as he was seated behind the wheel of his truck.

His call was picked up on the third ring without any call d
version, which meant that his cousin and company Commande
Blade Lombard, was carrying his mobile with him.

"Lombard," a gravelly voice snapped.

"Don't tell me I've caught you at a bad time again," Culle
murmured with real amusement. In the regiment, Blade's reputa
tion with women was legendary. If Blade was off duty, chance
were it would be a "bad time" to reach him.

There was a grunt of laughter, a rude suggestion concernin
where the cell phone should go from a feminine voice, followe
by a high-pitched squeal.

Blade came back on. "You'd better make it fast, mate."

"I'm getting married next week, and I want to take some unpai
leave—seven months, give or take a few days."

There was a stunned silence, then, "I take it this means you'r
not coming on exercise with us? The Australians *will* be ticke
They were really looking forward to taking you down after th
damage you did to their sabotage team last year. They're sti
trying to figure out how you managed to do it before they'd eve
made it to the target."

"I only got three," Cullen growled impatiently. "You and th
boys got the rest."

"West and I bagged one each," Blade murmured. "Carter ar
Ben had to fight over who got to take the last guy."

"Is the leave on?" Cullen asked curtly.

There was another small silence, and Cullen could almost hea
Blade's mind grinding through the regulations governing leave. "
take it there are extenuating family circumstances?"

Cullen briefly outlined the situation.

Blade muttered a string of inventive curses but, typically, didn't hang out for details. "When did you say this wedding is happening?"

"Next week. Saturday, I guess. Why?"

"Because I intend to be your best man. Ring me if there's any change of plan."

There was a brief garbled conversation in the background, some muffled grunts as if a struggle were in progress, then the phone went dead. Cullen stabbed the transmission button, snapped the wafer-thin phone closed and tossed it on the passenger seat. Darkness settled around him, along with the relative quietness of night. He glanced up at Rachel's flat. Her windows glowed with a soft radiance. He could hear music, classical music. She would be sitting down on one of those cosy sofas, maybe reading a book, eating from the fine porcelain he'd seen set out on her kitchen table.

A sudden vision of his house, his kitchen, replaced the gentle warmth of Rachel's.

He was going to have to make some changes. Damn, but his place was...rough. Clean, but rough. Suited to a bachelor who didn't spend any time there except to do the basics like cook, eat and sleep.

Frustration had his hands curling into fists as he gripped the wheel. He didn't know anything about making a house into a home. And that house was going to take a substantial injection of funds to make it into anything that resembled comfortable.

He had money. But the farm was soaking most of it up. He had access to other funds. Funds he'd never touched, and never wanted to touch, because it was his mother, Celeste Lombard's, trust money—her slice of the Lombard financial empire. Because he was her only child, it was legally his.

Cullen jammed his key in the ignition and started the truck. After his mother had abandoned him, he'd never wanted a thing from her that she wasn't there to offer in person. But she could help this baby, this child. It went against everything that he was to access his mother's fortune, but he would break the vow he'd made for Rachel and the baby.

He would take the money and use it for them.

Chapter 9

Rachel sat at the reception desk, enjoying the Friday afternoon sun and sipping a cup of herb tea as she used her coffee break to sort through the salon mail.

Over the past few days she'd managed to achieve more than she'd thought possible. The flowers for the church were ordered. She'd managed to find a wedding outfit, and had organised a removal firm to shift her furniture out to Cullen's house some time over the next week. Helen had quickly volunteered to take over tenancy of the flat. Cole had even agreed to come to the wedding.

She stopped at a letter that wasn't a bill. Curiously, she noted that it didn't have a stamp on it. It must have been delivered to the salon or somehow slipped directly into her post office box. Picking up the paper knife, she slit it open, pulled out a single sheet of paper and placed it on the reception desk. It wasn't the wedding card she was expecting.

Letters and words had been cut out of a magazine and glued onto a half sheet of paper, spelling out a crude sentence: "Cullen Logan is a murderer."

Rachel stared at the message, absorbing the ugly intent of it.

The nausea that was now her faint but ever constant companion roiled up. Closing her eyes, she forced herself to take deep, even breaths, sighing with relief when the sick feeling receded.

"Whoever has done this," she told herself, "is cowardly and malicious. And they've been watching too many television shows."

But she wasn't going to take it as a joke. Carefully, so as not to put any more of her fingerprints on the sheet of paper, she nudged it back into the envelope with the help of a pen. She put the envelope inside another larger envelope before storing it in her bag. She would hand it to Dan Holt just as soon as she could. Whoever had it in for Cullen in this town had just made a very big mistake. Rachel wasn't about to back down from this kind of intimidation, just as she wasn't going to let the furor of gossip surrounding her impending marriage, and the occasional nasty comment, get to her.

Many more people had wished her luck than had predicted gloom and doom, and she had a room full of cards and small gifts to prove it. The gossip *was* having an effect on the salon, but it wasn't the effect the person who'd sent the glued-on message would have hoped for. She and Helen were so busy with all the extra custom that she was seriously considering taking on an apprentice.

Helen sauntered breezily past, seeing one of their regular clients to the door, but instead of ushering her next customer to her work station, she stayed at the open double doors. The quality of her silence made Rachel look up, then join her.

"Oh, man," Helen breathed. "Look what just rolled into town. I think I just died and went to heaven."

Rachel saw the extended-cab truck pulled up outside the garage. Four men got out and started prowling around. A tall dark guy with military short hair took charge of the petrol pump, relieving weedy Sal Tremaine of the job with an abrupt, unquestionable authority. Rachel wouldn't have argued with that man, either. The way he was filling out his cutoffs and T-shirt, she would have given him way more room than old Sal had. A muscular blond guy disappeared into the shop, while the two others lounged against the truck and surveyed the town.

They were both tall and dark and built, and just as casually dressed as the guy taking charge of the petrol filler. The bigger of the two had sleek black hair caught back in a ponytail and an earring in one ear. All of the men had a restless, edgy aura of danger about them, but the one with the long hair kept drawing her attention. Something about him reminded her of Cullen. And it wasn't just the hair or the restless sweep of his watchful gaze.

She shook her head as the blond guy who'd walked into the garage shop sauntered out with several cans of soda. She must be farther gone than she'd thought. It was bad enough that Cullen dominated her thoughts and her dreams; now she was seeing his face in a stranger's.

"Yo, Blade, West," Carter said as he tossed two cans over the bonnet of the truck.

Blade caught his, more by instinct than sight; he was too busy looking around, *really looking,* and wondering what the hell it was holding Cullen in this totally ordinary country town. And what it was that had drawn Cullen into marriage and family when Blade had never known him to indulge in anything beyond the most casual of sexual liaisons. He'd assumed that Cullen was like him— and a lot of other special forces soldiers—damn poor marriage material. The very thought of commitment made Blade break out in a cold sweat. As much as he loved women—plural—he couldn't imagine settling down with one woman, in one place.

"See anything?" West drawled.

"Uh-uh," Blade grunted and tore the tab off the can before drinking most of it. He wiped lingering traces of moisture off his mouth with the back of his hand. "Do you?" he demanded.

West shrugged and crushed his can before making a potshot in the rubbish tin. "Nope."

"I see babes," Carter said, squinting toward what looked like the local hairdressing salon.

West groaned. Blade finished his drink.

"When don't you see babes, Carter?" Ben asked drily as he shoved the nozzle of the petrol pump back in its slot and peeled some notes out of his wallet for the nervous old guy who was standing around staring at them as if they were going to pull out a couple of sawn-off shotguns and start blasting. "Nice place you got here," he said, smiling. "Don't worry about the change."

West shook his head sadly. "Carter's problem is he's never been married."

Blade tossed his can in after West's. "He's too promiscuous for marriage."

Ben grinned. "Not to mention ugly."

"Ah, you guys are just jealous," Carter returned cheerfully, swinging into the driver's seat. "Cullen's about to have the noose tightened around his neck, Blade's the kind of husband material that would send any sane woman running, and you two shoulda stayed married to your guns instead of involving those poor females in your plans."

"Poor females?" Ben muttered. "Mate, I've felt safer jumping out of an aircraft at thirty thousand feet into pitch-black nothingness than trying to reason with my soon-to-be-ex-wife. What about you, West?"

West swung into the back with Ben and snapped the door closed. "She kept the house. She figured I didn't need it, since I was never there."

"See what I mean?" Carter drove slowly through the centre of town, staring around, amazed. Man, there was *no* traffic. It was kinda creepy, like some hick ghost town. "You guys should have stuck to 'relationships.'"

Ben eyeballed Carter in the rearview mirror. "Oh, very cool, Carter. Are we talking about one-night stands here?"

Blade indicated the next turnoff with a jerk of his thumb. "That *is* a relationship for Carter," he murmured.

"Ah, go on, then," Carter declared, taking the left-hand turn onto a rough gravel road. "Have your fun, but the fact is, one way or the other, you guys are all damaged goods. In the relationship stakes, I'm the only 'virgin' left in this sorry crew."

* * *

Cullen heard them pull up just as he tightened the last nut on the oil sump of his truck. He eased out from underneath, grabbed the bandanna holding his hair out of his eyes, and used it to wipe off his hands and the drips of oil that had hit his torso. As he walked toward the shiny new extended-cab, he ran his forearm across his sweating face. He didn't recognise the truck, but he knew who was in it. He'd only expected Blade, but he should have guessed the rest of the guys would wangle their way on this trip.

He couldn't keep the grin off his face as he watched them all pile out of the truck.

Blade said, "Good to see you, Cul," and something in Cullen's chest tightened up.

He hadn't realised how much he'd missed these guys, how much he'd missed being part of a team. "It's been a while," he agreed, shaking hands all around and getting pulled into a series of hot, sweaty hugs. "Hey, what is this? Male bonding? Next thing you know you guys'll be wanting to stick your tongues down my throat."

Carter made the sign of the cross with his fingers. "Easy, babe, just because you've snagged some poor, unfortunate woman, doesn't mean the rest of us are *that* desperate."

Cullen shook his head, his expression rueful. "As long as you promise to cook, you can all stay in the house."

"Carter ain't cooking," Ben said morosely. "We all wanna be alive when we wake up. Blade can be in charge of the food. I'll set up the bar."

He reached into the bed of the truck and hauled out a box of beer. Carter grinned, grabbed Ben's face with two hands and kissed him full on the lips.

"Oh, gross," Ben muttered, wiping his mouth on one arm and aiming a kick at Carter, before tearing the box open and tossing him a beer. "If you've gotta do something with your lips, man, plant them on that."

Blade prowled over to the truck and began hauling gear out. He aimed a pack at Cullen who caught it, staggering back under the weight.

"What's in here?" Cullen demanded.

"Ammunition." Blade snagged a rifle and tossed that at Cullen, too.

"Whoa." Cullen caught the rifle with one hand, easing the weight of the pack over his hip. "Just what kind of wedding do you think this is gonna be?"

"We're coming to the wedding, but we don't plan to stay. After you're bagged and tagged tomorrow, we thought we'd leave you to your privacy. We're heading north to do a little hunting." Blade jerked his head toward the towering, brooding bush-clad hills in the distance. "But next time we might try out those hills of yours. That's some of the meanest country I've seen in a long time."

After everyone was bedded down for the night, Cullen prowled restlessly in his room. He couldn't sleep. He wasn't going to even try.

Having the guys arrive like that had unsettled him completely. They were like family to him, and he wanted to be a part of their action, but suddenly there was this huge, yawning gap, and he didn't know himself. He didn't know what he wanted when this situation with Rachel was over. His career with the military had satisfied a lot of needs, but he just didn't think soldiering was going to do it for him anymore. He didn't know what would.

Beyond Rachel and the baby, that was.

A window shattered. The sharp report of a rifle punched through the sound of exploding glass.

Cullen was on the move, reaching for the sidearm he still kept in his bedside drawer, slamming the clip in place as he loped out into the passage and down the stairs. His mind was working coldly, quickly. The sounds had come from the south side of the house, facing the drive in. The vehicle he'd heard just minutes before meant that someone had parked, then walked to his house before firing a shot.

As he raced out the back door in a crouch, Cullen registered

he sounds of feet hitting the floor, weapons being snapped to-
ether, and then silence broken by the faint familiar sounds of
Blade and the rest of the team forming up in a tight patrol line
 behind him.

Cullen caught a flash of movement ahead and hand-signalled
back: two men. He could hear them, panting, out of breath, their
boots thudding on the gravel road. They reached their truck. One
swore as he stumbled and yanked on the door; then Cullen and
the rest of the boys were positioning themselves around the vehicle, guns brought up to bear.

"Put the weapon down," Cullen ordered curtly. "Then get
way from the truck, real easy. Move too fast and one of us might
et nervous."

One of the men swore, his hands shooting into the air. "Where
the hell did all of *them* come from?" he snarled at the unmistak-
ble figure of Frank Trask. "You said it would just be *him.* And
maybe some woman."

Blade stepped forward and picked up the shotgun. He motioned
en and Carter to move in and frisk the men. "You boys are
lucky it wasn't just Cullen," he said mildly. "We're all nicer than
im."

West and Blade covered the men, while Cullen sorted through
the contents of the truck and found a length of rope. "Anyone got
knife?"

Four hands shot into various stash places and produced gleam-
g blades. "Oh, man," Cullen muttered, "don't you guys ever
ke a break? I thought you were on leave."

"Bein' on leave doesn't mean we have to walk around naked,"
Carter muttered, flipping his fighting knife through the air. Cullen
aught it with smooth expertise, cut two lengths of rope, then
quickly and expertly tied the two men's hands behind their backs.

Carter spun the men around and pushed them into the side of
the truck. He wasn't gentle. "And seein' as how your neighbours
are so friendly," he continued, shooting a glance at Cullen,
"maybe you should be considering *your* wardrobe."

Blade pulled a cell phone from the pocket of his cutoffs. "Wh
do I call?" he asked Cullen.

Cullen gave him Dan Holt's number.

Blade stabbed some numbers, waited, then spoke tersely befor
flipping the phone closed and shoving it back into his pocke
"He'll be here ASAP."

Trask's head came up at the announcement. The glazed look o
both the prisoners' faces was fading fast, now that the banter wa
over and the prospect of an official end to their night's work wa
in sight.

After a tense interval, a vehicle sounded in the distance. Second
later Dan Holt's police car crunched to a halt. His eyes narrowe
on all the firepower surrounding the two cowering men. He centre
on Trask, then glanced sharply at Cullen. "Looks like a wa
zone."

"Just a few friends up for some hunting," Cullen replied.

Dan lifted his eyebrows. "Yeah, right. SAS I presume?"

Five faces went blank.

"Okay." He sighed, dragging a notebook out of his pocket an
flipping it open. "Fill me in, boys."

Cullen gave him a terse outline of events.

Dan produced handcuffs, looked ruefully at the expert rope jo
cinching the prisoners' wrists tight and stashed the cuffs in hi
back pocket with a fatalistic sigh. He herded the two men into th
back seat of his car and put the weapon they'd used in the boo
He nodded at Cullen. "I'll take these two into Fairley for the re
of the night. I'll see you there first thing tomorrow morning for
statement." Lifting his hand, he drove up to the house, turne
around, then drove back and out onto the road.

Blade gave Cullen a hard look as they all headed back to th
house. "I think you'd better tell us what's been going on her
Cul."

"I smell petrol," Ben said sharply.

"Yeah, you're right," West said. "Hey, Cul, those bastar
were gonna burn you out."

Carter examined the splash marks on the side of the house and scratched his head. "Then why the hell did they start shooting?"

Blade shook his head in disgust. "Accidental discharge, probably. Man, do I hate amateurs. Someone could have been hit."

Cullen located the petrol can the men had dropped in their panic. It's just as well they got careless," he said bleakly. "Otherwise we'd be watching this baby burn right now."

They were all silent, looking at the old house. Carter ambled off to get the hose and began watering down the areas that showed splash marks.

Blade jerked his head at Cullen and walked a short distance away from the others. "What's going on, Cullen?"

Cullen shrugged. "Some stuff's been happening. I got involved with trying to help the son of one of those men, and he didn't take kindly to my intervention. He beat up on the boy, then the boy's mother. And then he threatened Rachel."

"Doesn't seem motivation enough to risk something like this."

Cullen watched Carter turn off the water. Ben and West were systematically checking all the outbuildings, making sure there weren't any more surprises they should know about. Anger still vibrated through him, along with a cold, sick feeling he didn't like at all. Trask's sidekick had mentioned "a woman," which meant they'd been prepared to burn the house down with Rachel inside. "I haven't got to the bottom of Trask's motivations yet. I've got some ideas, but no way to prove any of it. And besides, it's a little difficult pointing the finger around here. I don't exactly have a pristine reputation."

"I know the kind of stuff you did. It wasn't that bad."

"Yeah, right," Cullen said drily. "Running with a gang, learning to survive on the streets. Just your usual youthful exuberance. Around here, you spit on the sidewalk and they consider putting you away."

"So, the town thinks you're some kind of bad boy come back to raise hell?" Blade shook his head. "Don't they know who you are? What you are?"

Cullen shook his head. "This is small-town New Zealand,

Blade, and these people saw me at my worst. To them, I *am* the bad guy.''

The next morning Cullen slotted his truck into a space outside the police station in Fairley. He gave his name at the reception desk before being ushered into an interview room.

Ironically, it was the same interview room he'd sat and sweated in fifteen years ago. Apart from a new coat of paint in a pale pink that was no doubt supposed to soothe the savage breast, it was unchanged. The same scarred furniture, the same feeling of claustrophobia—of being caged. The same stale smell of defeat.

Dan Holt joined him, along with another uniformed detective. The formalities only took a few minutes. The young guy in uniform took the paperwork and the empty fuel can Cullen had brought in, and left the room.

Dan sat back in his chair. ''You and Trask seem to have quite a little feud building up here. I'd be interested to hear anything you'd like to tell me about it.''

Cullen kept his expression blank. ''You talked to him about his claim that he hit my father?''

''Put the emphasis on 'I talked.' If Trask was as silent as that in the pub, a lot of folks'd be relieved.''

Cullen shrugged. ''Maybe he was just mouthing off. I didn't expect anything to come of it.''

''Anything, hell. What he did last night looks like retaliation.''

''So what happens now?''

''With the load on district court judges, it'll be months before Trask appears. He's been released pending trial, but I've slapped a court order on him. If he approaches you or Rachel, sets foot on your property, or tampers with any of your possessions, he goes into custody.''

Relief unlocked some of the tension in Cullen's muscles. ''Thanks. I appreciate the protection—for Rachel's sake.''

''But not your own?'' Dan met his gaze levelly. ''I can understand that. You haven't exactly had a lot to thank the law for

Believe me, if I could've found out what happened to your father all those years ago, I would have. I never thought you did it.''

"Thanks," Cullen said gruffly. He'd always thought Dan was fair, but he'd never expected him to offer anything more than guarded neutrality. Just as he was rising to leave, Dan put up a hand.

"Before you go, I'd like to get your slant on that letter Rachel brought in yesterday.''

Cullen's senses went on immediate alert. Letter? He could think of only one reason for Rachel to hand a letter to Dan. Fury tightened all his muscles at the thought of someone threatening Rachel. The fury increased when he considered that Rachel had clearly bypassed him with her problem. He found he didn't like that one little bit. Just as he hadn't liked her assertion that she could cope with being a solo parent just fine. "Rachel didn't mention any letter.''

Dan fidgeted with the file on the table. Cullen's eyes narrowed. Not much upset the middle-aged policeman. He had a cop's face, a cop's cynical eyes. Something unusual had to have happened to have breached that essential hardness.

Dan flipped open the folder and produced a plastic envelope with a sheet of paper displayed inside. "Rachel received this in the salon's mail.''

Cullen read the terse, precisely aligned statement and understood immediately why Rachel hadn't discussed the letter with him. She'd been trying to protect him. His fury condensed into a cold knot in his stomach. Ever since he'd reluctantly returned to Riverbend, he'd been encountering problems. Mostly it was just simple bad manners, sometimes a refusal to do business with him. The most frustrating difficulty was the ongoing problem of finding anyone to work for him. Consequently, it was taking him months to do what should have taken weeks. The sheet of paper was an abrupt escalation of his difficulties. Gossip and speculation, even anger about his past, were one thing, but apparently someone wanted him out of Riverbend badly enough to show their hand. But they'd just made a serious error, because Cullen wasn't eighteen and running scared. He was thirty-three and beginning to be seriously ticked off. "Did you manage to lift any prints?"

"Aside from Rachel's, not a one."

Cullen grunted. He hadn't expected to hear anything different. Just one look at the pristine paper, the carefully aligned letters provided the information that the person who'd put the letter together was careful and intelligent and unlikely to do anything a amateurish as leave prints.

Dan leaned forward. "Is there anyone who might have reason to...uh..."

"To convince Rachel that marrying Riverbend's bad boy isn' a great move? Take your pick, Dan. Half the town would like t see me gone."

"Not many of 'em would go this far. And I don't think Tras has got what it takes to produce something like this, either."

"It wasn't Trask," Cullen agreed. "Not this time."

Dan sat up straighter, his tired gaze sharpened. "If you've ge any ideas, I want to hear them."

"I have ideas. Nothing concrete."

"Damn it, Cullen, If you're withholding information—"

"If I come up with anything you can use," Cullen interrupted "I'll give it to you wrapped up with a bow."

"If someone's harassing you, it's police business," Da warned. "Don't try to handle it on your own."

"I won't start anything," Cullen promised grimly. "But if th son of a bitch who sent that letter to Rachel decides to get u close and personal with me, I won't be backing down."

When Cullen stepped out into the hallway, he almost walke into Trask and his cohort. And the elegantly suited figure of Ric ard Hayward. The lawyer looked right through him, but Tras didn't. His gaze was triumphant, as he strode past.

Cullen followed them out of the station and watched the me get into Hayward's expensive new Lexus and drive away. H wouldn't have thought Trask made the kind of money Haywa would demand for defending him. Or to make bail on attempt arson and firearms charges.

Unless he had someone with money backing him.

Chapter 10

When Rachel arrived at the tiny church just outside of town, she was glad she'd insisted they have the wedding there.

The church was beautiful, perched on the top of a ridge, commanding a wide view of the checkerboard valley that fell away at its feet and the hazy, blue distance of the hill country. With its peeling paint outside and hushed darkness inside, the old building possessed a timeless grace and peace that conferred a subtle blessing on her hurried marriage.

"You don't have to do this," Cole said bluntly, halting her at the front steps.

Rachel sent him and the other three brothers who had popped out of nowhere—minus girlfriends—an irritated look. She adjusted her small, defiantly white silk hat and half veil and ran a last-minute check on her simple white silk suit. "I want to do this," she said calmly. "Now, are you going to give me away, or do I have to do it myself?"

Cole released a strained sigh. "You could at least have waited til Dad could get here."

"He's in Japan for a month," she stated. "And I can't wa
There's no easy way to tell you this, guys, so...I'm pregnant."

Four jaws sagged. Then an excess of testosterone surfaced in
rush. Ethan bunched his hands into fists, Nick's eyes slitted, a
Cole had to snag Doyle as he made a violent move toward th
doors of the church.

"That's it," Cole said bleakly. "You're not marrying Loga
We'll look after the kid."

Rachel shook Cole's hand off and resisted the urge to ask if th
offer would still be open if she happened to have a daughter i
stead of a son? She stepped back, far enough away that she cou
stare each brother in the eye in turn. They were all Viking-blon
all gorgeous, and each one of them sported the stubborn Sincla
jaw. The one feature they all had in common. "I *want* to mar
him," she said firmly, not sparing herself. "This is all my doir
I've trapped him. He doesn't want me."

"Like hell," Doyle muttered, giving her a look of suprem
disbelief. "Why didn't he use a—"

"It just happened," she said flatly.

"Oh, yeah," Nick drawled. "It was still pretty damned carele
of him. He should have been prepared."

"Are you prepared...now?" she asked with delicate precisio

Nick's ice blue eyes narrowed to slits. "This is my only siste
wedding," he replied curtly. "I'm not planning on anything mc
strenuous than checking out this creep."

"Exactly," she agreed, holding out her arm to Cole and a
dressing him directly. "Do I go in alone, or are you coming w
me?"

Cole shook his head, a faint smile adding a rueful edge to l
simmering frustration. "Logan didn't stand a chance, did he?"

Rachel's cheeks heated up. "I told you, it *just happened.*"

"Yeah, like the time you manoeuvred Jamie Hanson into a da
corner and kissed him."

"That doesn't count. I was six years old!"

"And he was nearly twice your size and a manly eight, but y
herded him in that corner and planted one on him just the same

"I'm surprised you remember that."

"Oh, I remember," he said softly. "We all drew straws, and I was the one that got to beat the living hell out of him."

The smugness in Cole's voice was infuriating. "Then it's probably just as well I went to live in Auckland," Rachel retorted. "With you lot circling me like a pack of hungry Rottweilers, I never would have got to meet anyone."

"Yeah, well," he returned in a low, irritated rumble, "we tried our best, but we never could stop you. Witness what we're about to do now."

Rachel glared, jerking him with her up the first step. As they entered the open doors, the first strains of the wedding march filtered into the late afternoon air, and Cullen turned, his gaze immediately settling on her.

She barely recognised him. He'd cut his hair and was wearing military dress uniform, and the four men lined up beside him were similarly dressed. The church seemed packed full of soldiers. Maybe because they were all so big and the church was tiny.

She heard one of her brothers mutter something, and then they were walking down the aisle, Cole's forearm tense as corded steel beneath her fingers. Finally she was standing beside Cullen, all her brothers belligerently lined up with her, glaring across and through her at the soldiers. She could feel them each selecting who they would fight first. Doyle, who had always been hot-tempered, would be picking the two largest, meanest specimens. She recognised the soldiers. They were the same dangerous crew who'd stopped for petrol across the road from her salon yesterday. They were here for her wedding.

Her wedding.

Rachel forced a shaky smile for the nice old vicar. The same one who'd married her last time.

If anything, Cullen seemed even more remote in uniform, and her stomach tensed at the knowledge that he was still in the army, merely on extended leave. This whole cowboy routine was just a break for him, and his newly cropped military short hair, the crisp olive uniform with its distinctive SAS wings, the gleaming row of medals running across his broad chest, all served to remind her that her hold on him, despite this ceremony, was tenuous.

The vicar began to speak.

Cullen let out a slow breath. Now he knew he was living a dream.

She looked like a dream in a soft, silky confection of a suit, that veiled hat tilted on her satiny head while she watched him with dark, grave eyes, as if this were what she'd always wished for. Always dreamed about.

And God help him, but she was wearing white and fulfilling every one of his hungry fantasies. He hadn't expected that. Just like he hadn't expected her to be carrying flowers. White flowers. Roses, and something more heavily scented. Gardenias, maybe. The fragrance filled his nostrils, and he knew that whenever he smelt it he would be instantly reminded of this moment.

He'd only given Rachel a few days to prepare, but somehow, despite the opposition she must have faced—and the shock of receiving that anonymous letter—she'd managed to make this a wedding and not the expedient ceremony he'd wanted. Cullen's jaw tightened with a savage regret. Damn. This wasn't going to go away, no matter how hard he tried to lock it out of his consciousness. The images were too powerful: the graceful old church with the sun slanting through tall, arched windows; the massed white flowers; the echoing sound of the vicar's voice intoning words that were ancient, binding. The sheer beauty of the woman standing beside him. And the child she was carrying.

This shouldn't be happening. Just like his throat shouldn't be choking up, and his gaze shouldn't be locked with Rachel's as he drowned in her mesmerizing combination of vulnerability and fierceness.

He wanted to be able to forget this. He was pretty sure he was going to *need* to forget this or go mad.

Rachel barely noticed when the vicar finished the first part of the ceremony. She was too intent on Cullen and the unaccustomed softness in his eyes.

The vicar asked for the ring. The soldier closest to Cullen, the one with the long hair and the earring, dug in his pocket and presented a ring. Rachel jabbed Cole in the ribs with her elbow, then snapped out her hand. Cole grudgingly dropped a heavy ring onto her palm. Rachel placed the ring on the vicar's open bible alongside the other smaller one.

Cullen stared at the two seamless circles of gleaming gold. He'd bought a ring for Rachel, as was expected, but she'd got one for him, as well. The symbolism of the ring slammed through him. The perfect joining. Oneness.

No, he would never be able to forget this, and now he knew he didn't want to. It would hurt, but he would keep the ring. Always.

He could hear the boys shuffling uneasily, and Carter's whispered, "Oh, man, where does *that* one go? Through Cul's nose?" then Blade's terse, "Shut it, Carter." Then the ceremony was rolling on into the scary part. The part he knew he had no right to.

Rachel listened to the evocative power of the wedding vows, memories of her first wedding skating through her mind. She'd been filled with an innocent, carefree joy then. She'd been marrying the man she loved, the man she thought loved her. She'd believed they would be together all their lives.

The failure of that marriage pulled at her, made her stiffen her spine and square her shoulders. When the time came for her to respond, she did so clearly and firmly. Cullen's replies were firm, too, but quiet, rasping with the underlying strength that was so much a part of him.

When the brief ceremony was finished, he held her face between his hands and kissed her with a gentle purpose that brought tears to her eyes.

A collective sigh sounded from the soldiers, a kind of resigned exhalation from her brothers.

As the warmth of the kiss left her mouth, she began noticing just how many people there were in the church. Helen was near the front with her mechanic boyfriend, Gerry. Several of Rachel's customers and some longtime friends of her family had come. Dane was there—looking tanned and, after weeks of outdoor work, remarkably healthy—his eyes fixed on Cullen with something like awe and hero worship all rolled into one. Rachel hadn't formally invited anyone—there hadn't really been time—and she was profoundly touched by the unexpected support.

After signing the official documents in the registry, she and Cullen walked out into the softening light of late afternoon. This time her arm was enfolded by Cullen's. Even though she knew he was only doing what was expected of him, the warm clasp of his hand over hers was a bittersweet comfort.

As they reached the bottom of the steps, the SAS men lined up, two on each side. Blade barked an order, and they stood stiffly to attention. A shiver went down Rachel's spine at the sight of the big men forming an honour guard, their uniforms pristine, chests decorated with what she knew must be some of the highest military awards in the Commonwealth. As she and Cullen walked between them, they saluted.

Cullen groaned. "I didn't know they were going to do this."

Rachel surveyed the surprising gathering of people outside the church, all of them standing stock-still, quite a few of them with their mouths gaping at the military display. She smiled with grim satisfaction, thinking about the poisonous letter which Dan Holt was now investigating, and of all the malicious gossip and "advice" she'd been offered. "I'm glad they did."

The long-haired soldier, who Cullen introduced to Rachel as Blade, was the first to shake Cullen's hand, and after that there was a steady stream of well-wishers.

Blade kissed her on the cheek, and Cole, who'd taken up a position next to her, eyed him coldly. "I know you from somewhere."

Rachel jabbed Cole in the ribs again. Her brother's tone was deliberately goading. She would *not* allow him to start a fight. Cole ignored her, but Blade slanted her a surprisingly reassuring look. Surprising because he looked at least as untamed as Cullen did.

"I'm Cullen's cousin," he said in a soft, dark drawl that held just a hint of menace. "Cullen's father married my aunt, Celeste Lombard."

"Lombard," Cole echoed. "That's an unusual name around here. Any relation to the hoteliers?"

"My family have hotels, among other things."

"Yeah, right," Cole said drily.

"And of course, Cullen," Blade continued in that same soft drawl, "like every other member of my family, is a shareholder in Lombards."

Cole's eyes narrowed. "Is that so?"

"Cullen doesn't choose to have anything to do with the running of the company, but he could if he wanted to. If he ever sold out his shares—which he won't, because he's family—he could buy and sell this town."

"Point taken. He's richer than us."

Blade's mouth curled into a grim smile. "Considerably."

This time, when Rachel jabbed Cole in the ribs he paid her some attention. "You asked for that," she said tightly, suppressing her own dismay at the news. Cullen was a deeply complex man, but she'd thought she was coming to know him. Blade's information that Cullen was wealthy and connected to a powerful family seriously dented her perceptions. She was in love with Cullen, but the enormity of the vows she'd made still reverberated through her. Regardless of Cullen's intentions, she had meant every word, and she could no longer hide from what she'd done. She'd walked out of the ruins of one marriage and straight into another, and in doing so she'd linked herself to a stranger.

She almost groaned out loud. After what Cole had learned about Cullen's financial status, he and her other brothers were standing around, tense and thin-lipped, levelling cool sizing-up looks at Cullen.

And Cullen wasn't backing down.

"If you fight on my wedding day," she said, loudly enough for them all to hear, "I will cook every night for the next month, and you, Cole, will be invited over for dinner."

Cole groaned, and Cullen shot her a wary look.

"She can't cook," Cole said bluntly.

"I didn't marry her for her cooking," Cullen replied in a goading, rough-silk voice that made Cole go ominously blank.

Rachel could feel the close attention every single word was getting from the soldiers and her brothers. Helen's mouth dropped open. Every other conversation stopped as people tuned in to what was shaping up to be a brawl.

The look Cole and Cullen exchanged went on and on, the male aggression flowing with a tangible force. The soldiers bunched up behind Cullen, her brothers behind Cole. Then, so suddenly it felt as if someone had just flicked a switch, Cole nodded curtly, reached her in one long stride and kissed her on the cheek. Ethan, Nick and Doyle stepped forward, one by one, each kissing her cheek and quietly, curtly, offering their "services" if this marriage should fold.

"Keep in touch, Sis," Cole growled, slanting Cullen another meaningful look; then he jerked his head at his brothers, and they all strode away.

"What was that all about?" Carter asked as he watched Cole drive away, followed by another car packed with Sinclair brothers.

Cullen didn't reply. He was too busy watching Cole. Seeing him off the premises, Rachel fumed to herself.

"This is a wedding," she said with a delicate edge to her voice. Cullen's simmering metallic gaze swung back to hers. "My brother just gave me away—literally—to Cullen."

Carter nodded, as if that were perfectly logical.

Rachel could see he might never fully understand her point of view.

Blade smiled grimly. "Got a sister, Carter?"

"You know I've got one."

"Then just imagine her marrying a horny bastard like you, and you'll get the picture."

"Oh, yeah," Carter said, nodding, then, *"No way!"*

Rachel handed her small bouquet of flowers to Helen. "You'd better have these. Although I don't know why any sane woman would want to get married."

Ben turned to West and spoke in a considering voice. "Isn't the bride supposed to chuck those, West?"

West nodded sagely. "Aww, but you know how slow Carter is. I think she's afraid he might catch them, and then we'd be saddled with the job of finding Carter a wife."

"Oh, very funny, guys," Carter said. He smiled at Helen, dazzling her with a maximum wattage, killer-beach-boy grin. "Don't you go wasting your time with either of these old married men, darlin'. They had their shot at domestic bliss, and the sad truth is, they were both too wild to be tamed. Now take me." He planted a confiding hand on his broad chest. "I'm house-trained. I can do dishes, I pick up socks, I get takeout like you wouldn't believe, and," Carter's voice dropped to a gravelly whisper as he delivered his clincher, "if you stroke *me*, I purr...."

"Ah, geez, Carter," Ben groaned. "Give it a rest!"

Helen blinked at Carter's magnificence, then, without dragging her gaze from his flashing white teeth, mumbled, "I've got a present for you, Rachel. I'll get it."

She backed off a few steps, then turned and hurried off down the uneven path.

Cullen's arm slipped possessively around Rachel's waist. His eyes were narrowed, intense, wholly centred on her. Rachel's knees went weak when she identified his expression. He looked like that when he was making love. As if he were wild for her and couldn't get enough.

He gathered her in, his arm an iron bar at the small of her back, one hand gripping her nape. His mouth dropped on hers with the faintly cruel force of extreme arousal, parting her lips, forcing his entry in a kiss that claimed her completely and had her clinging to the lapels of his jacket. The furnace heat from his body burned through layers of clothing. When he finally lifted his mouth, Rachel had a fuzzy view of Helen standing nearby, holding on to a large parcel.

"Good luck," she said, as she handed the parcel over. "Although somehow I don't think you're going to need it."

Chapter 11

Rachel unpinned her small confection of a wedding hat as she walked up the steps and into Cullen's house. Her home.

She almost stumbled as the reality of her situation shifted into sharp focus. Up until this moment, she'd been solely concerned with the wedding; the future had been blurry, distant. Lifting her chin, she forced herself to survey her surroundings. She'd made her decision, and her needs were painfully simple: she wanted to love and be loved; she wanted babies; she wanted family; and she *needed* Cullen.

She'd been inside his house twice now, once to make coffee while Cullen had dealt with Frank Trask, then again just two days ago to drop off a suitcase of clothes and several boxes of kitchen utensils and crockery.

The hallway was long and unexpectedly wide, as if whoever had built it had had an eye for grandeur. And in its day the house *had* been grand. It was certainly big enough. And oh, so empty.

Cullen strode in behind her, carrying more of her possessions, which they'd picked up en route from the church—another suitcase of clothing and a bag of perishables from her fridge. His gaze lingered on her, and he frowned. Ever since they'd left the church, he'd been frowning.

"You look tired," he said. "I'll show you to your room."

Your room. Not *our* room.

A small lash of pain sliced through Rachel's carefully managed serenity as she watched Cullen off-load the bag of groceries on the floor. When they'd stood together in church exchanging vows, the emotion flowing between them had been a tangible thing. And later, outside, when he'd held her and kissed her, she'd almost forgotten that their marriage was a sham. She'd come close to forgetting her own name.

Cullen turned toward her, and Rachel drew in her breath at the purpose in his light gaze. She had the definite impression he was going to touch her, maybe place his arm around her waist and help her upstairs. But even as she watched, a subtle change took place, a closing out of emotion, and she realised he was deliberately distancing himself from her. His gaze glittered over her again; then he picked up the suitcase he'd just brought in and started up the stairs.

Abruptly, tiredness overwhelmed Rachel. She reached to steady herself against the rich wood panelling of the wall. She'd been running on nerves and little else lately. There had been so much to do, to arrange. So much to block from her mind so she could continue to function in a normal, rational way. She should have been prepared for Cullen's coolness. Despite that kiss outside the church, he'd made his position clear when he'd proposed this marriage.

Squaring her jaw, she kicked off her shoes and forced herself to move.

Cullen wasn't in the first room she came to. There was nothing in there. Like the rest of the house, the bedroom was bare. Sterile. He wasn't in the room opposite, either, although there was evidence of his occupation in the large, neatly made bed with his beret and uniform jacket slung over the end of it. She heard water splashing into a basin; then Cullen appeared at what must be the bathroom door.

He watched her critically as she padded toward him. Her chin
came up in automatic response. There was a brooding tension
about Cullen, an air of suppressed fury that she was at a loss to
understand. Or maybe it was just the short hair. He'd looked dangerous and untamed with long hair; now he looked even harder,
more remote.

Rachel didn't like the change. It emphasised his air of control.
He wore the veneer of civilisation as comfortably as he wore the
primitive, muscular beauty of his body, deepening the distance
between them in a way that sent panic flaring through her.

He was no longer wearing his wedding ring.

The absence of the gold band shoved reality at her again. She
hadn't known whether he would wear the ring or not. Some men
simply objected to wearing jewellery of any kind. But the ring had
been important to her; it had been a claiming of her own, a message that she hadn't given up on a real marriage.

She must have signalled her distress, made some kind of sound,
because Cullen uttered a low, succinct oath and covered the distance between them. His arms came around her as he eased her in
close against the hard, solid warmth of his body.

Time passed, and he continued to hold her. Rachel let her head
sink against his shoulder and wrapped her arms around his lean
waist while she listened to the heavy, regular beat of his heart.
Eventually he drew away.

"I'm a damned fool," he said quietly. "You're pregnant,
you've worked yourself into the ground organising the wedding,
and now you're dead on your feet. Why don't you lie down while
I bring the rest of your stuff in? Your room's down there." He
nodded at the far end of the corridor. "Take a nap. I'll make a
start on dinner."

Dazed and still tingling with the warmth of Cullen's embrace,
Rachel reached the doorway to her room. And stopped.

The rest of the house was bare, but over the past few days
Cullen must have worked night and day in this room. The wood
floor was polished to a high sheen and partially covered by a large
Turkish rug in warm, muted colours. The walls were painted a

similar tawny colour to the one she'd used in her flat, and the multipaned sash windows were draped in filmy muslin. There was bed. A romantic dream of a four-poster constructed from black wrought iron and hung with delicate folds of mosquito netting. Her suitcase sat on an antique chest at the foot of the bed. There was other furniture too: a dresser and dressing table, bedside tables—all with the glow of valuable antiques.

"How did you know?" she demanded.

"About the bed?" Cullen was directly behind her, his voice a velvety rumble just above her right ear. "Helen gave me a decorating magazine. She said you'd wanted the four-poster for the flat but it wouldn't fit."

"So you got it for me. Why?" she asked, weariness fading as she faced him.

Again the puzzling air of tightly condensed fury, of emotion locked beneath adamantine control. "I wanted you to be...comfortable."

"This is more than just comfortable." It was sumptuous, expensive and, under the circumstances, impractically extravagant. "But then, you can afford it, can't you? You're a member of the *Lombard* family."

"My mother was a Lombard," he conceded.

Rachel inhaled sharply at his deliberate evasion. There was, she decided, no point in being subtle. If she wanted information she would have to prise it out of him. "Okay, you're *related* to the Lombards. What I want to know is why you're letting this town put you through hell when you could pay someone to take care of everything for you?"

For a tense interval she thought Cullen wasn't going to answer, then he said bluntly, "It's my property, my responsibility. I'll be damned if I'll back away from it because the people of Riverbend are squeamish about a Logan being back in residence. I could hire a manager. I've got access to funds, but I've never wanted the money for myself. As far as I'm concerned, it all still belongs to Celeste."

"If she's dead, then she must have left it to you."

"Celeste didn't acknowledge me at any stage, and the Lombard family wasn't aware of my existence until after she died. I wa sixteen when they first contacted me, and by then I'd lived in mor places than I could remember." His mouth twisted. "And deal with agendas that swung from the pure profit motive to saving m soul. The Lombards wanted me because I was Celeste's son. Al I wanted was out."

"They didn't claim guardianship?"

"They tried. But by the time they got the paperwork done, was long gone. Gray Lombard, Blade's older brother, tracked m down eventually, but by then I was seventeen and working wit a construction crew. When he realised I wasn't going to go bac with him, he left. Gray used to turn up periodically, checking o me, and when I was being held in the cells at Fairley, he baile me out. I didn't call him. I don't know how he found out wha was going on." Cullen lifted his shoulders. "For Gray, I agree to meet with my grandparents, and I accepted the only thing I di want. The Lombards have some heavy-duty connections with th military. Gray pulled some strings, and I went into the army, even tually following both him and Blade into the SAS."

Rachel listened numbly to Cullen's clipped series of statement clearly outlining how ruthlessly single-minded he'd been, even a seventeen. He'd held off a powerful, charismatic family and ex tracted what he wanted from them. Then she grasped what h *hadn't* said. "You used Lombard money to do all this." Culle would wade through burning oil before he would use any of hi mother's money for himself. But he'd broken that tenet for he And the baby.

Cullen eyed her with a trace of wariness. "This farm, this house are not what you're used to—"

"You're right," she returned. "I'm used to an Auckland fla noise and smog and too much traffic. I'm certainly not used t that!" She gestured to one of the windows, at the view of wil country sweeping into endless hills, of the sunset refracting off distant, glittering fall of water, of a raw granite face rising out c darkness into light.

"It's quiet here," he agreed. "I'll give you that much. It's also lonely. I'm gone most days—all day. The nearest neighbour used to be Alistair Carson, but since he died, nobody's shown any interest in living in the shack he used to call home. You could visit your brother, but that's still a twenty-minute drive. On horseback, a good hour's ride." His gaze finally centred on her. "Not that you'll be riding."

Rachel's breath caught at the curt statement. She wasn't planning on riding, either, but she resented Cullen setting limits. So far they were playing by his rules, but no way was she going to be a doormat for any man. "I'll be working most days," she retorted crisply. "I imagine I'll get all the social contact I'll ever need at the salon."

Cullen's eyes narrowed, and suddenly the sense of tightly leashed control evaporated. He looked like he was spoiling for a fight.

Rachel's hands curled into fists. Ever since she'd met Cullen Logan, her life had gone from lonely and unsatisfactory to sheer, utter chaos. She was miserable without him. She was miserable *with* him. She was pregnant. A fight would be just fine by her.

Just when it looked like she was going to get her wish, awareness of how he was reacting dawned in Cullen's gaze. His hands bunched, released, and he went abruptly, oddly pale. Then Rachel was staring at his broad back as he strode out into the hallway. A door thumped closed. His bedroom.

She let out a breath that shook with temper and nerves, and discovered she was still holding her wedding hat. Grimacing at what she'd done to the expensive scrap of silk and gauze, she tossed it on top of her suitcase and began to pace. Her heart was pumping flat-out, and she was pretty sure she needed to break something, but, like the childhood temper tantrums, she'd left that behaviour behind when she was three.

His door opened a few minutes later. This time Cullen's step was louder, and she knew he'd changed into jeans and riding boots. When his footsteps faded, her nervous tension went with it, and she flopped down on the bed and stared at the ceiling, letting the swimmy feeling of exhaustion have its way with her. But along with stillness came the doubts.

She was married to a stranger.

Her sheer lack of knowledge about Cullen was daunting. He obviously had enough money to make a few phone calls and have some of the most expensive, exclusive retail shops in the country jump through hoops for him. He could probably make this whole empty barn of a house look like a decorator's paradise if he wanted.

That he'd decorated her room and nothing else jarred. She felt set apart—like a princess stashed in a tower—as if he wanted to shield her from anything unpleasant, even from the fact that she was living in his house. As much as she loved the room, she didn't like the sense of being separated from Cullen in such a way. It was what her family had always done to her, and she resented it fiercely.

Then there was the whole marriage thing. The possibility that despite separate rooms, Cullen might share her bed at some stage. She knew the battering force of his sexuality, the mind-numbing pleasure of his touch, but she also knew that wouldn't be enough. If they were going to make love again, she needed him to feel something for her. She needed him to want to be with her. And most of all, she needed some kind of real commitment from him.

When Rachel awoke it was full dark. Light filtered into her room from the hallway. She could hear distant kitchen noises: the chink of crockery, water hissing into a sink.

Pushing herself upright, she fumbled for the lamp on the bedside table, located the switch and flooded the room with a mellow glow. Her watch said it was eight. She'd slept for a good two hours.

When she'd changed out of her creased wedding suit and into snug jeans, a warm shirt and her favourite dark red sweater, she found the bathroom, splashed water on her face, then made her way downstairs to the kitchen.

Cullen was just removing a casserole from the oven. He glanced up as she walked in. ''I was just going to wake you.''

Her stomach grumbled as Cullen set the dish down on a heat pad on the table. Plates and silverware were already set out, as well as a bowl of steaming rice and a crisp, green salad. "You can cook," she said faintly.

For a second she could have sworn he was going to smile; then he shrugged. "It's nothing fancy. When you get dropped in a foreign country for weeks at a time with nothing to eat but army rations, you learn to improvise. Fast."

Rachel pulled a chair out and sat as Cullen pushed a plate laden with rice and casserole toward her. Normally the amount he'd just served up would have made her blanch. Now she helped herself to salad and barely restrained herself from starting before he did.

Before Cullen sat down he walked to the fridge, poured a large glass of milk and set it down in front of her. "For the baby," he murmured.

As Cullen pulled out his chair and sat, the enormity of what they were doing suddenly hit Rachel. They were married: Husband and wife. This was their first meal together. Normally the wedding breakfast was a ritualistic affair with speeches and ceremony. When she'd married Adam there had been over a hundred guests sharing in the ritual, toasting their good health and long life together, but in all the excitement the symbolic aspect of sharing a table, the intimacy of eating together, hadn't occurred to her. It did now. With the stillness of night closed in tight around the farmhouse, the shadows barely pushed back by the lone bulb screwed into the kitchen ceiling, the simple meal Cullen had prepared seemed more steeped in symbolism—more deeply linking—than that other, more formal, wedding breakfast.

Rachel picked up her knife and fork and tasted the casserole; it was plain, and it needed salt, but it was edible. Cullen didn't seem to notice the lack of flavour. He ate with a steady, relentless appetite that reminded her of her brothers. The food on his plate was needed fuel for his body; he neither liked nor disliked, and ate everything with an unbiased concentration. If he was filling his truck with petrol, he would probably have the same expression on his face.

Evidently he wasn't the least bit bothered by the symbolism
eating their first meal together.

By the time Rachel had finished her dinner, Cullen had polish
off his second impressive helping and was loading his plate in
a gleaming new dishwasher. Glancing around the kitchen, Rach
noticed that the stove matched the dishwasher, and the refrigera
and freezer also looked suspiciously new. She hadn't investiga
the laundry yet, but she would lay odds there were a brand n
washer and drier in there. A curl of hope started deep inside h
If Cullen had spent all this money on the house, then maybe, j
maybe, he had hopes for the future, too.

Rachel had just loaded her plate in the dishwasher when s
became aware that Cullen was leaning against the counter, thum
hooked in the belt loops of his jeans, watching her. "Dan H
showed me that letter you took in to him."

Rachel blinked at his bald statement and closed the dishwash
He'd said the words quietly enough, but she could hear the fo
behind his calm statement. So, this was what that air of condens
fury had been about. Cullen was intensely male, protective a
possessive. He hadn't liked it that she'd kept the letter from hi
"It was just a sick joke. I thought the police should deal with it

"You didn't think that I should know someone was ma
ing...allegations about me?"

"You're not a murderer. That piece of paper is a tasteless pra
by someone who should be seriously considering therapy."

Cullen didn't move from his relaxed stance against the count
but Rachel didn't mistake his stillness for indolence. He was coi
tight and ready to explode.

"You're right about the therapy part," he noted softly. "B
did you consider that this person might be dangerous? Baby
could shake you. Whoever put that message together means bu
ness. If anything like this happens again, I want to know abe
it."

"Aren't you making too big a deal out of this? Any schoolk
could have put that message together."

"If you really thought that, you wouldn't have taken the let in to Dan. That message wasn't the work of some schoolkid. There were no fingerprints on the paper besides yours, Rachel. It was absolutely clean.''

A cold chill went down Rachel's spine. No prints? He had to be joking. Of course, even if there had been prints, there was no guarantee of finding out who they belonged to. The perpetrator would have to have a police record for that to happen. But no prints at all?

Abruptly, Cullen pushed himself away from the counter and prowled the length of the kitchen. When he spoke, his voice was low and clipped. ''This morning I went in to Fairley to lay formal charges against Frank Trask for illegal discharge of a weapon and attempted arson. Last night Trask tried to burn this house down.''

''Burn the house,'' Rachel echoed, automatically following Cullen, feeling the same crawling sensation she'd felt when she'd first read the anonymous message. ''Why would he want to do that? Surely he's not still carrying a grudge about you helping Dane and his wife?''

''I don't know what thoughts go through Trask's head. But I'm pretty sure the arson attempt and the letter are related. Someone wants me out of Riverbend, and they're not too particular how they go about it, or who they hurt in the process.''

Rachel frowned. ''But why?''

Cullen's hands moved as if he were going to touch her. With a savage oath, he strode several paces away and gestured toward one of the chairs. ''Sit down, and I'll try to explain. Maybe when you've heard what I've got to say you'll make the sensible choice and go back to Auckland.''

Cullen watched Rachel sit down and jerked his fingers through his hair, cursing the naked feeling at the back of his neck, and wondering why he'd ever let Blade and the rest of the crew talk him into having his hair cut. Respectability had never bothered him a damn before, and it had always been too late to worry about it in Riverbend, anyway.

Just like it was too late for a lot of things. He'd never voluntarily talked about the hellish situation when his father had died. He didn't want to tell Rachel now. His first and strongest instinct was to tell her nothing, to keep her cocooned and as happy as he could through this pregnancy. But events had forced his hand. Rachel had to know what was at stake, for her own safety and that of their child. "You've probably heard enough gossip to piece my past together," he said flatly. "I'm going to give you the unadulterated version."

Taking a deep breath, he settled his hands on the back of a chair. "My mother left Riverbend as soon as she could after giving birth to me. According to my father, Celeste was wild, a drifter. He didn't know where she came from or where she went, or that she had money. Alistair Carson's wife, Mae, looked after me until I was old enough to move in with my father, and then..." He paused, his hands tightening on the chair. "I had what you might call a dysfunctional childhood. In lay terms, my father beat hell out of me whenever he'd had too much to drink. And sometimes just for fun."

"I heard you ran away," Rachel said softly.

"I made a career of it. I grew up fast, and I grew up hard. I was shunted out of this town when I was nine and didn't make it back until I turned eighteen. Riverbend didn't know what hit it. I was hell on wheels, literally. The whole place must have sighed with relief when I finally left. And when the cops picked me up and tossed me in a cell for the murder of my father, no one was in the least surprised. I was the perfect suspect."

The images sprang at him, as raw and hard-edged as if it had all happened yesterday. His knuckles whitened as he related the incident when he'd walked in on Caroline Hayward and his father, the ensuing fight, Ian Logan's death, the pieces of the puzzle—like the too expensive whiskey—that just didn't fit.

Rachel met his gaze levelly. "So, someone got your father drunk, beat him up, then left him on the side of the road, and now this person's scared you'll find out who he, or she, is."

"That's the only way I can figure it. There was no way my father could or would afford to drink a fancy whiskey like Chiva Regal." His mouth twisted. "He liked quantity, not quality."

"Then it follows that the attacker had to be someone who *could* afford to buy Chivas."

Cullen inclined his head. "I'd lay odds that whoever's encouraging me to leave town panicked when they heard we were getting married. Suddenly it looked like I was going to stay."

Rachel's gaze narrowed. "You know who left your father on the side of the road."

Cullen couldn't prevent a quick smile of approval, but even so, her quickness startled him. She was putting the pieces of the puzzle together almost as fast as he could give them to her. "I think Trask was involved, but only as hired muscle. The other person is more shadowy, but I'm pretty certain it's Richard Hayward."

Rachel's eyes widened. "My God," she muttered. "What a mess."

Cullen wasn't about to argue. It was one hell of a mess, and threatening to explode all over Riverbend. "I imagine Hayward wouldn't want any dirt rubbing off on his professional reputation. Being implicated in a murder investigation, even if he was never formally charged, would kill his business."

"He doesn't deserve to be practicing," Rachel said heatedly.

"That's if he *is* involved. All I've got is supposition and gut instinct. I don't have one shred of proof. I could run all this by Dan, but seriously, if you were a cop, who would you believe? A lawyer who has a solid standing in the community? Or a man who has no roots—who makes a living out of violence?"

A morepork hooted somewhere outside and was answered by a more distant cry, the fridge hummed steadily, and the sturdy old house settled in for the night with creaks and groans that were oddly peaceful.

The scrape of Rachel's chair as she got to her feet shattered the momentary quiet. "Is *that* why you won't let yourself get close to anyone?" she demanded, stalking around the table toward him. "The reason we can't have a normal relationship is because you'd sooner roll over for a creep like Hayward than prove how wrong everyone has been?" She jabbed a finger at his chest, and the smooth langourous flow of her voice metamorphosed into cool and

clipped. "Or maybe it's easier for you to believe your bad pre
than take a shot at commitment? I never would have labelled yo
a coward, Cullen."

Cullen caught Rachel's hand and clenched his jaw against th
need to jerk her against him and drown in her sweet scent, he
delicious softness. He'd touched her more today than he ever ha
except for the times when they'd almost made love, then final
had made love, and it was driving him crazy. "The hell wit
Hayward and his games," he rasped. "If I wanted to stay in Riv
erbend, he wouldn't stop me."

She blinked and shook her head. "So, why are you leaving?"

Cullen stared at her in open disbelief. "Haven't you heard
word I've ever said? I'm not the kind of guy you should be spen
ing any time with at all! I'm too rough, too damned hard to mak
good husband and father material."

Her tawny eyes flared, making her skin seem even creamier, he
hair richer, darker, and Cullen realised that despite Rachel's ap
parent calm, she wasn't backing off an inch. She was furious, bu
controlled with it, and the knowledge made his heart slam and h
blood pound thickly through his veins. He found he liked fightin
with her. The thought should have appalled him, sent him runnin
but instead he was aroused. It was all he could do to keep fro
taking her down to the floor, stripping her clothes off, shoving he
beneath him and doing the very thing that had got them in th
mess in the first place.

"And I thought I was dumb as a post about relationships," sh
drawled. "How would you know, when you've obviously nev
had one!"

Cullen should have expected the blow, given his knowledge o
Rachel's temper, but her fist shooting toward his chest took hi
by surprise. Even so, his hand shot up, catching her wrist befo
the punch could land. The movement swung her body into hi
Her breasts flattened against his chest, their knees bumped, an
her belly fetched up against the solid, aching ridge of his sex.
groan ripped from Cullen's throat. Before he could control th
primitive urge, his hips jerked, grinding himself even deepe

arder, against her soft warmth. Rachel wasn't moving; she was mply resting against him, accepting his hold on her hand and rist. Accepting the unruly pressure of his sex nudging her stomch.

Slowly, breathing hard with the effort, Cullen steadied her, then epped away. When he spoke, the words were scraped from his roat, guttural with the effort of forcing each dark syllable out. Fifteen years ago, on just about this precise spot, I hit my father ard enough to put a hairline fracture in his jaw. My knuckles ere bruised and split from that one blow.''

Rachel was breathing just as fast as he was, and he saw with a olt that she was aroused as well as angry. Another choking wave f lust slammed through him. Damn, this wasn't helping. She ould be staring him down with a haughty, patrician look instead f watching him with frank sensual hunger.

"He'd just hit a woman," she snapped. "He'd just hit *you.* nyone would have hit him back!"

"Not everyone would have enjoyed it."

The harsh words chilled Rachel. Moments ago Cullen had been scant breath away from kissing her, and more. She could still el the heated imprint of his body, the tingling pressure where is heavy arousal had rocked into her stomach.

"Sometimes," he continued tightly, "I wake up at night, sweat g, and I can *feel* what it was like to hit him. How much I wanted hit him again, and keep on hitting him. It makes me sick to my tomach. If I ever lost control—" His chest expanded. "I lost ontrol when I made love to you. I can't allow that to happen gain. If I can lose control and make love to you, I can lose control nd harm you."

"You wouldn't harm me."

Cullen cut her a look that was savage with impatience. "Can ou say that for sure? Will you be able to tell our child that he or he is safe?"

Rachel lifted her chin. "I *know* you. You would no more hurt e than any of my brothers would."

"I won't trust myself in a relationship," he said from between

gritted teeth. "I know how insidious violence is—I've read enoug
literature on the subject. If you need an example, look at th
Trasks. Generation after generation of families get caught up i
its cycle."

"You broke the cycle."

"Did I?" he asked bleakly. "Baby, I joined the SAS. In any
one's book, that's gotta be an escalation."

Rachel stared at Cullen, at the sweat sheening his skin, at th
implacable set to his jaw, and finally grasped the essence behin
every warning he'd ever given her.

He wasn't going to budge.

Cullen came from violence. He believed he would live with
forever.

Rachel didn't believe that. Not for a minute. From the first touc
of his hand on hers in the alley behind her salon, she'd sensed h
inner strength and gentleness. But Cullen believed it, and that wa
what counted. And he backed his belief with the granite will whic
was the very core of the strength she loved.

The magnitude of the risk she'd taken with this marriage h
her. She'd been certain that the emotion she sensed in Culle
would grow, that she could reach him. Now she saw that the odd
of her gamble succeeding weren't just long, they were almost no
existent. Cullen wanted her physically, but no matter what sh
said, what she did, he would go on believing that he was dangerou
to know. And way too dangerous to live with.

Panic and defeat cascaded through her, drawing her skin tigh
making her breath come faster. She'd told her brothers that she'
trapped Cullen into marriage. She'd been half joking at the tim
but now she knew just how much of a trap it was. He wanted he
yes, but her very proximity only served to remind him of every
thing he *thought* he couldn't have.

Her baby wouldn't have a father. The family she'd alway
yearned for would now only consist of two people, because ther
wouldn't be another man for her, and there wouldn't be any mor
children. Unless she could change the way Cullen saw himself.

God help her, but she couldn't give up. She still had time, about even months. But suddenly that didn't seem nearly long enough. he had the unnerving conviction that a lifetime would be too ort.

Chapter 12

Several weeks later Cullen met the engineer at his damage
bridge. Kevin Shortland was a tall, stringy man, with thick glasse
perched on the high, thin arch of his nose. He looked more suite
to academia than engineering, but the dark, tea-coloured tan of hi
skin proclaimed that he spent more time outside than he did in.

After trying unsuccessfully to get one of the local companie
out to assess the damage, Cullen had finally given up and con
tacted an Auckland based firm, which had meant further frustratin
delays and more expense. Like his difficulty in obtaining casua
labour or contractors, getting anyone local to come out had prove
to be near impossible.

"Don't drive on it," Shortland said bluntly. "The last series o
floods undermined the foundations. Everything else about th
bridge is fine. The timber's hardwood, all the beams are good, b
you're going to have to get a crew in to sink some new piles an
reinforce the old ones."

"We haven't been driving on it." Cullen straightened from hi
inspection of the cutaway bank. Luckily the bridge only provide
access to the western corner of the farm, where his land butted u

against Sinclair land. The grazing was limited because of the meandering nature of the river and the sudden onset of the high country which reared overhead. Dane had shifted all the cattle to the other side of the river and was using the lush grazing on the river flats for the mares and their foals. The bridge was a headache, though. He could dismantle it, since he was going to sell anyway, but the bridge in itself was valuable and would cost a great deal of money to replace. Anyone buying the farm would want it intact. Depending on how quickly the property sold, he would have to undertake the repair himself, or at least have estimates and plans available for any interested parties.

They clambered up the bank and strode across the broad, high structure.

Kevin shook his head and glanced up at the dark hills. "That's one hell of a watershed you've got up there."

Cullen studied the steep, wild terrain. The lower slopes were tawny with grass; the higher his gaze roved, the scrubbier the vegetation became, until the bush took over entirely. Here and there the rainforest had been ripped away by slips, the light scars stark evidence of the violent deluges that periodically plunged down the hillsides. His glance slid to the innocent chuckle of water tumbling beneath the bridge. "It's a real bitch," he agreed.

When Cullen pulled up at the house that evening, he was earlier than usual and too tired to find something else to fill his time. He'd changed oil and serviced machinery until everything was running more smoothly than it ever had. Every pump, every water trough, every electric fence, was working perfectly. And Dane had the horses in hand. The mares hung around him as if he were some prime stud they wanted to impress, and even the stallions had calmed down enough that he could halter them.

Pushing the door of the truck open, he swung out and instantly stiffened. He could hear music playing—soft classical music—and lights glowed in more than one room, giving the house a life and vitality it usually lacked.

Stepping up onto the verandah, he levered his work boots off

and carried them around to the mudroom. After tossing his socks
and shirt in the laundry basket and washing the dirt off his hands,
he made his way upstairs. And stopped.

Rachel was in his room.

Her hair was dragged back in a ponytail. She looked about sixteen in leggings and socks and an oversize sweater, and she was
measuring his window. His gaze shifted to the bed, with its plain
dark blue coverlet. It was rumpled, as if she'd sat on it. Or maybe
even lain down.

His chest expanded on a sudden intake of air as he tried to block
that particular vision out. How in hell was he supposed to sleep
if he kept seeing Rachel in his bed? If he kept smelling her scent
on his pillow?

Clenching his jaw against the startled, defiant look she directed
at him, he snagged fresh clothing from his drawer and strode into
the bathroom. He turned on the shower with a savage flick of his
wrist, then peeled his jeans off with considerably more care.

He hurt. Ah, God, he burned. And when he stood under the ice-
cold stream and soaped himself, he groaned out loud. Hell's teeth!
Her soap. Her shampoo. He could smell her on him night and day.
He was going to have to take a trip into town and buy soap that
didn't smell of Rachel. Something that didn't drive him crazy
every time he had to take a breath.

By the time he got out of the shower, she'd left his room, but
the bed was still rumpled, and he knew with savage certainty that
he wasn't going to be able to sleep in it that night. He could doss
down in the barn, but that held too many bad memories. He would
spend the night haunted by ghosts, reliving a past that should never
have been lived through even once. The couches in the lounge
were out; they were too short for his long frame. And, like the
bed, they smelled of Rachel.

Later on that evening, Rachel caught Cullen just before he went
into his study. He looked even grimmer than he had when he'd
caught her in the holy of holies, his room.

As if he had a thing to hide.

He lived as barrenly as a monk. No photographs, no knick-nacks of any kind, just that big gun in his drawer. Not that she'd done anything as intrusive as search through his personal things. He quite simply didn't have anything personal lying around.

"I want to paint the house," she said baldly, crossing both fingers behind her back, not because she was lying, but because painting the house wasn't all she hoped to achieve. From the first moment she'd seen the Logan homestead, she'd itched to do something with it. The big old house was just crying out for some attention. She intended to make it into the home that Cullen had never had. The home that *she* had always wanted.

Cullen's narrowed gaze met hers. "No."

Rachel bristled at the flat denial. Lately there was an air of compressed savagery about Cullen; he was like a big cornered cat waiting to spring, lending credence to his statement that he was lousy family material. He certainly wasn't adjusting well to living with her, if living together was what you called their odd, fractured existence. "What do you mean, no?"

Air hissed from between his teeth. If Rachel wanted to be generous, she would have said he sounded weary, that he'd been up before dawn and had worked sixteen hours straight—and all of it brutally hard physical labour. But he didn't sound tired. He sounded frustrated, impatient and downright bad-tempered.

"*You* won't be doing the painting. Or any climbing on ladders or lifting."

Rachel stiffened at the list of don'ts. For weeks now Cullen had ignored her. Most of the time she ate alone, which was probably just as well in the mornings, because she was still losing her breakfast on a regular basis. The few times their paths crossed he was polite, but did little more than acknowledge her existence. His avoidance of her cut deeply, even though she knew his reasons.

But something had changed in him. There was an edginess, a vibrating impatience, that sent shivers of alarm and excitement down her spine. "I redecorated the flat over the salon."

"That was different. You weren't pregnant then."

"So, you don't mind me redecorating as long as someone else does the heavy work?"

He was silent for a beat, then, "Someone else does *all* the work."

Her knees actually went shaky with relief. She sensed that this house was important to him, despite his determination to sell it. In the short time she'd lived there, she'd become increasingly attached to the house herself. It had an air of gentle waiting, a subtle sadness to the empty rooms, as if they longed to be filled with the sounds of family and children. She couldn't have borne it if he hadn't agreed to let her redecorate, and she'd been prepared to do battle for the right to do so. "You don't mind?"

He opened the study door as if he couldn't wait to be rid of her frustrating presence. "It's just a house. And when it's sold, it will be someone else's house."

"Fine," she snapped, fury building in her at his stubborn indifference and overriding any sense of alarm that she might be pushing him too hard. "I'll arrange for one of the local firms to do the work."

"Rachel," he said softly, as she was on the verge of leaving, "you will not pay for any of the work on the house, or any of the materials."

Guilt sent colour spreading across her cheeks. She didn't want Cullen to pay for something he so patently didn't want. It made her feel indulged, humoured. It made her feel sneaky. "I'm the one who requires the change, therefore I will pay."

"No."

She closed her eyes at his stubbornness. "I want to pay. I can afford to pay."

"I have money set aside for the house. It should be more than enough for your needs. I'll make it available to you."

When Rachel opened her eyes she found that his gaze had drifted to her mouth. A small, tingling jolt of surprise went through her. "What about your needs, Cullen?"

His gaze snapped back to hers, and she told herself she'd imag-

ned the faint mellowing. He looked about as mellow as a hungry
tiger.

"My needs are not at issue here."

"One day," she said, enunciating each word with a careful
precision, "I am going to get very tired of hearing about whose
needs are important and whose aren't. And when that happens, I
will probably break something. Over your head."

For the briefest moment his slitted eyes flared to hot metal. A
split second later the door was closed in her face.

Rachel stared at the rich wood grain in disbelief. She was furious and utterly frustrated, but she knew she'd already pushed
him far enough. She went in search of the telephone book and
found the listings for painters and decorators, as well as gardening
and landscape contractors. If Cullen thought that giving her carte
blanche to do what she liked with this place would negate any
need for his involvement, then so be it. But he was going to have
to be prepared for some changes. Some big changes.

A week later, Cullen rode in just as the last light was fading,
to find a minidigger parked in his front yard and the evidence of
its earthmoving capability scraped into mounds at regular intervals.
There was a van parked nearby, with a man who looked suspiciously like Charley Williams unloading pails of paint from the
back of it. Cullen bedded Mac down for the night and then went
looking for Rachel. He checked in the lounge. At first glance it
was empty. Rachel's warm overstuffed furniture had already altered this room, and with the jumbled disarray of magazines and
samples, a swathe of rich terra-cotta-coloured fabric—which he
assumed was curtaining—lying over one sofa, the room was trans-
formed even without any alteration to its walls.

A tightening pain squeezed at his chest. For the first time in
Cullen's memory, the house had taken on life. But the warmth and
rosiness only emphasised his own aloneness, reminding him of
everything he'd never had. And never could have.

A rippling movement caught his eye, and Cullen realised that
Rachel *was* in the room. She was halfway up a stepladder and

almost completely obscured by the heavy terra-cotta drape she was hooking onto a runner. He drew in a breath as she reached to attach another portion of drape, wobbled and muttered before regaining her balance. He was across the room before she could make another attempt.

Rachel had finally managed to relocate the slippery little hook she'd just dropped when the fabric was whipped out of her hands. She wobbled at the abrupt movement, nearly toppling straight into Cullen's irritable glare. Guilty colour flushed her cheeks. She'd promised Cullen she wouldn't climb any ladders or do any heavy lifting. Not that she considered two steps on a tiny stepladder *climbing*...

His hands clamped her waist as he swung her down. "Are you all right?" he demanded.

"Just fine. Why wouldn't I be?"

"What else have you been doing today?"

The last trace of remorse at climbing what could hardly be called a ladder evaporated at the raw demand in his voice. "The usual. I went to work."

"Then you came home and started this." His gaze jerked to the half-hung curtains, the piles of magazines and samples.

"*This* is hardly strenuous," she argued.

The look in his eyes said he didn't believe her. "Sit down," he commanded in the kind of soft, warning voice that she just bet made whole ranks of soldiers jump to attention.

"I've been sitting down half the day. Helen seems to think should spend more time answering the phone and doing paperwork than cutting hair. If I lift anything heavier than a cup of herbal tea, someone snatches it off me. The new apprentice I've taken on treats me like an elderly, slightly stupid grandmother who could inconveniently give birth at any moment. What I want to do now is hang curtains!"

Rachel was half prepared for the way he swung her up into his arms and carried her to the sofa. He dumped her down gently, but firmly.

"Stay there," he commanded. "I'll get you a drink."

"I don't want—"

His quicksilver glance silenced her as effectively as if he'd clapped his hand over her mouth, which Rachel decided he was quite capable of doing if she pushed him any further. He'd walked into his carefully controlled environment and found it turned upside down. Worse, she'd disobeyed one of his instructions and then had the temerity to argue with him.

Charley stuck his head around the corner to let her know he was off home. She heard Cullen's low distinctive tones as he passed Charley in the hallway; then Cullen entered the room, a glass of milk in his hand.

Rachel cleared a space on the cluttered coffee table. "If I drink much more milk, I'll not only look as round as a cow, I'll start mooing like one," she complained.

"You need to put on weight. The baby may be growing, but you aren't."

"And being a soldier, you would know a lot about pregnant women and babies."

His gaze measured hers. "I've had medical training," he drawled, confirming her own suspicions. He strode to the door, then paused. "I'll tell Dane to come and help you hang those curtains. I meant it when I said I didn't want you climbing ladders or doing any lifting."

Cullen's footsteps echoed down the hallway. The front door slammed behind him, sending a shudder through the solid old house.

"Well, you knew he wasn't going to purr like a pussycat right off," Rachel muttered to herself as she dutifully sipped her milk. "And you also knew he wasn't going to help you turn his life upside down when he fully expects to shunt you out of it in just a few months."

An infinitesimal flutter began deep in her stomach. Startled, Rachel replaced her drink on the table, her hand going to her abdomen. She'd felt flutterings before now, but nothing this definite. She held her breath as she waited for the next movement, then the next. The baby was kicking. Suddenly she was grinning, crying,

and the need to share their child's movement with Cullen was s
strong that she was on her feet and heading for the door befo
she reminded herself that he wouldn't welcome this. Just as l
wasn't welcoming the changes she was making to his house.

Swallowing her elation and the sadness that went with it, sl
sat back down on the sofa, waiting for another kick. The tir
flutterings started again, and her eyes filled with tears. She wasn
alone. She would never be alone again; she had that certainty,
least.

When the kicking finally stopped, Rachel made her way to tl
kitchen to start dinner. Cullen's tension was a heartening sign, sl
reminded herself. He was as moody as a restive stallion. The Cu
len she'd thought she knew didn't slam doors or behave irritabl
But then, he kept so much of himself hidden. Getting to know hi
was like lifting the lid on Pandora's box. She was playing a da
gerous game in recklessly pushing him for a response. When th
iron control finally snapped...

Rachel closed her eyes, seeing another room barely lit by lam
light. She swallowed against the memory of hot, wild lovemakin
of Cullen plunging so deep inside her that she shivered and burne
in his grasp.

Deliberately, she opened her eyes, blanking out the raw, di
turbing images, the automatic response of her body. She was *ban
ing* on Cullen breaking. Because if he didn't, she would have l
this gamble of a marriage.

Cullen prowled the piles of dirt that used to be his lawn. Fu
and desire twisted in him. He hadn't wanted to leave the hous
He'd wanted to stay and make sure that Rachel didn't climb th
dangerous excuse for a ladder again—three whole rickety step
damn it, if you counted that she'd been perched on the apex
the thing. He'd felt the thickening at her waist when he'd lift
her from the ladder, and the knowledge that she was growing l
baby inside her had made him weak at the knees. He'd wanted
carry her up to his bed, strip the clothes from her and *see* t
evidence for himself.

He still felt strange—dazed, disoriented. Cullen stopped and stared in irritable disbelief at the upheaval around him. A vision of a toddler crawling over soft, smooth lawn had his hands clenching into fists.

This would be someone else's house, he reminded himself. Someone else's garden. And children that didn't belong to either him or Rachel would play in the shrubbery.

Forcing the images from his mind, he strode over to the barn and began helping Dane load the truck with the fencing materials they needed for the morning. There was a substantial length of fence down in the high country, which meant they would have to scour the hills, mustering renegade cows out of the bush before they could close up the gap. It was going to be hard, dangerous work. He would be taking a rifle in case they had problems.

His gaze wandered back to the piles of dirt and the thought of children playing, and when he realised where his mind was drifting, he jerked his attention back to the repetitive physical work of lifting and stacking. But damn, he still couldn't shake the unsettling shifting sensation inside him, as if his centre of gravity had altered and he was still trying to find his balance.

Right at the start, he should have guessed Rachel would want to change the house. One look at what she'd done with her flat had told him that she was a natural homemaker, that of all the women who'd spent time in the barren empty house he called home, she would be the one to give it life and warmth.

But Cullen couldn't allow himself to be seduced by cosy domesticity. Not with the trouble he was having resisting Rachel anyway. And not with bastards like Trask and Hayward giving him a cold itch down his spine.

He couldn't be certain, but he thought that Trask was watching the property. A couple of times he'd heard a vehicle that sounded like Trask's. But each time he'd reconnoitred, he'd come up with nothing more than flattened grass where a vehicle had pulled off the side of the county road, parked, then driven off. He'd kept Dan informed, but without an actual sighting or physical evidence that Trask had trespassed, Dan couldn't do anything more than warn the man off.

Night closed in, leaching the last warmth from the air, bringing the winter brightness of stars and a cold stillness that intensified his feeling of aloneness, the aloneness that he'd always been comfortable with but which now didn't seem to fit him quite so well.

Tipping his head back, Cullen stared up at the blinking path of a satellite tracking across the sky and caught the faintest whiff of something savoury cooking, followed by the unmistakeable acrid scent of that same savoury stuff burning.

His mouth curved in an involuntary smile. Then he grinned. Once he'd grinned, he couldn't stop the laugh; it forced its way out of him, rough and unfamiliar. Cole had said his sister couldn't cook, and he was half right. She did the most hellacious things to red meat, although she didn't seem to have a problem with white meat or spicy dishes. And she made the best roast chicken Cullen had ever tasted.

If he hadn't had to leave so early that morning, he would have put on a slow-cooking casserole. It was never anything fancy, but it filled their stomachs at the end of the day, and he knew Rachel was relieved not to have to deal with the home-killed meat he deposited in the fridge and freezer.

The back door of the kitchen burst open. He heard a clunk as Rachel jettisoned whatever pot she'd been picking on tonight. The burning smell got stronger.

Dane drew up beside him, wiping sweat off his forehead with the back of his hand and grinning. With all the hard, physical work, Dane had filled out and now barely resembled the thin, desperate boy he'd been just months ago. Maturity had settled easily on his broadening shoulders. "Yum," he said appreciatively. "Smells like it's done."

"Oh, yeah," Cullen murmured. "It's done."

He was still chuckling as they picked their way around the side of the house, watchful of where they stepped in case they landed in the red-hot remains of whatever had been on the menu for tonight's dinner. They located the heavy cast iron frying pan with what looked like three steaks, shrunken and blackened and welded to the bottom of it by excess heat. Pulling on one of the heavy leather gloves he'd tucked into his pocket, Cullen carried the pan to the corner of the house where there was a tap, filled it with water and left it to soak. He would clean it in the morning, using a drill and grinding bit from the workshop if he had to. The way he'd done with the last pot Rachel had thrown out.

Chapter 13

Rachel eased herself carefully out of bed. She was in her seventh month of pregnancy, and her tummy had grown at an alarming rate. She didn't walk anymore. She waddled. And getting in and out of chairs was becoming a major feat.

She also tired easily, although that wasn't too much of a problem. Cullen and Dane had taken over most of the cooking in the evening, so when she got in from work she could usually slip up to her room and take a catnap. Happily, most of the interior of the house was painted. The house *felt* good to live in.

At least, it did to her. If Cullen's irritability level was anything to go by, he hated every change she'd made.

Rachel showered and dressed. It was raining. The unpredictable, squally rain of spring. Not that she minded. All that moisture was good for the newly planted gardens and the thick emerald fuzz of lawn that now surrounded the house.

She made her careful way downstairs, drank a cup of tea and cautiously nibbled her way through her usual piece of dry toast, and was just slipping her plate into the dishwasher when the expected wave of morning sickness hit her. Apparently not many women felt sick this late in pregnancy. She was one of the unlucky ones. Slamming the dishwasher closed, she clutched at the counter, taking deep, steadying breaths.

Just when she knew she would have to dash for the bathroom or disgrace herself in the kitchen sink, she heard the thud of Cullen's boots on the verandah, and the door to the mudroom burst open on a gust of cool air. Rachel groaned and wondered if she was going to make it to the bathroom without Cullen realising what was happening to her. Sweat beaded her brow and upper lip, and suddenly she doubted she could even take the one sorry step she needed to carry her to the sink.

Cullen's voice broke through the waves of nausea. "Rachel? What's wrong?"

She shook her head. She couldn't speak. God help her if she so much as opened her mouth... Instead she let go of the counter and began stumbling toward the door on the far side of the kitchen. Strong hands caught her around what used to be her waist, steadied her, and then she was swept off her feet.

Cullen carried her to the downstairs bathroom, then held her as the meagre breakfast she'd just forced down made its ignominious exit.

"All that work for nothing," she mumbled, mourning the loss of the dry toast. "My stomach hates me. It hates being pregnant."

Cullen smoothed her damp hair back from her face; then he lifted her up and away from the toilet bowl, pressed the flush, then settled her on his lap as he perched on the edge of the bath. The delicious sound of running water soothed her as she let her head rest against his shoulder. She noticed he was wet; she could feel the dampness penetrating her own clothing where she nestled against him, and it dimly registered on her that that was why he'd returned so unexpectedly.

He wet a cloth and gently wiped her mouth and face. When he was finished, he tossed the cloth into the laundry basket, then ran some water into a glass before holding it for her while she drank. When she'd had enough, he replaced the glass on the vanity and stood, cradling her with an easy strength. ''Just how long have you been throwing up?'' he demanded.

Rachel eyed him warily. ''Ever since about the sixth week.''

His chest expanded on a sharp intake of air. ''I'm taking you to the doctor,'' he said flatly, heading out of the bathroom and up the stairs.

''I'm okay,'' she protested, looking wistfully back at the kitchen. Now that she'd been sick, she could eat again. ''Lots of women get sick with pregnancy. I've already seen the doctor about it.''

Cullen shouldered his way through the door and into her room, then laid her down on the bed. ''There must be something he can give you.''

Rachel struggled off the bed despite his impatient glare. ''Once I throw up, I feel fine. And anyway, I can't rest. I have to get ready for work.''

''Screw work,'' he said bluntly.

Her chin shot up. ''I have to go. It's my business.''

''Then work less. You look tired.''

Unexpectedly, he reached out and touched the shadows she knew were beneath her eyes. She hadn't been sleeping well because she was spending her nights traipsing back and forth to the bathroom. Half the time when she was up, he was, too. If she didn't know better, she would have thought he was actually sleeping on that miserable chair in his study. He certainly didn't seem to spend much time in his bed.

The next day, her regular day off, Rachel had a doctor's appointment. Cullen had interrogated her until she'd told him about it; then he'd insisted on driving her in.

He parked the truck in the supermarket car park, which was next door to the surgery. ''I'll help you out,'' he said in a voice that didn't brook any argument.

Rachel watched him stride around the bonnet of the truck with an easy, muscular grace. The wind sifted through his dark hair and plastered his shirt against his broad chest and flat stomach. The ruck door swung open, but when she took his hand, he didn't just assist her, he pulled her forward into his arms and lifted her down, holding her until her feet were steady on the ground.

"Are you all right?" he asked in a low, soft rumble, his hands still on her waist, his head bent to hers.

Rachel drew in a breath at his nearness. After months of being carefully avoided, his sudden focussed attention was disconcerting. "Fine," she croaked, firmly squashing the dishonourable idea of pretending to be faint and making him carry her again. "When I'm finished at the doctor's, I'll start on the groceries."

"I'll meet you here in half an hour."

His hands dropped from her waist, and she felt an absurd sense of loss as he moved away. It was ridiculous how much she wanted to cling to him, and it wasn't just the unsettling vulnerability she was experiencing as a part of her pregnancy. It was the same need he'd had before she got pregnant. And it wasn't going away; it was getting worse.

The doctor's waiting room was full when she walked in. Mrs. Reese was there with a bandaged knee and a walking stick at her side. Her daughter Eleanor was vegetating beside her, reading a magazine. Rachel smiled and nodded, but Isobel pretended not to see her. Eleanor gave her a startled look, then jerked the magazine up high enough to hide her face.

An uncomfortable silence settled over the cramped room. Rachel gave her details to the receptionist then found a seat. The relief of sitting down surprised a long sigh out of her.

"Gets like that, doesn't it?" a voice said in her ear.

Rachel's head snapped around in surprise. A young pregnant woman was seated beside her. Rachel had seen her in passing but didn't know who she was.

"Kylie McLean," the woman said, holding out her hand and smiling.

Rachel clasped her hand, automatically smiling back. Something about Kylie McLean invited smiles. She had blunt features liberally sprinkled with freckles, rumpled chestnut hair and steady brown eyes. "Rachel Logan," she replied.

Kylie nodded as if this was information she already had.

One of the doctors came out and called Mrs. Reese's name. She hobbled past with the help of her daughter, still completely ignoring Rachel.

"Need a hand, Aunty Isobel?" Kylie called out.

Mrs. Reese glared at Kylie. Eleanor went bright red and refused to look at either Rachel or Kylie.

"She's your aunt?" Rachel murmured in disbelief.

A cheerful grin split Kylie's face. "It's a dirty job, but someone's gotta do it."

An older man sitting on Kylie's other side, chuckled.

"By the way," Kylie said. "This is my dad, Andrew Hogarth. He's Aunty Isobel's brother."

Rachel shook hands with Mr. Hogarth, who looked so thoroughly normal and innocuous that she couldn't imagine anyone less likely to be Isobel Reese's brother. "I'm afraid Mrs. Reese has taken a fairly strong dislike to me."

"Oh, don't take it personally," Kylie said airily. "Aunty Isobel has barely talked to us since before I was born, ever since Dad married the 'wrong' woman. It's a very peaceful state of affairs."

Several minutes later, Rachel was in the consultation room, lying on the high examination bed, having her tummy listened to and measured.

Dr. Dalziel pulled Rachel's shirt back into place. "The baby's healthy but a little on the big side, which isn't so surprising. Your husband's a big man."

"Will size be a problem?" Rachel asked, accepting the doctor's help as she got down from the bed. Slipping on her shoes, she took a seat beside his desk.

"As long as the baby doesn't get too big, you should be able to give birth naturally. Your pelvis is small, but lots of small women give birth to big babies. But I'm a little worried about your blood pressure. It's up, and the last blood test indicated that you have a very mild case of preeclamptic toxaemia. Your mother had the same condition, but it's nothing we can't control with diet and plenty of rest." He made an entry in her file. "I'd like you to have weekly blood and urine tests. Just to be on the safe side. I'd also like you to finish work.''

Rachel suppressed a pang of alarm. Dr. Dalziel went on to outline the various conditions that had led to her mother's death, reassuring her that the toxaemia was the least of them and not an uncommon problem. When he'd finished, Rachel asked the only question that mattered. ''What happens if the condition progresses?''

''We put you in hospital for bed rest and observation. If your condition deteriorates, we'll operate and take the baby out early.''

Rachel barely noticed the short walk to the supermarket. The day was warm with the increasing heat of spring. She hardly noticed that, either. Her hand strayed to her stomach—her baby was so unutterably precious to her that the thought of not being able to carry him or her to term was devastating.

She'd already decided not to tell Cullen. The chances were her condition wouldn't progress, and Cullen was under enough strain without having to worry about possible pregnancy complications.

Collecting a trolley, she began walking blankly down the aisles. She was halfway around the supermarket before it registered that she hadn't put anything in the trolley. Muttering beneath her breath, she pulled out the list she'd made at home and backtracked. She was reaching for the milk when she became aware that she was not only being followed, but talked about in sneering tones.

''I beg your pardon,'' she said politely to the rough youth who appeared to be the leader of the three boys following her. ''Would you like to repeat those words?''

He did.

Rachel picked up a small milk carton, ripped it open and dumped the contents down the young punk's front.

''Hey!'' he yelped. ''Did you see that? She just poured milk on me!''

Rachel heard Cullen's measured tread a split second before she felt his warmth at her back. Anger dissolved in the heady strength

of his presence, and she gave in to the need to move back into the
shelter of his body.

His hands settled around her upper arms, fingers moving with
a subtly caressing stroke that was as sensual as it was protective.
But his words when he spoke to the dripping youth were soft and
edged with menace. "And I thought you were just wet behind the
ears."

The youth backed up, his pale, stubbled features going even
paler. "Didn't mean anything, man. Just joking."

"Don't apologise to me. Apologise to my wife. She's the one
you just insulted."

"S-sorry, Mrs. Logan. I'm really sorry."

Cullen's hands slipped from her arms in slow, lingering sweeps
that left her bare skin tingling. He stepped around the puddle of
milk, cutting off the youth's escape route. A box of tissues was
conveniently placed near the meat chiller; he gestured toward it.
"Clean up the mess you made."

The boy swallowed, took a wad of tissues and began hurriedly
blotting the milk. The puddle wasn't that big; most of it had soaked
into his greasy clothing.

The supermarket manager, a thin woman in her fifties, hurried
down the aisle to see what was going on.

Cullen didn't take his gaze off the youth. "You want these boys
in your store, Mrs. Fields?"

"Not unless they're actually planning on buying something,"
she said drily.

Cullen directed a flat, hard stare at the shuffling group. "You
heard the lady. If you're buying you can stay, if not..."

They shifted restlessly, then backed off, muttering. Cullen nodded curtly at the store owner.

"Mr. Logan," she said, just as he was about to turn away.
"Thank you."

Cullen's expression didn't change, but Rachel sensed his surprise. "It was no problem," he said quietly, and then added, "I
hear your husband died a couple of years back. I was sorry to hear

that. Archie was a good man. If you need any help dealing with these sorts of situations, don't hesitate to ask.''

Stacey Fields flushed pink with pleasure. The sudden relaxation of her features made her look at least ten years younger. "Thank you, Mr. Logan, I might take you up on that offer. Those boys have been plaguing me for months, shoplifting and harassing people. Dan Holt tries to help, but he's so busy, and we haven't been quick enough to catch them red-handed with anything.''

Rachel held up the empty milk carton. "I'm afraid I was the one who made the mess. You can add this to our bill.''

"Not in this life," Stacey Fields said briskly, relieving her of the empty box. "If a little spilt milk is all it takes to pull those boys into line, consider it on the house.''

When they were finished shopping, Cullen insisted on carrying all the groceries. As they left the supermarket and began walking across the car park toward the truck, Rachel noticed the group of boys huddled in a tight knot. One of them turned to stare; then a movement over by Cullen's truck caught her attention. It was only a flicker, and she couldn't be sure, but the back of the man's head as he stood from a stooping position looked a little like Frank Trask's. The man disappeared behind a large delivery van.

Cullen had noticed him, too, but his attention was reclaimed almost immediately by the boys, who were now drifting across the car park in front of them, swaggering and talking loudly.

"Having some trouble?" Cole's voice enquired from directly behind them.

"Nothing we can't handle," Cullen replied, as Cole drew level.

Cole glanced at the departing boys, then back at Rachel. "You're looking...round," he said, giving her stomach the kind of respect an unexploded bomb commanded. "When's my little niece due?"

"Nephew," she retorted.

"Niece," Cullen contradicted.

Cole grinned. "Okay, when's my little *relation* due?"

"Any day now," Rachel muttered.

A glint of amusement eased Cullen's expression. "Eight weeks, give or take a day."

Cole frowned, then pierced Rachel with a look. "He looks too relaxed. Have you told him?"

Rachel glared back. Cole had been checking on her periodically, and he was especially fond of enquiring about her health. He didn't know about the toxaemia, but he'd been fussing for weeks now about the problems Rachel's mother had experienced before and during Rachel's birth. He also knew she hadn't discussed any of this with Cullen.

"If you don't tell him," Cole said mildly, "I will."

Rachel glared harder at her brother. "Tell him what?" she said in a meaningful voice, wishing he would shut up and go about his business. Of course he wouldn't. It had always amazed her how her family could conveniently cut her out of their lives but still reserve the right to interfere whenever they saw fit.

"That your mother had complications when she had you."

Rachel shot a glance at Cullen, then wished she hadn't. Any trace of amusement was gone. His jaw was firmly set, his mouth a straight line, and there was nothing cool about his eyes—they burned with a leashed intensity that made her drag in a breath.

"Your mother died," Cullen said softly.

"Yes, she did," Rachel said, thinking furiously. "But that was twenty-seven years ago, and *her* condition was severe. She also had a weak heart that no one knew about."

"Her *condition?*"

Rachel realised she'd given herself away. She shot Cole another irritated look. "My mother suffered from toxaemia when she was pregnant with me. The doctor thinks that because we're physiologically similar, I may be at risk." Her gaze dropped. She studied the bulging bags of groceries that Cullen was holding with sudden interest. "And, as it happens, I do have a mild case of toxaemia."

For an endless moment the whole town went quiet. The wind actually stopped blowing, the bland music that usually oozed from the supermarket sound system ground to a halt, and the drone of traffic, never a predominant sound in Riverbend, was noticeably absent. When Rachel finally looked up, both men were staring at her as if she'd just grown an extra head.

Predictably, Cole swore.

"What—in—hell—is—toxaemia?" Cullen asked in a low, taut voice.

Rachel studied the grocery bags again. She didn't want to tell Cullen, but she knew that if she didn't he would go to a library, or to Dr. Dalziel himself, and find out anyway. "It's got something to do with increased blood pressure and fluid retention. If it gets bad enough it can mean a premature birth and...problems for the mother, as well. But that's not likely to happen. My blood and urine are being monitored. If there's a problem, it will show up early."

Cullen didn't reply for a long time. He looked so grim that Rachel expected him to explode right there in the car park. When he finally did speak, he didn't say a word about the toxaemia.

"Let's go home," he said, spun on his heel and strode toward the truck.

Cole was still standing beside her like a spare part.

"You shouldn't have told him," Rachel said, trying not to panic as she watched Cullen stow the groceries, certain that something was wrong. Something beyond what she'd just told Cullen.

Cole looked as impervious and unrepentant as usual. "You weren't going to. He needs to know."

Chapter 14

The drive home was achieved in silence. Cullen's jaw was tight and a telltale pulse flicked in the lean hollow of his cheek. Rachel still couldn't shake the feeling that something was wrong, something important.

Tyres crunched on gravel as Cullen parked near the house. He helped her down, his touch frustratingly brief and impersonal, then collected the bags of groceries. Rachel followed him into the kitchen and watched as he set the groceries on the table. Cullen didn't look at her or acknowledge her in any way.

"I always wondered what it was like to be invisible," she commented as he stacked frozen items in the freezer.

No response.

Cullen returned to the table for another bag of groceries and began unloading cans and dry goods into the pantry. His refusal to speak to her, to even acknowledge her presence, snapped something inside Rachel. She'd been so worried about the baby, so afraid, and he wouldn't so much as look at her. Hand shaking on a rush of temper, Rachel picked up a container of milk. It occurred to her that emptying two litres of milk on someone you were

rious with would probably be a whole lot more satisfying than
e miserable half litre she'd emptied on the punk in the super-
arket. "Are you going to talk to me?" she asked in a cool,
markably even voice.

Sleet grey eyes pinned her. Cullen's gaze shifted to the milk in
er hand. She had finally gained his full attention.

"About what?" he drawled with all the sensitivity of a rock.

Rachel considered unscrewing the lid on the milk. "About
hatever it is that's bugging you."

Now that she'd got it, his concentrated attention made her pulse
ammer. There was a brooding quality to his regard, a glimpse of
ark shifting currents and savage tensions she could only guess at.

He shrugged, an indolent movement of his shoulders that was
abtly dangerous, as if energy were coiled tight inside him, waiting
r his control to slip. "You weren't going to tell me."

It wasn't a question. Rachel placed the container of milk on the
ble and rubbed her still-shaking palm down the side seam of her
ggings. "No."

"Did you know about your mother's medical history?"

"Not all of it."

He was silent for a beat, then said, "The hell of it is, it doesn't
atter whether you were going to tell me or not. The fact still
mains that by the very act of making you pregnant, I've put you
danger."

Rachel's eyes widened at the way Cullen had interpreted the
tch in her pregnancy. There it was again, the granite wall she
pt running into. Cullen wouldn't budge an inch from his stub-
rn belief that he was dangerous. The sheer force of his will beat
r every time, and imagining what it would be like to have all
at intense, immovable focus trained on her, on making a life
gether as a family, only made the hurt cut deeper. The urge to
sh out, to make him see that he was twisting events to fit his
liefs, and that in doing so he was *hurting* her, was too much.

"Don't take it so personally," she snapped. "It's true that you
d get me pregnant. But I'd planned to have children anyway. I

would have faced the same medical problems regardless of wh
fathered my child.''

Cullen's eyes narrowed at her last statement, but his expressio
remained stonily impassive.

Rachel snatched up the milk and marched toward the fridg
Cullen watched with a trace of wariness as she put the contain
away, and she briefly entertained the milk-dumping fantasy agai
''And as for you putting me in danger,'' she stated coolly, ''I'
not in any, unless I ignore medical advice.'' Gently she closed th
fridge, then placed herself squarely in front of Cullen. ''Toxaem
is not uncommon. In the unlikely event that something does g
wrong, the doctor's clinic is fifteen minutes away, the hospita
half an hour.''

He moved his head impatiently. ''Rachel—''

''Rachel, nothing,'' she interrupted, stepping forward, for on
ignoring his keep-out signals, intent only on making her point. H
hand lifted in unconscious appeal and brushed his chest. She fe
the hot sharp shock of the contact on her skin, the shudder th
moved through him.

His hands shot out, clamping her upper arms, preventing h
from getting any closer. He'd moved so fast that she was startl
by his speed.

The breath left her lungs in a rush. ''I hope I never get on th
wrong side of any war *you're* fighting.''

A dark humour surfaced, softening the hard intensity of his eye
''The feeling's mutual.'' He shook his head again, but this tim
there was an intimacy to the gesture. ''Baby, you scare the he
out of me with some of the risks you take. I'd never consider
hair spray and milk as weapons. If you ever managed to lay yo
hands on anything with an edge, you'd be lethal.''

Despite all her efforts, Rachel could feel herself responding
the rueful warmth in Cullen's voice, the heat radiating from h
palms. It was painfully sweet to be held by him, in any capaci
but giving in to the delight of his touch only made her longing f
intimacy more acute when he went back to avoiding her.

On cue, the amusement disappeared from his expression. ''N

that you're going to be taking on any more gangs of young thugs. You were lucky they didn't hurt you."

"I think they were more interested in insulting me."

It was the wrong thing to say; it reminded Cullen of all the reasons why he shouldn't be touching her, teasing her. His hands tightened, then fell away.

"You haven't been sleeping well," he said abruptly.

Rachel blinked at the change of subject. She'd expected Cullen to go back to ignoring her, to shoving groceries away with the ruthless male efficiency with which he went about most tasks. "That's because the baby sits on my bladder all night. I have to keep making trips to the bathroom."

Cullen's expression darkened. "No wonder you're looking so damned fragile."

The baby chose that moment to kick. Hard. Rachel gasped and rested her palm on the vigorous, undulating bulge moving across her tummy.

"What's wrong?" Cullen asked sharply.

"There's a foot at least as big as yours inside there, and I swear it's got a boot on it."

Before Cullen could rationalise that laying his hands on Rachel again would be a very bad move, and that if he had any sense at all he would get out of the kitchen—*now*—he'd slipped his hand beneath hers.

Rachel stiffened at his touch. Cullen took a moment to register her surprise; then the energetic jabbing against his palm transfixed him, wiping his mind clean of anything but the woman he was touching and the baby nestled inside her. He felt as if he'd been the one who was kicked. In the chest.

Their child. His and Rachel's.

"Two more months," he said thickly, still absorbed by the antics of the baby, the miracle unfolding within Rachel. "How much bigger can she get?"

"He," Rachel corrected tightly. "And a lot bigger. He's hardly started growing."

Cullen wasn't about to argue about the sex of the baby, but for some reason there was no question in his mind. There was a little lady in there. What really worried him was that the baby already looked about as big as Rachel's fine-boned body could handle. "And you're certain the doctor's okay with your progress?"

Rachel's hand fell away from his, and she moved restlessly beneath his touch. "What is it with you and Cole?" she demanded. "I'm pregnant, but that doesn't mean my IQ's decreased. If I needed medical help, I'd get it."

Cullen's gaze lifted to Rachel's. With a sharp pang, he recognised her physical and mental withdrawal from him. Fury tightened every muscle in his body, and he had to steel himself against a purely instinctive desire to reach out and draw her into his arms. He had no right. He'd consciously refused to consider himself in the role of husband and father. He'd shut Rachel and the baby out, immersed himself in the brutally hard work of restoring the farm's roads, fences and drainage systems, in between times trying to second-guess Hayward and Trask. But somehow the feelings had sneaked up on him and ambushed him when he least expected it.

The thought of holding his child turned his legs to putty and his mind to mush. He suddenly knew what the term *clucky* meant, and why tough, hardened soldiers could literally spend hours staring at their kids' baby photos.

The ruckus beneath his palm subsided. Rachel stepped away from his touch. Again the instinctive need to have her close had Cullen tensing; then his own needs ceased to be important as Rachel sighed and began rubbing her back. Cullen frowned and forced himself to examine her critically, noted the translucent quality of her skin, the heaviness of her movements. Rachel looked more than tired; she was exhausted.

"You need to lie down—now," he said flatly.

Rachel glanced at him, eyes wide, dark, and Cullen felt as if he'd been slugged again. His chest tightened on a wave of self-condemnation. Damn, what was wrong with him? Despite the way she'd played down the toxaemia, she was worried sick, and he'd been too concerned with his own personal fears to pick up on it. Cullen cursed himself for being every kind of fool there was. Rachel didn't wear her emotions on the outside; like him, she contained them, keeping the things that hurt the most locked deep inside.

Without waiting for her to agree or disagree, and not giving himself time to rationalise that holding his wife was the last thing he should be doing, Cullen swung her up into his arms.

Rachel grabbed at his shoulders and hung on, but her body was stiff, resisting. "Let me go, Cullen." Panic spiked the honey-warm flow of her voice. "I don't *want* to lie down."

Rachel's raw panic stunned Cullen. He couldn't bear the thought of Rachel sick or hurt by the pregnancy. And he couldn't accept her rejection of his touch. He *needed* her touch. He hadn't realised how important that small link was until she denied it to him—the brush of her fingers, his hand at her waist when he helped her out of the truck, the casual bump of her shoulder against his arm in the kitchen....

His arms tightened, holding her more securely against his chest despite her refusal to relax against him. Maybe he would get used to being without her in time, but not now. Not yet.

Ignoring Rachel's continued protests, he carried her up the stairs, shouldered his way into her bedroom and set her down on the bed. His mind was working furiously, assessing the damage, looking for ways past the vulnerability he'd just discovered. He would have to learn to do without those small touches, and the sooner he started, the better.

But when he tried to remove his arm from beneath her shoulders, Rachel cried out, her hand flying to her scalp.

Cullen went instantly still. Her hair must have caught on his watch strap. Cursing beneath his breath, he bent over her and began working the strands of her hair free from the buckle. Murphy's law, he thought savagely. This was it, in spades. Just when he didn't need it to, everything that could go wrong was going about as wrong as it could. Right now he needed distance, and lots of it.

Rachel's nearness, the intimacy of leaning over her while she lay on her bed, hammered at him. The room was warm, sunlight spreading across the floor and the bed, washing everything in hot gold and intensifying scents. He could smell the cedar chest at the end of the bed, the perfume Rachel used. Cullen sucked in a short, sharp breath and almost groaned out loud. He could smell Rachel's skin. A bead of sweat eased its way down his spine. He cursed silently as his fingers slipped and pulled on her hair.

Finally he was finished. "If you lift your head, I'll get my arm out."

Rachel slid both hands around his nape. Her grip tightened as she pulled herself up. When his arm was free, she didn't let go as he'd expected. His gaze locked with hers. He was bent over Rachel, hands braced on either side of her on the bed, and her face was so close that all he needed to do was move a bare inch and his mouth would brush her forehead.

A tremor moved through him. He knew how close he was to kissing her. To doing a lot more than just kissing. "You need to rest," he said bluntly, warningly. "If you don't let go, I'll join you on the bed."

"You're the one who decided I needed to rest," she reminded him. "If you hadn't carried me up here, I'd be unloading groceries right now."

Rachel's voice was as clear and direct as her eyes. Cullen sucked in a breath when he realised that he would have to be the one to unlatch her hands from his neck, because she wasn't going to. He also knew with a sudden unquestionable clarity that the reason she'd recoiled from his touch before wasn't because he physically repelled her, it was because touching him hurt her as much as touching her hurt him. Cullen's gaze dropped to her mouth, and his whole body tightened on a sweet, savage rush of need.

God help him, but he didn't want to take her hands from his skin. He wanted to stay with her on the sun-drenched bed, immerse himself in the dark longing in her eyes, the soft fullness of her mouth. He wanted to strip away her clothes and acquaint himself with every curve, every change the pregnancy had made to her body. He wanted to push himself inside her, make love to her unti they were both shaking and exhausted, and then start over. But most of all, he just wanted to lie with Rachel and hold her.

"At least there's no danger I'll get pregnant," she said huskily. "Unless you're planning on making medical history."

Reaching up, she brushed her lips across his. Once, twice, a third time. A shudder went through Cullen, and his mouth opened, capturing hers. She accepted his tongue into her mouth with a hunger and intimacy that shattered him. Her fingers thrust into his hair, gripping, tugging insistently, pulling him even closer as she settled back on the pillows. Then, just as Cullen was tensing himself to pull free, she began raking her nails lightly down his scalp, his nape, across his shoulders, stroking and petting him the way she'd done when he'd first kissed her at the Hansons' barbecue. He'd never forgotten the sheer mind-blowing sensuality of her touch then, but now the stunning, raw pleasure of her nails against his skin drove him to his knees beside the bed.

A groan rumbled from his chest as she continued to stroke him, knead him. God help him, but he needed Rachel's hands on his skin. He needed her naked. And he wanted her beneath him, her legs coiled around his waist, body fusing damply with his while he took her slowly, sweetly. Endlessly.

Cullen broke the kiss and tried to block out the graphic vision. It was like trying to stop fire with an empty bucket, but he had to try. Rachel was too damned fragile; the last thing he wanted to do was hurt or scare her.

He loved her.

The realisation speared through him as strongly, as inevitably, as the first touch of morning sunlight striking through cold, clear water. A tremor followed that had nothing to do with lust and everything to do with fury and despair. Sweet hell. This wasn't supposed to happen.

"Cullen?"

Rachel's voice was low, husky. He could see the question in her eyes, the vulnerability, the chance she'd taken in opening herself up to him, and he knew he couldn't leave her. He was going to do what he'd promised himself he wouldn't. He was going to make love to his wife.

Bending his head, Cullen placed his mouth against Rachel's. He absorbed her taste, the exquisite way her tongue curled around his, then slipped past his own lips to explore his mouth with an intimate delicacy. They'd made love, he'd penetrated her body and made her pregnant, but somehow this kiss was more intimate, more deeply piercing, than the brief, explosively passionate encounter that had consumed them both. Rachel's kiss reached inside him and twined around what passed for his soul, and when she took her mouth from his, she had it all. He knew he loved her with everything he was. Everything that he could be. There would never be another woman for him.

And he could never tell her.

When she pushed his shirt from his shoulders, he also knew he wasn't capable of pulling back—if he was damned to a dark eternity without Rachel, then he would take a taste of her exquisite light, her fierce sweetness, with him and hope that what he had to give in return would help heal some of the hurt he'd caused her.

With fingers that felt thick and clumsy, he unbuttoned her shirt. Even so, fabric tore and a button flew, but he hardly noticed; he was too consumed with the changes in her body. Her breasts were very full, the creamy flesh spilling out of her white bra, the enlarged areolae clearly visible even through the cotton. A stunned sense of the child growing inside her filled him.

His jaw clenched with the effort it took to hold himself still, to keep his touch gentle. Her skin was moonlight pale. He didn't want to bruise her, and his whole body was too big, too brutal. He couldn't help but mark her.

Her eyes challenged his stillness; then she slid her hand down between them and began undoing his belt buckle. He felt the touch of her fingers, cool and firm against him, heard the chink of metal, the slide of leather, felt the unintentional caress as she unfastened his jeans.

Cullen groaned at the hot pleasure as she stroked and measured him—possessed him. Sweat sprang out on his forehead. With a harshly restrained movement he unfastened her bra. The pure, feminine beauty of her breasts stunned him. Her skin was silky, delicate and translucent against his callused palms, the dark velvet peaks enlarged in readiness for the child. "I feel like the Beast touching Beauty," he murmured hoarsely.

"You're the one who's beautiful," she whispered.

And then she moved. Her fingers clasped, then glided hotly over him, and Cullen felt his own inner tightening, the powerful gathering sensation that urged him to thrust against the light stroke of her hand. With a barely suppressed groan, he clamped his hand over hers, cursing the raw demands of his libido, cursing his fumbling lack of control.

"This is for you," he growled softly. "Only for you."

Rachel went still, transfixed by the savage beauty of the man looming over her. Even kneeling, Cullen was still overwhelming.

And he was still in control. Fury and desperation curled through her when she realised what he was doing; he was going to make love to her, but on his terms. He was going to watch her come undone, expose her helpless vulnerability, and then walk away.

She watched as he got to his feet and systematically removed his boots, his pants, and her breath came in roughly. She'd never seen all of him before. She'd had him inside her, touched the muscular, hot-satin flesh rising from between his thighs, but the reality of him was...startling. Apprehension feathered her spine as he came down on the bed beside her; then she forced herself to release the breath she was holding. She'd taken him before; she could take him again.

And then there was no more time to think. The heat of his long sleek body as he lay beside and over her seared her. His musky scent filled her nostrils as he began to remove her clothes, his hands lingering on the rounded swell of her stomach with something akin to reverence. And with every brush of his fingers, Rachel realised that the pregnancy had affected her in a way she hadn't expected. The rasp of his fingers as he eased her shirt from her shoulders and arms, the warmth of his palms as he smoothed her leggings off, tingled through her. The pleasure of his lightest touch was almost unbearably amplified.

When she was naked, his gaze swept her body with a slow deliberation, as if he were memorising every part of her, drinking her in. And something about his very intentness, his steady determination, started tremors deep inside her. He wasn't touching her but his frankly hungry gaze was hot on her skin, altering her pulse rate until she ached with the slow, heavy throb of a sensuality more compelling than any she'd ever felt before.

He began stroking her, gentle, featherlight touches that shivered and burned like fire and ice combined. When Rachel couldn't stand it anymore, she wound her arms around his neck and pulled his mouth to hers. He gave in to the pressure, and, despite the fact that she could feel the heavy heat of his arousal against her stomach, the gliding caress of his lips was gentle, careful, almost clinical in its briefness. With a sound that was part fury and all desperation, Rachel held him to her mouth. He was fully in control while she was a mess of inflamed, clamouring nerve endings. This time she used her tongue, stroking his lips until he opened his mouth over hers and slid his tongue inside her.

The demands of the kiss brought him so close that his hot restless vitality seemed to thrum through her with every slam of his heart. One thigh slid between hers, the abrasion of hard muscle and masculine body hair against her ultrasensitive inner thigh making her gasp. He cradled her breast, his thumb rasping across her tender nipple, sending her arching while tremors shook her body. His mouth travelled down her jawline, her neck. Then he was poised over her, his arms supporting his weight, caging her as he dipped and took the aching tip of one breast into his mouth.

The rough, wet heat of his tongue curling around her, drawing her in deeper, had her clutching at his arms and arching, climaxing with a suddenness that left her dazed.

She heard Cullen's quick intake of breath, felt him cup the damp curls between her legs, one finger sliding inside her, gauging the tight, clasping aftermath of climax. The intrusion initiated another series of shock waves. Then he was gently holding her against him. For comfort.

It wasn't what she wanted. Rachel sensed that, given the chance, Cullen would take nothing for himself. Like that time at the water hole, he would set his own needs aside. But in denying himself, he denied her, and his withdrawal was beyond bearing. Emotionally, she felt as naked and vulnerable as her body was. She loved Cullen. He was her chosen mate, and she gloried in his blunt, uncompromising masculinity, his ability to protect her and their child from any and all threats, but now she needed him shaking and weak in her arms, just as she shook and trembled for him.

With movements made short and sharp by anguish and frustration, she freed herself, placed a hand on Cullen's chest and pushed him flat.

He watched her warily, eyes slitted, jaw taut. "What are you doing?" he asked in a voice that was guttural, thick.

A rivulet of fear, purely primal and completely feminine in source, eased its way down her spine. With his eyes glittering, his big body tense with arousal, Cullen looked both predatorily hungry and tightly controlled. He'd leashed his sexual need to meet hers, but it wouldn't take much to make him shed that control completely. The way he had when they'd made love before.

Rachel's jaw squared stubbornly. With a deliberately sensual movement, she slipped her palms down his chest, stroking his sleek coppery skin, the deliciously rough pelt of hair. His muscles leaped and hardened beneath her touch. "Do you believe in male-female equality?" she asked huskily.

His nostrils flared as he drew a harsh breath. "You're on top. Is this a trick question?"

Her hands slipped lower, and his stomach muscles jumped. He growled a low, grating curse.

"No. Just a statement of intent."

He tensed as if ready to spring, and Rachel knew a moment of sheer panic. He wouldn't allow her to keep teasing him. Bending forward, she laid her mouth against his small male nipple and drew him into her mouth, her tongue licking across the tight little nub.

His whole body arched at the overtly sexual caress, but he didn't push her away. She could hear the rasp of his breathing, feel the air jerking in and out of his lungs.

Cullen knew he was going to die. But he'd never thought it would be of pure, searing pleasure. Rachel's mouth on him was soft, tentative, and driving him *crazy*. She stroked him, tasted him. She catalogued him as thoroughly as he'd done her. And then started all over again.

His hands bunched into fists. He was shaking, sweating, his jaw clamped so tight it ached, and just when he knew he couldn't take any more, she spread his thighs and knelt between them. Before he could stop himself, his hands were on her hips. "What do you think you're doing?" he demanded hoarsely.

Rachel stared at him with the peculiar dreamy absorption that filled her face when she was making love and continued to stroke him. He'd been trying to wipe that particular expression from his memory for months, and he knew with a furious certainty that now he never would. And any second she was going to put her mouth where her hands were, stroking and tormenting him, and then he would— His breath exploded from his lungs when she did exactly that.

Biting out a lean Anglo-Saxon phrase, Cullen surged upright and reversed their positions so that Rachel was lying beneath him and he was poised over her, his arms taking all his weight. Sunlight poured across the bed, turning her eyes to gold, her skin to rich ivory, as she lay quiescent in his grasp. With a look that was as sweetly beckoning as the exquisite centre of some rare, delicate flower, she wrapped herself around him and Cullen knew he was lost. When he entered her, he did so with an agonising gentleness, the breath lodged at the back of his throat as she took him sleekly, tightly. Perfectly.

"I don't want to hurt you or the baby," he said on a soft rumble as he withdrew slowly, then pushed in again deep enough to send a small sound rippling from her throat. "I'll stop if it's too much."

Her eyes closed, then opened again. "I don't want you to stop."

Cullen shook with the frank sensuality of her expression and with the effort of holding back, of keeping his movements slow, shallow. Rachel wasn't helping. Her hands were on his shoulders, her nails raking, sliding, tormenting him even now, and she kept arching up, catching him by surprise, taking him deeper each time.

"Easy," he groaned as she shifted restlessly beneath him; then his hands were soothing her, holding her still as his thighs pressed hers wider apart and he penetrated her with such completeness that she caressed and clung to every inch of him.

And then he couldn't think, only move and drown in the dark gold of Rachel's eyes, the small sounds she made every time he filled her. Pleasure rolled through him, pounded him, pressed the air from his lungs. The languorous scent of their lovemaking filled the air. The sun seemed to increase in intensity, shafting across the bed, lying hotly on his skin, outlining Rachel in a passionate nimbus of light. She lifted her legs, pulling him deeper, cried out, and then her internal muscles shivered around him, tightening almost unbearably.

Heat slammed through Cullen. A hoarse cry ripped from his throat. Then nothing existed but incandescent, burning pleasure and the woman coming apart in his arms as they fell into the sun together.

Moments later, or it could have been hours, Rachel pulled herself from the drag of sleep. She was pinned by one brawny arm and thigh, her back snugged in against Cullen's chest.

"Did I hurt you?" he asked in a voice that was edged with alertness and oddly flat.

Rachel understood his wariness immediately, and she braced herself for the hurt she knew would follow. No matter what happened, she wouldn't allow their lovemaking to be diminished by regrets. "You were...perfect."

He didn't answer. The euphoria of lovemaking gradually seeped from Rachel, leaving in its place an acute awareness of Cullen holding her but still separate and alone. "I'm not made of candy floss," she said calmly. "I'm a woman. I want to be made love to, not...indulged like a child."

Abruptly Cullen rolled away, got to his feet and began pulling on his jeans and boots. "I was rough," he said bluntly. "And I'm too damned big. You need someone who can offer you all the things I can't."

Rachel dragged the quilt over herself, instinctively trying to capture the remnants of Cullen's warmth. "A family and home that will always be there?" she said quietly. "A husband who will stay with me?"

Cullen flinched, and she felt a moment of remorse for flinging her own particular losses, her own needs, at him when he was already burdened with the weight of more hurt, more desolation than she could imagine. But it was hard to be civilised when she could see her future slipping away. She watched as he picked his shirt up off the floor. "I'd rather bring this baby up solo than live with a man I don't love," she said shakily. He went still, and she knew she was going to hurt him even more. "It beats me why you won't have a crack at the biggest thing your old man failed at."

He looked at her across his shoulder. "And what would that be?"

She saw grim knowledge in his eyes. He knew what she was going to say, but she said it anyway. "Fatherhood."

His hand tightened around the already crumpled fabric of his shirt, and when he spoke, his voice was low, gravelly. "I know about fatherhood. I know how to kick and hit. I know how to swear and yell and break a child down until there isn't anything left but betrayal. I know how to put a child on the school bus for the first time, sending him off to an unknown destination with an apple and some stale bread in a brown paper bag. That kid hadn't known where he was going, or why." Cullen stared down at the bunched-up shirt, seemingly unaware that he'd shifted his words into the context of memories. "And when older kids beat up on him because he was dirty and impossibly dumb, he felt right at home with the bloody nose and smashed lip. So at home that pretty soon he was dishing it right back. And he was a big kid, with big strong hands. Just like his old man."

Abruptly Cullen pulled on the shirt, leaving it hanging open. "Maybe I could be a good husband and father. And maybe I couldn't. But I can't take the risk with you or our child."

Chapter 15

The early summer heat had given way to the slow, grey buildup of a northeasterly blow. The Hansons' annual barbecue would no doubt be held inside this year.

Rachel slipped on a dress she'd sewn herself. It was made of layers of delicate lilac-sprigged cotton voile and left her arms bare. She smoothed the soft fabric over her stomach, grimacing wryly. With her shape, she definitely missed out on elegance, but at least she felt cool and, after months in leggings and shirts, feminine. Not that that would make any difference to Cullen.

Ever since they'd made love, he had been both more distant and more attentive. He stayed around the house and made sure she kept her feet up, and wouldn't allow her to cook. But he didn't touch her if he could help it. The few times Rachel had been reduced to requesting his help, the resulting strain between them had made her regret asking.

She coiled her hair into a loose knot at her nape, slipped into flat comfortable shoes and picked up a straw clutch purse. A hollow, shivery sensation tightened her stomach as she descended the stairs and headed slowly, cumbersomely, for the lounge. She was becoming used to the unsettling shiver. It wasn't caused by the baby but grew out of the panicked feeling that time was running out, that he would be happier without her. If it wasn't for the baby and her inner conviction that Cullen needed both of them as much as they needed him, she would do as he wanted. She would take herself as far away as she could, leave the house she'd come to love, the community that, despite its faults, was *hers,* and give him back his lonely, disciplined life.

Cullen had his back to her when she entered the lounge. His head swung around, his gaze landing on her with familiar intensity, then running the length of her body in what she knew was an instinctive check on her health and well-being, not a sexual inventory. He was dressed in a lightweight black jacket and matching trousers that fit him like an expensively tailored glove. A white T-shirt clung to his broad chest, making him look both lazily dangerous and sophisticated.

He didn't look in the least like the outlaw Riverbend had branded him. He looked successful, self-assured. He looked like he didn't need anyone or anything.

"You look beautiful," he said quietly. "Why don't you wait here while I get the truck? I don't think we should take your car. If the rain sets in, the road'll turn to slush."

Rachel glanced out at the light rain. "I'll get something to sit on and a couple of towels, just in case."

"Grab a jacket, as well. It's warm now, but it's going to get colder."

The rain became heavier, and the wind increased in velocity, as they turned onto the winding county road that led to the Hansons' drive. The windscreen wipers raked back and forth, and the headlights stabbed into the slanting rain as Cullen deftly negotiated the muddy road. A set of bridge abutments loomed, ghostly bright, just as a gust of wind hit the truck side-on. Rachel gasped, but Cullen swung the wheel, correcting in time, and they swept across the bridge, water spraying from the tyres.

A large pothole where the bridge joined the road jolted hard enough for Rachel to reach up and grab the hand support above the door, and then they were weaving through the final treacherous series of switchback bends.

Cullen swore beneath his breath as the wheel went sloppy in his hands. He'd felt the difference as soon as they'd cleared the pothole. He braked gently, then drove into the skid as the truck slewed sideways. Another controlled pump on the brake and they cleared the corner safely.

The wheel went dead in his hands.

"Hang on," he said curtly.

They were going slowly, but the road was slippery. If he braked too hard, he could send them into a spin. Their momentum slowed, slowed. The bank grew out of greyness, spreading until it filled the windscreen. Cullen jerked on the hand brake and the back end of the truck slithered around. They lurched to a halt, rear wheels lodged in the ditch, headlights probing up into rain and thick, swirling clouds.

Cullen hit the hazard lights, killed the engine, then snapped on the interior light. It wasn't dark, but the heavy cloud had created a preternatural gloom. Rachel was still clinging to the hand support, one arm draped protectively across her stomach. The angle of the truck had thrown her against her door. Cullen would have fallen onto her if his seat belt hadn't held him in place. Before he could think, before he could stop himself, he reached out and touched her face, felt the coolness of her skin, the fine tremors running beneath it. He dragged in a breath, sealing away the raw, possessive need to haul her onto his lap and run his hands over every part of her body—to check for himself that she was all right.

"Are you okay?" he asked quietly.

"I'm still in one piece," she said with a trace of dry humour that, perversely, made him want to shake her.

He was still scared as hell.

"What happened?" Rachel asked.

"The steering went." Grimly, Cullen opened the glove box and retrieved the flashlight he always kept there. "I'm going to have a look underneath the truck."

Seconds later he was directing the torch beam at the truck's chassis. It didn't take long to find the problem. Even with muddy water dripping, he could see the hanging tie rods and the bright gleam of metal that had been partially sawn through.

The sound of a vehicle had Cullen straightening. It was Cole.

"What the hell happened?" Cole demanded as he slammed his car door and pulled on an oilskin.

"Cut tie rods," Cullen said succinctly. "Two of them."

Cole's eyes narrowed at that information. "Is Rachel all right?"

"She's fine. A little shocked." Cullen opened the truck door so Cole could see for himself that his sister was okay, and as he listened to Rachel reassuring Cole, his heart contracted with ho rage that anyone should try to hurt her. Although whoever had tampered with his steering hadn't seen Rachel as the target. They had been after him. Tossing his soaked jacket behind the seat Cullen retrieved his mobile phone from the glove box. He glanced at Cole. "If you want to help, take Rachel on to the Hansons' and keep a close eye on her to make sure she really *is* all right. I'll deal with this."

Cole swept an impatient hand over his wet hair. "I'll give you both a lift. Pass me the phone and I'll get a couple of my men to come out and tow your truck in."

"I'd appreciate the tow," Cullen said flatly, handing the phone over. "But I'll wait with the truck until your guys arrive. I want Dan Holt to take a look at it first."

There was a small silence filled by the steady beat of the rain then Cole stabbed out some numbers. He spoke tersely into the phone before handing it back. "If you get Rachel out, I'll fetch an umbrella."

Cole came back with a large golfing umbrella just as Cullen lifted Rachel free. After he'd settled her in the comfort of Cole's mud-spattered BMW and watched them drive away, he phoned Dan Holt and settled back to wait.

It was possible that each attack or incident that had been perpetrated against him was done by someone different, but Cullen didn't think so. Tipping his head back, he let the rain hammer his face—let the relentless cascade douse some of the rage coursing through him. A memory slotted neatly into place, like a damn cue card. A partial view of a head bobbing up beside the truck while it was parked outside the supermarket. Cullen had been distracted. First by the boys who'd insulted Rachel, then by Cole, and finally by the news of Rachel's pregnancy complications. And then they'd made love.

He cursed as heat and longing rolled through him at the memory. He could have prevented this accident if he'd followed up on his unease and checked the truck over. One glance would have revealed the amateurish hack job Trask had done. Cullen's jaw tightened with disgust. Only trouble was, these days his instincts were all located in the same place his brains were, somewhere not too far south of his belt buckle.

The Hansons' house was packed. Isobel Reese was holding court from the most central sofa. Dane was there, his handsome face alight with laughter and male satisfaction, his arm slung territorially around the waist of Rachel's apprentice, Sara. People flowed cheerfully through the rooms, talking, arguing, but mostly laughing.

Cole found Rachel a seat and a glass of lemonade, then sat asking questions about her health until she glared him into silence.

"You must be okay," he muttered irritably.

He glanced around the room, and Rachel sighed at the fury tightening his jaw.

"It wasn't Cullen's fault," she said, certain that Cole was seething about the accident.

"No," he replied, surprising her. "It wasn't Cullen's fault." He glanced around, then got to his feet. "I'll be back in a few minutes. I need to make sure that Cullen got through to Dan Holt."

Dan Holt? Rachel watched Cole stride through the shifting groups of people, an entirely new sense of alarm filling her. She kept remembering the sudden loss of control *before* Cullen threw them into a controlled skid. And Cullen had immediately wanted to examine the underside of the truck.

Rachel held the frosted glass against her temple. Anger sent heat flooding across her skin. The only reason Cullen would need Dan Holt to look at the truck was if it had been tampered with. Someone had wanted to hurt Cullen. It was sheer chance that she'd been in the truck; normally she used her car. If the weather had been better, they both would have used her car tonight, and the next time Cullen used his truck would probably have been around the farm. He could have lost control on a hairpin bend. He could have been killed.

A cultured drawl rose above the general hum of conversation. "I don't think there's any real doubt that Cullen Logan killed his old man." A soft laugh followed. "In my opinion he deserves a medal for doing the town a favour. Of course..." There was a pause while the conversation around the expensively suited man fell away. "One wouldn't want to encourage someone like that to stay."

"Someone like what?" Rachel demanded as she levered herself to her feet and looked for a place to plonk her glass down before she gave in to the impulse to heave it at Richard Hayward's handsome, smirking face.

There was a small shocked silence, then a rustle of approving noises that sent a dull flush running up Hayward's neck. The lawyer clearly hadn't expected Cullen to have supporters. And then Rachel remembered what Cullen had told her about the events surrounding his father's death. She knew that the only reason Cullen had speculated aloud had been to make her careful about where she put her feet—in case she stepped on a rat. But when all was said and done, she was a country girl at heart, and she wasn't the least afraid of rats, just wary of the kind of damage the vermin could inflict. "What brand of whiskey do you drink, Mr. Hayward?"

The question flabbergasted him. He answered without thinking. "Chivas, of course."

"Of course," she murmured with a tight smile. "How much does that cost a bottle?"

"I wouldn't know," he retorted. "My wife takes care of those details. A lot, I imagine."

"More than most drunks would be prepared to pay. And from what I've heard, Ian Logan wouldn't have been able to afford Chivas even if he'd wanted to."

A rustle went through the gathering. Wariness entered Hayward's expression.

Rachel swept her gaze around the room. "Ian Logan would have drunk something a lot cheaper and more available."

Several people made assenting noises.

"Then one would have to wonder why he was drinking Chivas the night he died. The same night someone left him unconscious on the side of the road."

The sharp sound of breaking glass shattered the moment.

Caroline Hayward was standing in the doorway that led to the kitchen, staring at her husband. Her face was pale, the pink lipstick she was wearing suddenly too garish for her pretty, elegant face. Her gaze flickered around the room, and with a mumbled apology she crouched beside the mess and began clumsily gathering up the shards. One of the pieces sliced into her finger. She dropped the glass bits to the floor and stared at her shaking hand, watching the blood drip and splatter onto her pristine white trousers with a silent, rigid fascination.

A lean, tanned hand curled around her wrist, urging her to her feet; then the man who'd walked out of the kitchen behind Caroline gently wrapped a tea towel around her bleeding finger before helping her to a chair just inside the kitchen.

The man was Cullen.

Conversation built like a slow breaking wave, and with it came the clearly audible words, "You bitch."

Rachel lifted her chin and met Hayward's incensed gaze. Had she ever thought he was benign and rather boring? A too smooth ladies man? The cold fury that shone in the lawyer's eyes was calculating and decidedly cruel. He'd been busily slinging mud at Cullen, accusing him of the murder of his own father, but if anyone in this room was capable of doing deliberate harm, it was Hayward.

Cullen reappeared in the doorway, his eyes locating her immediately. The sound level dropped to nothing. Cullen's gaze narrowed at the silence, grey eyes flaring to hot metal as he prowled the gathering with the smooth shift and glide of a big hunting cat, cutting a path straight to Rachel.

He'd changed out of his wet clothes, but he was still dressed in black, black pants and a black crew neck sweater that was so thin it clung to his chest, emphasising the muscular power of his build. He suddenly looked like exactly what he was, an ice-cool, highly trained and disciplined special forces soldier. Too many people had been content to judge Cullen on outward appearance alone, and now they were getting a firsthand taste of the real man. And if the outlaw had been wild and untamed, the warrior was infinitely more dangerous. Heat and vitality and danger throbbed from him. He made every other man in the room look pale and lifeless.

Cullen's single-minded focus as he strode toward Rachel sent bittersweet emotion twisting through her. He was looking at her as if she were the only woman in the world, and she was his. No one here could be in any doubt that she was Cullen's woman. Cullen's bride.

He took her hand and squeezed it gently. "You all right, babe?" His gaze roved over her, checking for any signs of stress or pain.

Rachel didn't even try to stop the giddy rush of pleasure that just having him near started. Her fingers twined with his, soaking in his touch. "I am now."

He smiled a gentle, sinfully sweet smile; then he looked up and over her shoulder, and all the warmth leached from his expression as he took in each and every person in the room in one slow, sweeping glance. His gaze stopped, locking on Richard Hayward. He smiled again. Unlike the smile he'd shared with her, this was a warrior's smile, radiating disdain and a lethal confidence. The kind of expression that made men shuffle back a step and start looking for the way out.

Richard Hayward was the first to the door.

"I wouldn't leave just yet," Cullen warned softly.

Hayward whipped around. Suddenly he didn't look elegant or handsome at all—he just looked scared.

"According to my calculations," Cullen continued in his low, rough-silk voice, "right about now you should be apologising to my wife."

Hayward's adam's apple made a run for his throat, then dropped back down, disappointed. "Sorry," he croaked.

"Sorry...?" Cullen relinquished Rachel's hand, suppressing his regret at not being able to prolong that small, sweet contact for longer. But right now he had to put everything he wanted aside. The strategies in the campaign waged against him had always been dirty, but now that Rachel had been included on the list of casualties, the rules of engagement had just gone wild. Cullen wasn't planning on taking any prisoners.

He strode close enough to Hayward that he was invading the man's personal space. His hand went flat against the partially opened door, easing it closed behind Hayward with a gentleness that was subtly threatening.

Hayward's throat convulsed again, his eyes darting Rachel's way. "I'm sorry if I offended you. I'm sorry I mentioned anything about Ian Logan's death."

"Ah, yes," Cullen murmured. "My father's untimely death. Not many people in this town turned up for the funeral, and I can't say I blame them. He made a lot of enemies. Some of you might even say I was one of them. Only problem is, I know damn well I wasn't the one who provided him with a bottle of whiskey that was more expensive than the brand he usually drank, then knocked him out and left him on the side of the road. He may have stumbled into that ditch all on his own, and the cause of death may have officially been drowning, but the son of a bitch had help. If you don't tell them, Hayward, I know someone who will."

Cullen gambled on a woman's hurt eyes and the inner lacerations they revealed. Lacerations that were more damaging than the outward, physical ones his father had enjoyed inflicting, but had the dubious advantage of not showing on her sleek, expensive hide. "Tell them, Caroline."

Caroline had just sidled into the room, a bandage around her finger. A flush ran along her cheekbones. She looked guilty and scared, and Cullen regretted having to use her. But there was no one else, no other choice. He had to put a stop to these "accidents" before someone got killed. And maybe, if she faced up to what was being done to her, she would make some changes in her life that were long overdue.

When she didn't answer, Cullen ran another slow glance around the room. "Someone tampered with the steering on my truck. When Rachel and I were driving here tonight, both tie rods sheared through. We could have been killed. Tell them, Caroline."

Hayward shifted uneasily. "I didn't have anything to do with that!"

"No," Cullen agreed evenly. "The hands-on stuff isn't your style. Dan Holt should be talking to the prime suspect right about now, and knowing how ticked off Dan is with all the paperwork this particular person has caused him lately, I'd be willing to bet he'll lean on him. Hard. I don't imagine it'll take Trask long to figure his odds. With the assault charges his wife's brought against him, the firearms and arson charges he's facing, he doesn't have a lot of leeway—he'll pull time anyway. But then, you should know. Trask is one of your clients."

"Cullen didn't kill his father."

The words were quietly spoken. They dropped into the tense silence like stones hitting the surface of a deep pool, then sinking all the way to the bottom. Caroline wrapped her arms around her middle and stared at the floor. "Someone hit Ian Logan, but it wasn't Cullen."

"Who was it, Caroline?" Cullen asked gently.

"Caroline—" Hayward said on a low, warning note.

"*No.*" She cut him off, face twisting. "Richard hired his thug Frank Trask, to do that particular job!"

There was an angry murmur from several people. Cole muttered a curt promise that, if he ever managed to carry it out, would keep him in prison through this life and the next, and would put paid to any future generations of Haywards.

Hayward took a step forward, jaw tight, mouth a thin line.

"I wouldn't," Cullen said casually.

Hayward did as he was told.

But then he did something that made Cullen's skin crawl. Hayward stared flatly, intently, at Caroline, his eyes brimming with cold promise.

A flicker of pure rage started deep inside Cullen, and suddenly he was eighteen again and facing his father. The series of harsh, frozen images from fifteen years ago jolted through his mind. The farmhouse kitchen. His father standing casually with a bottle in his hand. The bottle coming at Cullen's face. A moment of spinning, cascading colour when the blow connected. Then the explosion of years of anger and fear, culminating in a moment of surging triumph as he hit his father. Became his father.

Cullen shook his head, trying to clear the old ugliness, the tight, building rage coiling in his gut. He hadn't realised what he would be walking into when he'd gone after Hayward; he'd only considered the safety of Rachel and the baby. He'd never stopped to think about how close this situation could come to duplicating his worst nightmare.

A familiar scent filled his nostrils, flowers and freshness, and the subtle earthy warmth of woman. Rachel. She touched him, sliding her hand over one bunched fist, stroking his fingers. Cullen's breath sifted between clenched teeth. Some of the tension drained from him. He heard her shaky sigh, felt her warmth all down his side, then she laced her fingers with his.

As quickly as that, Hayward ceased to be important—although Cullen couldn't dismiss his fury entirely, because Rachel's safety was at stake. Now Cullen needed to touch her, to pull her close and reassure himself that she was all right. He'd let Cole care for her after the accident only because Cullen had needed to brief Dan and ensure that no one tampered with the sabotaged tie rods before Dan had a chance to examine them. Cullen didn't give a damn that the room was crowded with interested spectators; he centered on Rachel, drinking in her dark, level gaze, her vulnerability. The fear.

He'd frightened her. Cold washed through him, dousing the last hot flickers of fury. She'd finally seen who, *what*, he was. And

Cullen knew that if Rachel hadn't touched him at that moment, if she hadn't dissipated the anger welling deep inside him, he would almost certainly have lost control. He would have hit Hayward and enjoyed doing it. And with the knowledge he now had, the physical power he possessed...

Rachel's hand tightened. Cullen returned the pressure, but gently, gently. A soft touch on his arm had him staring into Caroline Hayward's ravaged eyes.

"I never did thank you," she said softly, holding up her bandaged finger and almost succeeding with a rueful smile. "That's twice you've had to patch me up." She turned to face her husband, only feet separating them, and when she spoke, she lifted her voice so that while it was still soft and husky, the whole room could hear. "Fifteen years ago Richard was having an affair."

Hayward uttered a harsh phrase.

Caroline flinched, but went on. "We'd only been married for a short time, but it wasn't the first affair, and it certainly wasn't the last. I decided to have one, too—with the biggest, baddest wolf I could find. Ian Logan. I wanted to punish Richard and ended up punishing myself instead. Things...went badly wrong. It all got out of control, but Cullen got me out of there."

She stopped, took a deep breath. "Unfortunately, I couldn't hide the mark on my face. Richard found out everything and arranged for Ian to...run into a door. After conveniently getting him drunk, of course. Ian wasn't supposed to die. When he was found the next morning, Richard panicked—he couldn't afford to be implicated in a murder investigation. The fact that Cullen just happened to be back in town and raising hell was...convenient. Any hint of scandal would have ruined Richard's business, and his old man wouldn't have stood for it. Irvin Hayward would have kicked Richard's butt so hard he'd still be travelling. The old man had already threatened to sell the business if Richard kept up his womanising." She laughed unevenly and sent her husband a bitter look. "Which of course he did."

"Shut up, damn you," Hayward snarled beneath his breath.

"No," Caroline snapped. "I've stayed quiet long enough. Ever

nce Cullen's been back in Riverbend, Richard's been sweating
p a storm, worrying that Cullen would find out what really hap-
ened. When Cullen got involved with the Trasks, Richard freaked
ut. He's been trying for months to get rid of Cullen, one way or
nother.''

''You can't prove anything,'' Hayward said tightly. He glanced
round, searching for support. ''She's drunk. She's been drinking
nce three o'clock this afternoon. I'm surprised she can string a
ntence together.''

''Caroline looks just fine to me,'' a low-pitched feminine voice
bserved. Janet Hanson appeared beside Caroline. ''That was my
omemade lemonade on the floor, Hayward. You got some prob-
m with your wife drinking lemonade?''

The breath hissed between Hayward's teeth. His cold glance
iced around the room, which just happened to be filled with some
f the wealthiest, most powerful landowners in the district, along
ith a large percentage of businesspeople. Most of whom were—
r, Cullen reflected with grim satisfaction, had been—his clients.
ith a last stabbing glance at his wife, Hayward wrenched the
oor open and slammed it behind him.

There was a moment of stunned silence while they listened to
ayward's receding footsteps, the eerie howl of the wind, the
rumming rain, then the faint sound of a car being gunned too fast
own the Hansons' drive.

''Good riddance to bad rubbish, I say,'' someone sniffed.

Isobel Reese rose imperiously from the sofa. ''Eleanor, get Car-
line another drink,'' she commanded. ''Then bring her over here
efore she falls down. And you, Cullen Logan. Take that little
ife of yours home. She's carrying that babe awfully low.''

Cullen met Isobel's fierce glare, saw the coins of colour burning
igh on her cheeks and remembered that Hayward was her
ephew. Then Isobel's words sank in, and he fixed his attention
n Rachel.

She did look tired. And the baby *was* low—whatever that meant.
e broke out in a panicked sweat at the most obvious answer.
amn. She kept rubbing her back, too. It was too early—three

weeks too early for her to be having the baby. She wasn't read
to have the baby.

And Cullen wasn't ready to let her go.

"I'm taking you home," he growled next to her ear.

Without giving Rachel time to object, he slipped his arm aroun
her waist and guided her through rapidly recovering groups
people, evading most of the well-wishing, the concern for Rachel
advanced pregnancy, and the increasing numbers of determine
women who'd rallied around Caroline.

Cole intercepted them as they reached the hallway. "Goo
You're taking her home."

Rachel stirred indignantly.

Cullen forestalled her protest with a gentle squeeze that pulle
her more firmly against his side. "We've both had about all th
excitement we can handle for one night."

Cole nodded. "I thought I might put a call through to Dan.
His expression turned distinctly wolfish. "It'll take Hayward
good twenty minutes to hit the main highway in that fancy car
his, so we've got time to stop him. If Dan needs back up, I ca
despatch some of my guys to give him a hand."

"Dan might not have enough evidence to move on Haywai
yet," Cullen warned.

"But there's no harm in trying," Cole drawled softly. H
sketched a quick salute and disappeared back into the lounge.

Cullen released Rachel. "Wait here. I'll drive as close as I ca
get to the door, then come and get you."

"Do we have a vehicle?"

"Cole lent us one of his four-wheel drives. And if this weath
worsens, we're going to need it." Cullen didn't add what scare
him most. If Rachel went into labour early, they would need
four-wheel drive to get through the inevitable floods and road dan
age and to the hospital care she needed.

"I don't care if this *has* been the party from hell," she sa
abruptly. "I'm glad everyone knows what a rat Hayward is. Wi
he face charges?"

Cullen lifted his shoulders. "Trask's not likely to take all th heat on his own. He'll talk. If Caroline agrees to testify, Dan won't hesitate to indict Hayward for harassment, at the very least. But even if none of the charges stick, Hayward can still kiss his career goodbye. He'll never work around here again, and it's likely he'll face disbarment."

"He deserves everything he gets," Rachel said fiercely, touching his arm. "What you did for Caroline..."

Cullen had to restrain himself from laying his hand over hers. Her fingers were pale and smooth, elegant and impossibly fragile against his scarred, muscled forearm. Beauty and the Beast. The analogy hit him forcibly. He felt like the Beast. Even now, his instincts were primitive. He wanted to haul Rachel close and keep her beside him so that she and everyone else would know that she was his. But he had to deal with her fear first, no matter what it cost him. Gently, he withdrew from her touch. "I frightened you."

"You didn't *frighten* me! You've never frightened me. Now Hayward..." she said deliberately, "I'd say that's one very frightened man. If I looked apprehensive it was because I knew what that situation in there cost you."

"Then maybe you *should* be frightened, because if you hadn't touched me when you did, I would have hit Hayward, and the way I was feeling, I wouldn't have wanted to stop."

With a last shuttered look, he turned and strode out into the darkness.

Chapter 16

When they reached home, Rachel made sandwiches and coffee for Cullen while he put the truck away. Every part of her body throbbed and ached in subtle ways, as if she'd been sandpapered from the inside out. She was exhausted, but it was as much a tiredness of the spirit as the physical strain of late pregnancy. Three weeks. That was all she had, and it was going too fast. Soon she would have a baby in her arms, a child to love and cherish, but they would be alone. She could feel herself breaking inside, a slow splintering of all her hopes and dreams, and she wondered how she could possibly survive it. Not that she would have any choice. She would have to survive, for the baby's sake.

The mudroom door opened and closed on a burst of wind as she lowered herself into a chair at the table. She could hear Cullen shedding his oilskin and boots, the sound of water running as he washed his hands; then he padded in.

Instead of taking his seat, he went down on his haunches beside her. His hand settled gently on the curve of her belly, sending minor shock waves through her at the unexpectedness, the tingling heat, of his touch.

"Are you sure you're all right?" he demanded. "If you think e baby's on its way, I'll take you to hospital now."

Rachel met his gaze with calm determination. "I'm not in la-ur. The baby isn't due for three weeks. All my tests have been e. Dr. Dalziel said I'd have to expect to feel tired. And that's I I'm feeling. Tired."

She didn't say what was uppermost in her mind. Once she went hospital, she would relinquish what little contact she had with llen, and she *wouldn't* give up on his love until she knew she'd st.

In a move that was as unexpected as his hand caressing her mach, Cullen touched her cheek, then the delicate skin beneath r eyes. "I'm sorry," he said huskily. His eyes locked with hers r a long, drawn-out moment; then he straightened and turned the dio on.

The storm had been upgraded to a depression, and cyclone arnings were being broadcast at regular intervals. Often big eather systems headed their way but dissipated, swallowed by e vast expanse of the Pacific Ocean before they ever reached the rthern tip of New Zealand. This one was early in the season and d been discounted because of that. But instead of the innocuous izzle that had been expected, the system was holding, building.

By twelve o'clock the next afternoon the windspeed was gale rce. Rachel paced into the kitchen and stared out the window. loud crack jerked her gaze around in time to see a branch of e big old puriri tree next to the garage break off and tumble wn the corrugated iron roof of the building. The sound of glass attering punctuated the steady howl of the wind.

She was alone in the house. Dane had stayed in town for the eekend, and Cullen was shifting stock out of the lower river flat stures before the whole area flooded. He hadn't wanted to leave r, but Rachel had insisted. She felt perfectly fine, and the mares d foals needed to be moved. The wind wasn't as violent as it uld have been, but with the torrent of water that would pour wn off the hills, flash flooding was expected. Her final argument,

that she could always ring Cole if she couldn't get hold of Cull
on his mobile phone, had finally convinced him.

Another strong gust battered the house, and abruptly the pow
went out, plunging her into gloom. A piece of iron that must ha
been dislodged by the falling branch peeled off the garage ro
with a shrieking sound and whipped away, leaving a hole in t
roof and other pieces of iron flapping.

Rachel rubbed her arms. Goose bumps roughened her skin, ev
though it wasn't cold. It was lunchtime, and Cullen should ha
been back by now. He'd rung twice earlier to check on her, t
she hadn't heard from him for over an hour. He could be in dang
trapped by a flood or unconscious under a fallen tree. She pick
up the phone and stabbed in his number—it took her a mome
to realise the line was dead.

Of course. The power was out, so why should she expect t
telephone lines to remain intact? Panic settled low in her stoma

"Get ahold of yourself," she said sharply. "Just because t
phone's dead, it doesn't mean Cullen is. All it means is that he
taking longer to shift stock than he'd planned and he can't g
hold of you."

But even though she'd said the admonitory words aloud, th
didn't comfort her in any way. Cullen was strong, but the relentle
power of the storm was frightening.

Rachel paced the house, staring out different windows, straini
to see past cascading water, to hear more than rain and moani
wind. The helplessness of being trapped alone in the house wh
Cullen was outside in *that* filled her with frustration. If the wi
showed any signs of abating, she decided, she would take her (
and check on him. The decision to act instantly made her fe
calmer, more in control. The road to the river flats was high, w
metalled and clear of trees—the chances of getting stuck we
almost nonexistent. She would take a thermos of coffee and so
sandwiches. She shivered at the monotonous flapping of the loc
iron on the garage roof. She would take the first aid kit, too.
she parked with her lights on, Cullen would see her and con
and then she would know he was safe.

Quickly she filled a thermos with hot coffee and slapped peanut
butter sandwiches together. She stuffed everything into one of the
ancient canvas day packs that Cullen kept on a peg in the mudroom, then made herself sit down and wait.

The wind was supposed to drop through the day, and no matter
how restless and downright scared she was for Cullen, she
wouldn't risk her baby in dangerous conditions. Half an hour
passed, and the wind did seem to lessen. She hadn't heard any
more iron rip loose, and the torrential downpour had abated to a
steady light rain driven by wind.

On impulse, Rachel grabbed the phone and punched in Cole's
number, then remembered the phone was dead and let the receiver
drop back onto its cradle.

She couldn't wait any longer.

Dragging one of Cullen's oilskins on over her cotton sweater
and leggings, Rachel stamped her feet into gum boots, awkwardly
managed to shoulder into the day pack, then grabbed her car keys
and braced herself to go out the door.

Even though she expected it, the wind nearly tore the handle
out of her grasp. Gritting her teeth, she forced the door shut and
walked gingerly down the steps, holding on to the railing with one
hand, keeping the hood of the oilskin anchored to the top of her
head with the other. When she rounded the corner of the house,
the wind hit her full force. She staggered back. Had she thought
the wind had lessened? Bowing her head, she did her best to shield
her face from the stinging, driving rain.

Getting into the garage was an unexpected problem. The wind
was blowing against them, making the heavy, reinforced doors
almost impossible to open. Gasping for breath, Rachel forced herself to think. She had to wait for a lull in the gusts, then quickly
pull the door open and fasten it, otherwise it would slam back and
hit her.

Not for the first time in her life, she cursed her feminine weakness. Cullen could have done this one-handed without breaking a
sweat. If only the wind would drop for just a split second.

Agonising seconds ticked by; then finally a lull came. Rachel

wrenched at the door, got her shoulder in the gap, then used
weight of her body to lever the door back against the shed. Fu
bling and breathless, she located the hook and jammed it i
place, anchoring the door open. Wiping rain and wet hair off
face, she rested while the wind pounded on her back and the r
drummed a staccato on the stiff oilskin. Time seemed to stre
out while she waited for her chance at the other door, and wl
the drop in the wind arrived, she almost didn't react. Stepp
clumsily, her stomach suddenly feeling tight and heavy, she st
gered to the other door and put her weight against it, almost fall
over when it swung with unexpected speed. Latching it open,
stumbled into the dark interior of the garage, which was lighter
where the battered roof was now open to the weather.

The baby chose that moment to kick.

"Don't you start," she muttered, massaging the place the li
tyke was abusing and feeling the lumpy outline of a foot.

After shrugging out of the pack, she unlocked and opened
car door, tossed the pack inside, then gingerly hauled herself i
the driver's seat.

The engine fired immediately. Breathless but relieved, Rac
backed out into the gravel turnaround area. Flicking on the ligl
she eased out onto the farm road and began to drive slow
searching the murky daylight for any sign of another vehicle.
nally she brought the car to a halt and stared down at a landsc
she hardly recognised.

The bottom paddocks were almost completely underwa
There was no stock in sight, so Cullen must have got them
away in time. Even as she watched, the water encroached on m
pasture. The river itself was a boiling mass of brown, w
branches and trees being railroaded along in the current.

Movement caught her attention. There *was* an animal stran
on one of the last pieces of land still above water. No, there w
two. Three. And one of them wasn't an animal, it was Cullen
his horse, Mac. He was attempting to pull another horse out
what looked like a ditch, and a lanky foal was in imminent dan
of miring itself, as well. Cullen must have got the rest of the h

out, then come back for the stuck animal. But he didn't have much time left. Within a matter of minutes the whole area would be flooded.

Rachel inched the car down the hill, then came to an abrupt halt. Cullen had left the truck parked in the centre of the road, above a bridge. There was no way she could drive around the truck without bogging her little car down.

She could take the truck. The bridge still cleared the water by a foot or more. It would only take a minute or two to haul the mare out with the sturdy vehicle.

Snatching up her pack, Rachel eased from the car, holding the door against the slamming wind. When the wind dropped, she made for the truck, using both vehicles as support.

The truck was cumbersome after her small hatchback, but not unfamiliar. When she was old enough to drive, her brothers had made sure she knew how to use four-wheel drive vehicles during the holidays she'd spent at the farm. As she inched across the bridge, Cullen wheeled Mac and arrowed toward her at a reckless canter. She glanced down at the deep, narrow creek. Debris was packed up on the banks, crowded against the bridge timbers. She felt a shuddering vibration as a particularly large log rammed into one of the piles.

It was a relief to be on solid ground again.

She brought the truck to a halt just as Cullen slid off his horse and wrenched her door open. His face was taut, eyes narrowed against the wind and rain that hammered around him as he filled the doorway with the width of his shoulders. "Thank God," he muttered, then cupped her face with his cold, wet fingers, forced her lips apart with his and plunged his tongue into her mouth. The kiss was deep and hard and possessive. And over so fast that Rachel was still spinning when he pulled away.

"What was that for?" she said into the relative calm of the cab.

He closed his eyes briefly, and when he opened them, he looked furious as well as grim. "The bridge is unsafe. The road barrier and reflective tape were all blown away by the storm. When I saw you driving down the hill, I didn't think you were going to make it across.''

Rachel's stomach clenched, tight and heavy with dread. ''*That* was the bridge you told me about?'' she asked, thinking back to what had seemed unimportant when mentioned over dinner one night.

''That was the bridge,'' he echoed flatly. ''Shift over.''

Rachel moved awkwardly onto the passenger seat, while Cullen hitched Mac to the fence. Then Cullen swung in behind the wheel and manoeuvred the truck into the paddock so he could use the winch on the front. He attached the rope to the harness he'd already strapped on the mare before inching the truck backward. The mare neighed a protest, her foal bugled shrilly, but she finally began to slip free. When she scrambled up the bank she was slimy with mud and trembling. Cullen led both horses through the gate, untied the harness and rope, and slapped the mare's rump, sending her shambling toward the relative safety of the hills, her foal close behind.

Cullen backed the truck out of the paddock. The deeply notched mud-grip tyres slid in the wet, then bit solidly into gravel as he gained the road. The water followed them in a lapping tide, easing over the place where the horse had been stuck only seconds ago.

Rachel glanced at Cullen's set face. ''Now what?'' she asked, knowing in advance what he was going to say.

He drove his fingers through his hair, slicking it back from his face. ''We wait,'' he said grimly. ''If we take the truck over the bridge now, the whole thing will probably go.''

The water had risen in the short time since Rachel had crossed the bridge. As they watched, a tangle of tree branches caromed into the side of the debris piling up against the bridge timbers, creating a dam effect. The water began to spread on either side, onto the road.

''I can't believe I drove across it,'' she said numbly.

''Why do you think I went so crazy when I saw you? Damn it, when I said I wanted you to stop taking risks, I meant it.''

''You needed help with the horse,'' she countered stubbornly.

"The hell with the horse."

"There's no need to yell! I wanted you out of that paddock. If I'm going to lose you, it won't be to a flood."

Cullen made a rough sound. His hand curved around her jaw; warm hard fingers stroked her skin. "You are one crazy woman. It would take a lot more than this to bring me down."

Rachel rubbed her cheek against Cullen's palm, unable to resist the shimmering delight of his touch, even if he was mad at her. "A tree branch smashed into the garage. When that happened, I couldn't stop thinking about the same thing happening to you. I couldn't bear to stay inside when I thought you might be hurt or drowning."

"You shouldn't have gone outside. If something hit you..." His fingers tightened on her chin. "How in hell did you get the garage doors open by yourself? And what were you doing in there with trees falling on the building?"

"Not trees," she corrected, irritated by the way he'd homed in on what she'd already privately acknowledged as a miscalculation on her part. "One branch. And I opened the doors in the usual way."

"The usual way." He said something terse beneath his breath. "The wind was slamming in hard against those doors when I secured them this morning."

"I managed."

His expression said he believed that only because she was here now. "You're supposed to be resting," he said in the controlled tones of one talking to a particularly dense child.

"I've been resting for months! I'm sick of resting. I'm sick of you saving me, too. It was going to be my turn to do the saving."

Cullen's eyes narrowed at her outburst. A bubble of silence seemed to grow and expand to fill the cab of the truck, pushing back the sounds of the storm. He released her chin and raked his fingers through his wet hair. "Oh, baby," he said softly, his mouth curling in a way that made her bones melt. "What am I going to do with you?"

Rachel blinked and looked away before she made a couple of

pertinent suggestions that involved the next fifty odd years. Before she gave in to the need to reach out and touch him in the way he'd been touching her, to demand a kiss that would involve a lot more than longing and regret.

"I brought you coffee and sandwiches," she said instead, reaching for the pack she'd dumped on the floor when she'd shifted seats. Just as she unscrewed the cap of the thermos, there was a loud cracking sound. Her head jerked up. She was just in time to see the bridge tilt, skew, then half submerge as the water gained momentum and punched through the gap where the supports had once been.

Cullen swore with an earthy, somehow reassuring, fluency.

"What do we do now?" Rachel whispered.

"What we were going to do anyway. With the water running so high, we can't use any of the fords. Aside from that bridge there's no other way out of this part of the farm other than to head up into the hills, then down onto Sinclair land. I'm going to call Cole on his mobile and tell him where to meet us. Then we drive as far as the road will take us, ride Mac along the stock routes until the going gets too rough. Then we walk. Or rather, I walk—you're not doing one more thing if I can help it, except breathe."

Rachel stared at him with unfeigned horror. "You mean you're going to carry me?" Blessedly, in the past few weeks the nausea had stopped. Unfortunately, her appetite hadn't.

Cullen didn't answer, which meant he was going to carry her. Rachel stared in dismay at her very pregnant body as Cullen swung out of the cab and hitched a sodden Mac to the rear of the truck.

When Cullen clambered back into the cab, he jabbed a number on his cell phone and spoke tersely, then handed the phone to her. "Cole wants to talk to you."

Rachel took the receiver and listened to a furious catalogue of brotherly anxiety and abuse. She noticed almost absently that Cole didn't blame Cullen as he once would have. He placed the blame securely where it belonged—on her shoulders.

"I love you, too," she said wryly, when Cole had run out of sensible reasons for his sister's irrational behaviour and had started on the insane ones. Then she gave him the only reason that mattered. "I couldn't stay in the house when I thought Cullen might need help."

After a few more gruff words, this time in a more reassuring vein, Cole let Rachel terminate the call. Cullen started the truck and headed up into the greyness that she knew hid hills, hills and more hills. Rugged country cloaked by a dense coverage of bush and broken by sheer rockfaces.

He stopped the truck at the base of a particularly steep piece of road. "This is as far as we go on wheels."

"Couldn't we four-wheel drive up there?"

Amusement took some of the grimness from his expression. "We *could* rock and roll over these hills, but somehow, I don't think junior would appreciate it."

Rachel touched her stomach. "I'm sorry. I came to help, but all I've done is cause you more trouble."

His hand covered hers in what was now a familiar gesture. "You did help. Without the truck, I couldn't have got that mare out, and we would probably have lost the colt, too. If this is anyone's fault, it's mine. I should have had the damned bridge either repaired or demolished by now."

Rachel stared out at the rough country, where the tussocky grass disintegrated into brooding bush and dark, towering peaks. She couldn't help thinking that if Cullen hadn't sacrificed so much of his time to help her, he would have finished the work on the bridge weeks ago.

"Don't worry," he said, misreading her expression. "We'll make it out of here. We've got hours of daylight, and we'll take it slow. The first thing we need to do is check on the weather. The wind's eased, but I'd like a report before we leave the truck."

Cullen turned on the radio and they both listened, frustrated at the static that fuzzed up the reception so badly that they could hardly hear what was being said. The hills cut off or disrupted the radio signals.

"There goes Plan A," she muttered. "Do we have a Plan B?"

Cullen switched the radio off. His gaze drifted to the pack she'd brought. For some odd reason, he smiled. "We eat. What did you cook me?"

She plunked several spongy packages in his hand.

"Peanut butter. Mmm. My favourite."

He handed her one of the thick, doorstop sandwiches.

Rachel's stomach twinged in protest. "I'm not hungry."

"Eat it for her," he murmured, glancing at her tummy.

Rachel took the sandwich and nibbled at a crust. It disgusted her that once she began to eat, she developed a hearty appetite and polished the whole sandwich off. "How do you know she's a she? She could be a he."

He gave her a complacent, very male look. "There's a little lady in there. I could tell by her foot."

Another annoying twinge tightened her stomach, then shot up her back. She shifted her position to ease it. "Before you got the boot off or after?" she demanded irritably.

Cullen frowned. "What's wrong?"

Rachel rubbed at her back. Now that she'd eaten, she felt slightly nauseous. And she needed to go to the bathroom something fierce. "The usual. My back feels like it's got a knife stuck in it, and I need the bathroom. Now."

"I'll help you." Cullen screwed up the sandwich wrapping, shoved it back in the day pack, then came around to her side and opened the door.

"What do you think you're doing?" she asked weakly, knowing very well what he intended.

"Taking you to the bathroom."

"I can hold on."

His brows lifted. "For how many hours?"

She closed her eyes and held out her arms. He lifted her out of the truck, cradling her against the angled, driving rain as he walked as if she weighed nothing.

"This is as sheltered as you're going to get," he said into her ear. Cullen set her on her feet, his big body shielding her from the worst of the weather. His hands slipped up beneath the oilskin, firm and gentle as he began pulling her leggings down.

"I don't need any help," she protested, grabbing at her leggings as a cool, moist draught blew up her legs. She knew the sensation of exposure was ridiculous; she was draped in enough oilskin to make a tent, and they were standing in the middle of nowhere, with wind and rain howling around them. There was no one for miles, and no reason to blush. Biting back a disgusted groan, she gave in to Cullen's gentle pressure and squatted. Her back protested the movement, and the sudden stab of pain made her sag against his chest.

"That's it," Cullen murmured into her ear. "Lean on me."

His thighs were on either side of hers; he was all around her like a muscular supporting framework. Rachel gave in. Not that she had much choice. Her face burned as she voided a ridiculously small amount of liquid. When she was finished, Cullen helped her back to the truck. Once they were inside, he stripped them both of their oilskins, rolling one up so that the dry lining was on the outside—a crude, but usable bolster that he positioned in the small of her back.

"See if you can sleep for an hour. By then the wind will have dropped even more and the going will be easier."

Rachel tensed on another tightening pain.

"Damn," Cullen muttered, grabbing a cloth from beneath his seat and mopping up a trickle of moisture. "The rain must have soaked through the oilskin."

Rachel bit her lip. "Cullen," she said softly. "That's not rain. I think my water just broke."

His gaze locked on hers, pupils expanding with shock, but he said quite calmly, "How long have you been having contractions?"

"I didn't think I was! I've been having the usual back pain, and some twinges that I put down to muscle strain."

"Muscle strain?" he repeated with a dangerous quietness.

"The wind was pinning the garage doors closed. I had to get in the garage."

Cullen stared out at the grey, relentless hell of the storm. At the sheer, brutal force of the weather spinning off from the Pacific hurricane belt. Weather that killed, scything down on land just as wild. Even though the storm was diminishing in intensity and would blow itself out overnight, they were still cut off, isolated from any form of help. And Rachel needed to be in hospital. Now.

Adrenaline surged white-hot through his veins, tearing a low, rough sound from his throat. Sweat leaped from his pores. Suddenly he couldn't block the emotion that beat at him from all directions. Sweet hell. He'd never felt such fear.

Rachel's mother had died giving birth. Rachel and the baby could die because of him.

He was the one who had allowed this impossible situation to develop. He'd gotten her pregnant, risked her health with the burden of bearing his child, brought her to live on his wild property with its dangerous propensity to flash flood.

Ever since he'd returned to Riverbend, events had careered out of control. In the SAS, if there was an enemy to overcome, his options were as clinically precise as black on white. In Riverbend, the rules were wild, and the shadows of his past reached forward and touched everything with grey. And even though he now knew that most of the trouble and bad feeling had been deliberately manufactured by the man who'd been indirectly responsible for his father's death, he still had his own personal demon to deal with.

And that demon seemed determined to give him a guided tour of hell. He loved Rachel more than his next breath, but all he seemed to bring her was trouble and danger, then more trouble and danger.

Rachel met his gaze unflinchingly. Despite the discomfort and uncertainty she must be feeling, her eyes were clear, trusting. Trusting him. Pain spasmed in Cullen's chest. He picked up one of her tightly clenched hands and folded it in his. "The weather's too bad to airlift you out. The rescue services would never get a chopper in the air, even if they were willing to try. Our original plan is still our best option." He didn't add that it was their only option. "I'll get you to the hospital. It'll take two, maybe three hours to get above the mouth of the river, then it'll be downhill all the way until we hit Sinclair land. Cole will be waiting for us with a four-wheel drive.''

As he catalogued everything he would have to do, everything he would need to take, Cullen's thought processes sharpened, clarified, shifting into the disciplined cadences of tactical planning. He let out a slow breath, deliberately relaxing his muscles, then reached for the phone. He knew the extent of his strength and endurance; he'd been tested often enough and in worse conditions than these. Ironically, now that Rachel was in trouble, she couldn't be in better company.

After he'd spoken with Cole, Cullen began filling the day pack with everything they would need. He retrieved a small tarp from the back of the truck and rigged that, along with the rope he'd used to rescue the mare, behind Mac's saddle. If they didn't make it to the rendezvous with Cole before the baby came, they were going to need every bit of shelter he could contrive.

When everything was ready, Cullen deposited Rachel's oilskin-draped figure on Mac's back, then swung up behind her. When he was settled, he turned her so she was sitting across the saddle, her legs to one side, her head cradled in the curve of his shoulder. Her arms slid around his waist as if they belonged there, filling him with the intense pleasure of her nearness and another grim jolt of determination.

Mac's hoof-falls thudded steadily through the wind and rain as Cullen guided the horse, sometimes by memory, sometimes by pure instinct, through pathways, gullies and bush-shrouded slopes he hadn't seen since he was a half-wild boy running from a violent father. The higher they went, the steeper the country got, but Mac was as as agile as a cat. They stopped periodically, to rest Mac and ease Rachel's discomfort when the contractions began to strengthen.

Cullen kept clear of the thickest bush as long as he could, but when the river blocked their path, they were forced beneath the dark canopy. Although they were now sheltered from the worst of the wind, water cascaded through branches and dripped from fronds. Woody roots and rotting vegetation made the ground treacherously slippery, and some groves of trees were too thickly tangled to penetrate on horseback.

Cullen brought Mac to a halt before a particularly dense stand of trees. "This is where we get off."

Rachel roused herself from the semiaware state she'd instinctively retreated into when the contractions eased. "You can't carry me through *that*."

Cullen helped her from the horse. "I routinely carry packs and equipment that weigh more than you."

Rachel held on to the branch of a small sapling as Cullen untied a tarp and rope from Mac and rigged it to his pack. "But you'll need both arms free to—"

Dropping the pack, Cullen bracketed her face with his hands and kissed her, his mouth moving with a gentle hunger over hers. The wind and rain receded, the forest ceased to exist, and warmth flowed through Rachel on a wave of sweetness that was cut abruptly short by another contraction.

He lifted his mouth from hers. "The baby?"

Before she could answer, he unbuttoned her oilskin and slid his hand beneath her sweater and shirt to the tightening muscles of her stomach. "How long?" he asked tautly.

"Could be hours, could be minutes," she muttered, her voice tense with the effects of the contraction. "If there was such a thing as a practice run, maybe I could tell you something different."

"If there was such a thing as a practice run, I'd be damned I'd let you go through it," he said as he refastened her buttons. "You're already in too much pain."

"How much is too much?" she retorted with a touch of asperity. "I've got a feeling this is only the beginning."

Cullen's arms came around Rachel, enclosing her. She breathed him in, almost tasting his heady, hot vitality, feeling some of his strength run through her in the subtle uplifting of her spirits, the rock-solid certainty that he would keep her and the baby safe no matter what.

His fingers stroked her jaw, tilted her head back until she was

ce again locked in the clear, metallic purity of his gaze. "If I
uld, I would take the pain for you. Always."

Tears sprang to Rachel's eyes. Damn, she was raining from the
side out now. "I know," she said huskily. And suddenly she
ew she couldn't hold back how she felt. If she didn't tell him
w, she might never get another chance. "That's just one of the
asons why I love you."

Cullen went absolutely still. His fingers trembled against her
w. "Rachel," he said hoarsely.

"Don't," she said, afraid he would express regret and not sure
e could bear that. "Don't say anything."

A rough sound tore from his throat; then he pulled her close,
rapping her in so tightly that she could feel the shudders running
rough his big body.

Minutes later Cullen slapped Mac on the rump, sending the
orse mincing indignantly back the way they'd come. He lifted
achel into his arms. "Hold on around my neck, and I'll be able
use one arm to clear branches when I have to. Tell me when
ou feel a contraction coming on, and I'll stop."

Rachel settled her head on the curve of his shoulder. As they
imbed higher into the steep hill country, Cullen's breathing deep-
ed but never faltered. She could feel the smooth bunch and shift
f his muscles beneath her hands, the relentless rhythm of his
round-eating stride. He was sweating, and a startling amount of
eat radiated from his body, but he only stopped when she needed
, and he only altered his pace for her comfort.

"I *am* too heavy," Rachel protested when Cullen had to take a
articularly long detour around a sheer rockface.

He didn't answer. His breathing was still deep and even, but
achel didn't know how long he could keep it up. With a rigorous
iorning's work behind him and the rain soaking his pack and
oots, adding to the weight he had to carry, even Cullen's strength
ad to have its limits. But then again, maybe not. His strength and
ndurance, his fierce will, awed her. In many of the men Rachel
new, those qualities were present, but subdued and perhaps sel-

dom tested. In Cullen, they burned with furnace heat, blastin
through normal barriers.

After a period of time, she realised they were going downhil
The wind and rain had dropped considerably, but the afternoo
was darkening toward an early dusk. Finally they walked free o
the bush. Cullen stopped, setting her on her feet while he scanne
the area.

He grunted with satisfaction and pointed out a glow in the dis
tance. "Cole's waiting. Twenty minutes and we'll be on our wa
to hospital."

Hospital. She went still as a pain that had nothing to do wit
the baby poured through her. That was where she wanted to go
but Rachel was suddenly reminded of exactly what the hospita
meant. The end of her marriage.

Cullen mistook her tension as the beginning of another serie
of cramps. Rachel didn't disabuse him.

The last few hundred metres seemed to take forever. Culle
cradled her with exquisite care, but the contractions were close
together and had strengthened, arching Rachel like a bow ever
time one struck. Leaving her breathless and trembling when the
finally ebbed.

Cole was waiting beside a four-wheel drive. There were sever
other vehicles and an array of neighbours, presumably gatherin
to form a search party if needed.

Cole opened the passenger door of his extended-cab truck
"You're early," he said roughly.

Cullen lifted Rachel onto the rear passenger seat and strippe
her oilskin away before stowing it in the covered back of the truc
along with his own. He climbed in next to her, belted them bot
in, and settled her in the curve of his arm. "Forty minutes, forty
five at the outside, and we'll have you in hospital."

His molten gaze seared into Rachel with such force that she ha
to believe that if it were possible to keep the baby from bein
born by will alone, then Cullen would achieve it. But Cullen's wi
was so very strong, strong enough to push her and the baby ou

f his life no matter how hard she tried to break through his bar-
ers. No matter how much they needed him.

No matter how much he needed them.

Cole reversed the truck, then turned it, pointing them in the
eneral direction of the road. Powerful lights cut through rain and
vind and darkness, picking out a fence line, an open gate and
nally the lighter outline of the farm road. Despair seeped through
.achel, even as Cullen's warmth, his magical touch, sank into her.
he could measure the time she had left with Cullen in hours,
inutes. Ten minutes to the main road. Ten minutes into River-
end. Half an hour at the outside to get to Fairley. And no time
t all until the baby was born. Once this baby was out, any hold
he had on Cullen would be gone. The years stretched ahead bar-
enly, and Rachel knew with dull certainty that she wouldn't be
ble to stay in Riverbend. Not only had she lost Cullen, she'd lost
er home.

Another contraction began its relentless stretching and squeez-
ng. Rachel gasped, wrapping her arms around her taut belly and
rying to breathe through the pain. Even so, a keening note escaped
er, etching out her grief. With an effort of will she reached for
ontrol, for the dignity not to beg Cullen to stay with her, not just
or now, but forever. When the pain ebbed, she lay against Cul-
en's chest and closed her eyes.

Cullen stared at Rachel in blank anguish. He touched a finger
o the pulse in her throat. Her skin was cold, her heart rate much
oo fast. "Step on it, Cole," he said quietly.

Cole looked at the big man cradling his little sister like a piece
f precious porcelain and drove.

Chapter 17

Rachel was whisked away for an examination as soon as they arrived at the hospital, and since she was in the middle of another painful, wracking contraction, Cullen didn't have any chance to speak with her.

The only other person in the waiting room was a small bald-headed man who was holding an ice pack to a red swelling on his cheekbone. He nodded at Cullen. "That your wife they've just taken in?"

Cullen inclined his head, barely paying attention to the man, just as he was only peripherally aware of Cole shadowing his every move. Fury at his own helplessness consumed him. He could see why expectant fathers paced—there was no other way to siphon off all this frustrated urgency.

The man bobbed his head knowingly, then winced, reapplying the ice pack. "Thought so," he said. "My wife's in there, too. On her fifth. Your old lady hasn't got a weapon anywhere on her, has she?"

Cullen stared at the man blankly, his mind almost solely occupied with what was happening to Rachel and whether or not any

ne in there knew what they were doing. Whether the bored young
octor who'd taken charge of her knew how desperate her situation
as. And, most of all, just how damned much the next contraction
as going to hurt her.

"Better check," the man said sagely. "Women get mighty un-
asonable on the delivery table."

A nurse pushed through the waiting room door. "You can go
," she declared sunnily.

Cullen's head jerked up. "Is the baby all right?"

"The baby's hours away yet," the nurse said drily. "First
ne?"

"How many hours?" Cullen asked.

"If it's a first baby, chances are it could take a while." She
niled brightly. "But you never know, your wife could surprise
s all. Some women deliver so quickly they never even make it
a doctor's surgery."

Cullen felt the blood drain from his face.

Cole came to stand beside him. "Is she well enough to have
e baby?" he demanded, abrasive as ever. "Shouldn't she have
urgery?"

The woman glanced distractedly at her wristwatch. "We've
aken a urine sample, administered a painkiller, and the doctor's
hecked her over. Mrs. Logan is quite relaxed. She's reading a
aagazine and listening to some soothing music. I'm sure she's
uite capable of having the baby naturally."

Disbelief combined with the fury already shuddering through
ullen. After hours of intense physical effort, of ruthlessly keeping
is fear for Rachel's safety—for her very life—at bay, no one here
eemed to be providing her with anything like the attention his
vife should be receiving.

The two men watched the nurse walk briskly away to deal with
nother patient. They exchanged a look. Music? Magazines? For
nce they were in perfect accord. If the nurse wasn't going to give
achel the attention she needed, then they would.

* * *

"Do you need another painkiller?" Cullen asked Rachel three hours later in a voice taut with strain.

A young nurse who didn't look old enough to be out of school, let alone caring for a pregnant woman, gave him a patronising smile. "No more painkillers."

"Damn it, you gave her some before. Why not now, when she really needs it?"

"It's bad for the baby this close to delivery. The drug's only for the early part of labour."

Rachel gripped Cullen's hand as another contraction began. He was sitting on the bed, and she was leaning against him; he could feel the excruciating tautness of her muscles, the fine tremors that kept running through her.

Cole was pacing. He'd become good at it during the past few hours.

Rachel whimpered, almost arching off the bed.

"Get a doctor," Cullen snarled. *"Now."*

Cole strode through the swing doors of the delivery room and appeared seconds later with a dazed woman, then disappeared as rapidly as he'd arrived.

"Are you a doctor?" Cullen rasped.

She nodded.

"Good. See to my wife. She's having a baby."

The doctor raised her brows, shared a look with the nurse, asked some questions about Rachel's condition, then pulled on a pair of tight, thin rubber gloves before proceeding with her examination. Cullen watched with narrowed eyes. He knew the doctor had to do an internal examination, but that didn't mean he had to like it. As gentle as the woman tried to be, she still hurt Rachel, and frustration raged through Cullen at his inability to help her when she needed it most.

"Won't she need assistance?" Cullen asked. "Won't you need to do surgery?"

The doctor smiled reassuringly, stoking Cullen's fury. Why didn't they take this business seriously? Were all the women in this hospital power crazy?

"Your wife is almost fully dilated, Mr. Logan. She's quite capable of having this child unassisted. Surgical procedures are for when something goes wrong, not a routine birth."

Routine. Cullen carefully unclenched his jaw. There was *nothing* routine about his wife having a baby.

"Now, Mrs. Logan, did you want to be in any specific position to give birth?"

"Hands and knees," she gasped. "I've heard it helps to push the baby out."

"Right then. Mr. Logan, you can help us out here. Why don't you put all that restless energy to some use and help your wife turn over? The baby should be born sometime during the next few minutes."

"Help be damned," he muttered. Cullen gently lifted Rachel and turned her over himself, arranging extra pillows so she was kneeling and resting at the same time, and able to hold on to the bar at the head of the bed for extra support.

Rachel gripped his hand. "Stay with me. Here. Where I can see you."

"I can't help you," Cullen returned from between gritted teeth.

"Yes, you can," she said fiercely, her eyes linking with his. "I need you. Only. you."

Cullen felt as if he'd just had all the air squeezed out of his chest. Rachel needed him. Only him. Not Cole, not the doctor, not some other man. Only him. The ferocious tension of the past few hours tightened, making it even more difficult to breathe. He covered her hands with his, trying to ease her white-knuckled strain with the stroke of his fingers, willing her through the last violent birth pains with the only thing he had to offer: the love that twisted inside him, knotting up his gut almost as hard as hers every time she had a contraction. And this time—instead of holding to what he couldn't do, the ways he couldn't help—he answered the hunger, the need, in her eyes and poured his strength into her. She'd endured more than any woman should have to over the past few months, stoically accepting the difficulties of their relationship and awing him with her capacity to hope.

She loved him.

He broke out into a renewed sweat at the wonder, the reality, of her love. She needed him. He swallowed, cursing thickly. Damn it, he wanted to take the burden from her, take her pain, and something broke in him then, an internal shattering that made his head spin.

Nothing mattered but Rachel.

Not his past. Not his fears for the future. Nothing but Rachel.

"I love you," he declared hoarsely, just as she cried out on a different note. Her eyes, wide, almost wholly absorbed with the business of giving birth, flared with shock, and then, incredibly, a smile spread across her mouth. With her hair clinging damply to her forehead and cheeks, and sweat sheening her pale skin, she was the most luminously beautiful creature Cullen had ever seen.

"One more push, Mrs. Logan," a distant voice intruded. "The head's crowning."

"Cullen. Oh, God, Cullen..."

"Sweet heaven," Cullen muttered, as she cried out again. She grasped his hands, her nails slicing deep enough to draw blood, but he barely felt it; his whole being was locked on Rachel. Locked on the incredible miracle of the woman he loved giving birth to their child. And he knew with stunning clarity that he couldn't let her go. Ever.

"Would you like to catch the baby, Mr. Logan?"

"Do it," Rachel said between controlled breaths. "Hold our baby, Cullen."

Cullen relinquished Rachel's hands. Awe shuddered through him again as he positioned his big, scarred hands under the tiny glistening head of the child. A few seconds later the warm, wet body slid into his palms, and his daughter screwed up her delicate red face and waved her tiny fists and feet at him. Her dark hair was plastered to her head, and she was so defenceless, so utterly vulnerable, that his heart shattered again.

Cullen felt as if he were dying. Being born again. Adrenaline slammed his heart into overdrive. He went cold, then hot, and his hands began to shake. Dimly, he recognised that he'd gone into mild shock.

His mother had never held him as a baby. He'd heard the story from his father often enough—she'd given birth and left without a backward look. Rachel's mother had never had the chance to hold Rachel before she died; then her father and brothers had kept their distance, uncomfortable with the responsibility of bringing up a fragile girl child.

Cullen wanted to hold *his* baby. And in that moment he accepted the responsibility for her and all the love and anguish that bringing up a child would entail. No way was he going to use fear of the future as an excuse to walk away from his daughter. He knew he could never harm a child as his father had done.

Just as Cullen had never harmed a woman.

That one damaging moment fifteen years ago, when he'd found out just how like his father he could be, was abruptly shoved into perspective. He *had* broken the cycle of abuse.

His fear that he'd been on the verge of exploding into violence and hitting Hayward was nothing more than a fear. Maybe he would have hit the lawyer if Rachel hadn't touched his hand, and maybe not. The important thing was that the touch of Rachel's fingers had been all it had taken to stop him. Cullen's father would never have let a woman stop him from doing anything he wanted.

Gently, he bent and kissed his daughter, breathing in the scents of birth and Rachel, of warmth and love; then he turned gingerly so that Rachel could see, afraid of jolting or jarring the baby in any way. Rachel had turned over with the nurse's help, and her face was radiant, aglow.

"I love you," she whispered as Cullen settled the tiny scrap against her breast, and Cullen knew he'd been given gifts and richness beyond belief. Rachel's strength and love. His baby girl. His family.

She cradled their baby, catching Cullen's hands and holding them against the wet, warm skin of the child. Her smile was like the sun coming up.

"Who's going to cut the cord?" the midwife demanded.

The doctor and student nurse snickered.

The midwife attached clips to the cord in two places and, using a sterile napkin, slapped the handle of a pair of surgical scissors into Cullen's big hand. "We've got a rule in this hospital. You know it's kind of like when the little lady does all the hard work to produce a meal, the men get to clean up. Well, this is where men get to be useful in the delivery room."

Rachel allowed herself to be distracted from her dazed joy that Cullen had finally admitted he loved her and the giddy conviction that when she'd given birth to their daughter, her family had been born, too. She glanced at her husband. For a healthy outdoors type, he was looking decidedly green around the gills.

He stared at the surgical scissors in his hand, his jaw working. "I guess since you ladies need us at the start of this baby business, we should be there at the finish," he allowed.

"So true," the doctor drawled sweetly. "We haven't quite figured out how to circumvent that first part yet, but we're working on it."

Cole clapped Cullen on the shoulder. "You have my sympathy, mate."

Cullen dragged his gaze away from his absorption with his daughter. He was busy watching her, making sure she was all right while Rachel had a shower.

The nurse had expected Rachel to walk to the ablution block. Cullen had insisted on carrying her. He would have washed her, too, if she hadn't reminded him to get back to the baby. And when he'd looked in on the tightly wrapped little bundle, for a moment he'd been sure his daughter had stopped breathing. He'd been on the verge of panic when one angry, pink fist had shot out of the folds, quickly followed by another. Cullen's knees had gone weak with relief. He couldn't blame her; if he was wrapped up that tight, he would be fighting to get out, too. Muttering beneath his breath, he'd loosened the swaddling clothes, and then his daughter had smiled at him.

Well, he thought it was a smile. He'd definitely seen her gums—

then she'd jammed her fist in her mouth and nearly knocked herself out.

Cole's words finally penetrated his haze of parental devotion. "Sympathy?" Cullen echoed.

"Yeah." Cole bent down and touched one fingertip to the baby's tiny fist. She clutched his finger with the surprising strength Cullen had already discovered. "It's some responsibility having one of these little sweethearts around. If she's anything like that wildcat mother of hers, you'll be on guard duty for the rest of your life. Better try to make it a boy next time."

"There won't be a next time," Cullen growled. He didn't ever want Rachel to go through all that pain again, no matter how wonderful the result was.

"Yeah, right," Cole said with a grin. "Next time. Welcome to the family. Rachel always said she wanted to have at least four, and to my clear and certain knowledge, she always gets what she wants. One way or the other."

"I hope they never succeed," Cullen said several weeks later.

Rachel's heart skipped a beat, as it always did when she watched Cullen with their tiny daughter. He'd just changed Kate's nappy and put her down for the night in her bassinet.

"Never succeed at what?" she asked as she walked into the bedroom they'd redecorated as a nursery.

Cullen adjusted the lightweight quilt so Kate wouldn't get too hot. The contrast of his big, tanned hand against the delicate apricot cotton brought a lump to Rachel's throat. Partly because the contrast symbolised his strength and gentleness, but mostly because he was wearing his wedding ring. He'd been wearing the plain gold band when he'd come to see her and Kate in hospital the day after Rachel had given birth. Cullen hadn't directly mentioned the ring, simply picked up her left hand with his, laced their fingers together and kissed her. Something akin to an electric shock had travelled through her at the reverence of the caress. She'd felt a powerful sense of déjà vu. If they'd been back in church, repeating their vows, the sense of emotional commitment couldn't have been more intense.

"At cutting men out of the procreation business," Cullen replied absently. He turned and drew in his breath when he saw what Rachel was wearing. "Where in hell did you get that?" he asked thickly.

It had been six weeks since the birth, the cyclone, and Hayward's ignominious end in a police cell, and in all that time he hadn't seen Rachel in anything other than loose shirts and bike pants. This lacy creation revealed more than it covered, and just the sight of it turned him to pure steel.

"I bought it last week. It's for our honeymoon."

"Honeymoon?" he echoed roughly.

She brushed past him. It was deliberate. He actually felt her hardened nipple against his arm. There was perfume, too, something softly sweet and sensual that tore up his insides.

She bent over the bassinet, fussing with the covers and incidentally giving him a great view of the way the lace ran out and turned to transparent gauze just above the delicious flare of her buttocks.

Now, that was definitely deliberate.

"Rachel." He gritted his teeth.

She straightened and turned. Her hip grazed the throbbing ridge that was fast rearranging the front of his jeans. One tiny little shoestring strap slipped off her shoulder, leaving a ridiculously fragile piece of lace clinging to her breast. Rachel's breasts were round and full from breast-feeding, and driving him crazy. He'd never thought about how attractive a woman could be through pregnancy and afterward, but he'd found his hunger for Rachel increasing by leaps and bounds with the new lushness of her body.

She placed one fingertip on his chest and worked a button loose. "Kate and I had a check-up today. The doctor said that if I feel ready we can...you know..."

His hands assumed a life of their own, coming up to hold her arms. "We can make love?"

She smiled.

Cullen drew in a harsh breath, swung her up into his arms, strode into their bedroom and laid her gently on the bed. He stripped his clothes off with rapid, jerky movements, then came down beside her. And stopped. Rachel was softer, even more deliciously feminine, than she'd been before. The differences enchanted him, but he'd deliberately kept from touching her, exploring the changes to her body, because he just couldn't trust himself that close to her. And Rachel would have invited him into her body whether she was ready or not. "Are you sure?" he asked in a voice that was little more than a whispery rumble.

Her hands found him, and his heart almost stopped. "I was sure months ago."

"I can't wait," he rasped.

"I don't want you to. *Cullen*," she breathed, gripping his shoulders as he pushed the filmy nightgown up to her waist and mounted her with exquisite care. "I need you. Love me. Really love me."

He moved into her with a smooth, careful stroke, and the relief of feeling her moist internal clasp shuddered through him. Unconsciously he'd been waiting for this, the chance to claim her physically as his own. He was acutely aware of the need to seal the bond of their love in the most primal way there was, to start the process of overlaying the grim events of the recent past with memories that were sweeter, hotter, and burned more brightly, than the darkness and despair they'd both faced.

The past few weeks had been a time of intense adjustment, but the shattering intimacy of sharing a bed, a bathroom and a baby had been the most deeply satisfying experience of Cullen's life. He'd brought the same focus and determination to the process of cementing their relationship that he'd brought to avoiding it in the first place. He wanted to wrap Rachel in satin and silk, cuddle and cosset her, chase the last sombre remnant of uncertainty from her eyes. If he had to spend the rest of his life reassuring her that he would never leave, then he would, willingly. "I need you," he said deeply. "I love you. Always."

Cupping her face, he moved his hips that final last increment,

burying himself hilt-deep inside her. The tender, exquisite heat of
her body welcomed him, and her eyes glowed with a soft radiance
that sank into his very soul. In that moment he gained the certainty
he needed. She was his, just as he belonged to her.

Rachel's fingers bit delicately into his shoulders, then twined in
his hair, tugging. With a shattered groan he gave in to her unspo-
ken demand and joined his mouth to hers. Warmth and sweetness
exploded through him, healing old wounds and even older fears.
He wasn't alone; he would never be alone again. And neither
would Rachel. It didn't matter what difficulties they faced, where
they lived.

As long as they had each other, they were home.

Epilogue

he next morning, as they were eating a late breakfast, a car
ove up. Rachel would have recognised Mrs. Reese's ancient
over anywhere.

"Want me to get the door?" Cullen asked, coming up behind
r and nuzzling her hair aside to kiss her nape.

Rachel raised one brow at Cullen's Sunday-morning-sleepy eyes
d unshaven jaw, his naked chest and tight, faded jeans. The
by, naked except for her bulky diaper, was plastered sound
leep over one brawny shoulder. "You're hardly dressed for vis-
rs."

His mouth curled in a slow, sinful smile. "As soon as I get this
tle sweetheart in her bassinet, I wasn't planning on being dressed
all."

A crisp knock sounded. Cullen's smile turned into a lazy grin
he ambled past Rachel on his way to get the door.

When the door swung open, the last thing Isobel Reese expected
see was Cullen Logan, more man than was decent and looking
e the devil incarnate with that sweet, innocent angel of a baby

propped over one of those oversize shoulders of his. Isobel jerke
her chin up a notch. Not that it was likely to make any kind o
difference. From where she was standing, the man was as big a
a mountain. "I hear you're giving up the army and you're goin
to stay in Riverbend and try your hand at farming?"

His eyes narrowed at her question. "That's right."

Isobel sniffed. "Well, it's about time. We came to see th
baby," she announced, noticing the wicked glint in Cullen's ey
and trying not to let her old eyes dwell overlong on all that prim
muscle on display. Despite the flash of a wedding band on hi
finger, he still looked more wild than tamed. Lord, but that littl
Sinclair girl had netted herself a live one here. "Eleanor," sh
commanded, elbowing her daughter in the ribs.

No response.

She expelled an irritable breath and turned to see Eleanor starin
at Cullen Logan with her eyes wide and her chin near draggin
on the ground. With a sigh, she detached the parcel from Eleanor
limp hand and shoved it at Cullen's washboard flat stomach. "F
the baby."

His eyebrows shot up in a way that made her feel faintl
ashamed she hadn't called in sooner, but she ruthlessly pushe
that emotion aside. She was here now, wasn't she?

He was silent for a beat, then asked, "Would you like to ho
her?"

Isobel's eyes flew wide, but she shook her head with regre
"She's sleeping. I wouldn't want to disturb her."

"I was just going to put Katie in her bassinet. Would you lik
to come in and visit a while?"

A blush warmed her cheeks at his smile, the velvety rasp of h
voice. And those strange, light eyes. Good lord, but the man wa
too sexy for words. Reminded Isobel of her Harold. Her thro
tightened as it always did when she thought of her husband.
hardly seemed like twenty years since he'd died. Now *there* w
a man who knew how to make a woman feel like a woma
"Maybe another time, when that little girl's likely to be awake
she said gruffly. "We'll be late for church if we stop any longer

Cullen smiled again, white teeth flashing wickedly against his
*t*nned, stubbled jaw. "Thank you for the gift. And don't forget
to stop by. Rachel enjoys company."

On the way to the car, Isobel fanned herself. "Whew, it cer-
*ta*inly is boiling today, isn't it?"

Eleanor settled into her seat with a dreamy look on her face.
*"*That man is downright beautiful."

Isobel set the car in gear, the tyres spitting gravel as her gammy
*le*g pressed just a bit too hard on the gas pedal. The burst of speed
*ce*rtainly had nothing to do with her irritation at her daughter for
*li*ving in such a dream world and not supplying her with a whole
*bu*nch of sweet babies like the one draped across Cullen Logan's
*sh*oulder. "You had your chance at him, girl," she muttered, peer-
*in*g at Cullen's battered cattlestop and aiming for the centre, "and
*yo*u messed it up big time. You can't expect to catch one of those
*wi*ld ones if all you ever do is look with your mouth open!"

Cullen snagged Rachel's hand as he walked down the hallway.
*"*Bed," he said as he towed her upstairs to their room.

Instead of putting his little darling in her bassinet, he simply lay
*do*wn on the sunny, tangled bed and let her sleep on his chest.
*Sh*e seemed to like that best of all and usually slept twice as long,
*w*hich, since she was such a lively little critter at night, meant that
he and Rachel could catch up on some sleep of their own.

"Cullen?"

He tore his wondering gaze from the tiny, snuffling scrap of
*ba*by splayed all over him, her diapered rump stuck up in the air.
*Ra*chel settled in next to him, snuggling into the curve of his arm.
*ri*ght where she belonged. "Hmm?" he rumbled lazily, running
*hi*s fingers up Rachel's arm, then letting them sift through her
*go*rgeous, silky hair.

She smiled, putting the sunlight in the shade. "Did you see what
*th*e Reeses brought?" She unraveled a large T-shirt and held it up.
*A*nother tiny matching T-shirt fell out.

"The old devil," Cullen said, chuckling.

The T-shirts both read, Made in Riverbend and Proud of It.

* * * * *

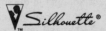

Looking For More Romance?

Visit Romance.net

Look us up on-line at: http://www.romance.net

Check in daily for these and other exciting features:

Hot off the press

View all current titles, and purchase them on-line.

What do the stars have in store for you?

Horoscope

Hot deals

Exclusive offers available only at Romance.net

Plus, don't miss our interactive quizzes, contests and bonus gifts.

PWEB

INTIMATE MOMENTS® Silhouette®

invites you to go West to

Cameron, Utah

Margaret Watson's exhilarating new miniseries

FOR THE CHILDREN...IM #886, October 1998
Embittered agent Damien Kane was responsible for
protecting beautiful Abby Markham and her twin
nieces. But it was Abby who saved him as she
showed him the redeeming power of home
and family.

COWBOY WITH A BADGE...IM #904, January 1999
Journalist Carly Fitzpatrick had come to Cameron
determined to clear her dead brother's name. But it's
the local sheriff—the son of the very man she believed
was responsible—who ends up safeguarding her
from the real murderer and giving her the family
she's always wanted.

Available at your favorite retail outlet.

Silhouette®

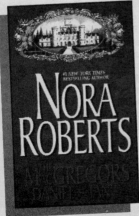

COMING NEXT MONTH

#919 THIS HEART FOR HIRE—Marie Ferrarella

Given the threats against him, Logan Buchanan knew he had no choice but to hire private investigator Jessica Deveaux, but seeing her again only reminded him of how much he'd once loved her. Now it was up to Logan to prove he'd changed, before someone took away his one last chance for happiness.

#920 THE FUGITIVE BRIDE—Margaret Watson

Cameron, Utah

FBI agent Jesse Coulton was having a hard time believing beautiful Shea McAllister was guilty of doing anything illegal on her Utah ranch. As he worked undercover to discover the truth, Jesse desperately hoped she was innocent—because the only place she belonged was in his arms!

#921 MIDNIGHT CINDERELLA—Eileen Wilks

Way Out West

After being accused of a crime he hadn't committed, Nathan Jones was determined to put his life back together. And when he met and fell for his sexy new employee, Hannah McBride, he knew he was on the right track. But then their newfound love was put to the test and it was up to Nate to prove that he was finally ready for happily-ever-after.

#922 THE DADDY TRAP—Kayla Daniels

Families Are Forever

When Kristen Monroe and her nephew Cody knocked on his door, Luke Hollister knew his life would never be the same. As she hid from Cody's abusive "father," Kristen shocked Luke with an incredible secret. And the longer they stayed, the more Luke fell in love—with the woman he desired and the son he'd always wanted....

#923 THE COP AND CALAMITY JANE—Elane Osborn

Bad luck seemed to follow Callie "Calamity Jane" Chance everywhere. But when she met sexy detective Marcus Scanlon, she knew her luck had changed. He was hot on the trail of suspected catnappers, and Callie was hi only witness. Once the culprits were nabbed, would Callie accept Marcus's proposal—for a disaster-free future?

#924 BRIDGER'S LAST STAND—Linda Winstead Jones

Men in Blue

Detective Malcolm Bridger never thought he'd see Frannie Vaughn again after their one memorable night together. Then Frannie got mixed up in his current case. Suddenly Malcolm was falling for this forever kind of girl, and their near one-night stand was slowly becoming a one-*life* stand